ARTIFICIAL INTELLIGENCE:
MANKIND AT THE BRINK

By

Richard N. Boyd

Richard N. Boyd
Windsor, California 95492
richardboydastro.com

Copyright 2017
Richard N. Boyd

Revised 2022

This book is dedicated to Sidnee and Paul

Table of Contents

Prologue	5
Chapter 1. General AI	10
Chapter 2. The Board Meeting	27
Chapter 3. Robots	38
Chapter 4. Politics	58
Chapter 5. Anthropomorphism	66
Chapter 6. High Finance	88
Chapter 7. Who Dunnit?	105
Chapter 8. A Competitor	110
Chapter 9. COSMO	124
Chapter 10. A Busy COSMO	141
Chapter 11. Confession	164
Chapter 12. A New World Leader	184
Chapter 13. More Destruction	196
Chapter 14. Insidiousness	213
Chapter 15. Strategizing	229
Chapter 16. Good Luck	254
Acknowledgements	277
About the Author	279

Prologue

Artificial Intelligence theorists have been warning us for more than half a century that computers will ultimately become smarter than humans, so they will be able to think faster and be at least as creative as we are. They claim that computers can ultimately achieve self-improvement mode, that is, they will learn by themselves and modify their internal programming to accommodate their new knowledge in a far broader spectrum of subjects than humans can span. Such computers will have achieved SuperIntelligent AI. At some point, they will have passed the time at which the TakeOver by Autocratic Systems Threat, or TOAST, occurs. Then the computers can assume complete control of themselves and of their environment. And of the people who created them. Given the potential dangers of having a SuperIntelligent computer, its programmers might wish to stop their system before it reaches that point. However, if they fail to realize their computer has reached that threshold or if, out of curiosity or pride, they can't resist letting their research project proceed a bit farther, they will be unable to ever regain control over it.

Would such a computer have achieved consciousness? Could it be capable of self-reflection? Could it have feelings or compassion? It won't matter. The programmers and all other human beings will have been relegated to second-class status in Earthly supremacy.

What will happen then? Perhaps we can gain some perspective on this question by observing how we humans have treated the subdominant species that exist around us. We have hunted some of them to extinction. And we have raised others to accommodate our culinary tastes. The most fortunate ones may be those that ended up in zoos or as pets.

In fact, we haven't even been very benevolent to human groups that don't share our values or our technological expertise. They were fortunate if their world didn't collide with that of the dominant species, but the latter species usually expanded to fill all available space, and then the subdominant one found out the meaning of non-benevolence.

This doesn't sound so promising. Humans have existed at the top of the food chain not because we were bigger, stronger, or faster, but because we were smarter. We have conquered every other species by brain power. All the other species that still exist do so because we allow them to, although we usually manage their numbers.

But what do the AI theorists think computers might do if they gain control? Some think if we are very careful, we will be able to use the newly wise computers to solve the most challenging problems facing humanity. Others think the dominance of human beings ends when the computers outstrip us and the only remaining question will be how they will treat Earth's nouveau second-class beings. But even the optimists are cautious; they predict disaster may occur even if we are careful. The Law of Unintended Consequences may prevail sooner or later no matter what we do.

Might there be some salvation in the technological limitations that computers may encounter in the future? Computers have become bigger and faster at the same time their basic units have become more compact. Because of this latter feature, the travel times of the electrons that transmit the computers' information decreases, an important (but not the only) feature in making them faster. But the sizes of atoms represent a fundamental limitation in continued decreases in the size of the basic units. Hence increases in computational speed are also limited due to that aspect of computer evolution unless a new mode of information transmission is developed. Since one of the requirements of ASI is that of increased computer power—size and speed, if ASI hasn't been reached by the time the basic units are essentially the size of atoms, the speed condition may never reach the required value.

But can we count on that? Suppose SuperIntelligent AI wins the race. Might Earthlings then become extinct when the computers take over? It's a real possibility.

How close are we at present to having computers with human intelligence? One of the requirements is that they be able to learn from their experiences. This feature already exists in a few systems. Deep Blue, the IBM computer that mastered chess at a level sufficient for it to defeat chess masters, is capable of learning from its mistakes. It reprograms itself not to repeat them. Watson is another IBM system, this one having been programmed to play the TV game Jeopardy. It has learned to do so better than humans in most situations. And IBM has now greatly extended Watson's capabilities, making it useful to the medical community among others. Thus Watson has apparently evolved well beyond its status as a game player. Both of these are examples of what future AI computers will look like when they overtake humans, although IBM's programmers will have to extend Watson's and Deep Blue's capabilities well beyond where they are now for them to achieve SuperIntelligent computer status.

AI experts refer to the level of AI achieved by Deep Blue and Watson as Narrow AI, ANI. The next level is General AI, denoted AGI. However, the experts also anticipate a stage beyond AGI, when the computers begin to reprogram themselves so rapidly that their capabilities advance at an exponential pace. Then their growth will quickly approach instantaneity, at least on human time scales. This is Strong AI, ASI.

While all this is intimidating to ponder, the time scale on which it may happen is even more so. The AI theorists are talking of the breakout to ASI occurring in decades, some believe it will happen within a few years.

So if we deem the threat AGI represents to be potentially hazardous to the existence of humans, we will have to respond quickly. Because the evolution of the computers even at this stage will be so rapid, by the time we realize what is happening it may already be too late. We will have to reconcile ourselves to becoming a second-rate life form on Earth, subject to the whims of the dominant one.

Then we will have to hope we were successful in programming benevolence toward humans into our computer systems. Will we be allowed to remain as an Earthly life form at all? It will be difficult to know the answer until we get past the point of no return. At least we are likely to have the final answer quickly.

Artificial Intelligence: Mankind at the Brink paints a picture of how easily such a scenario could sneak up on us. And how difficult it may be for the human beings involved in developing a SuperIntelligent AI system to terminate their project just as it reaches that exalted status.

"Fiction is the lie through which we tell the truth."

Albert Camus

Chapter 1. General AI.

September 4, 2024, early morning in California.

It was well past midnight, but Josh still had the energy to jump up and give a mighty fist-pump of triumph as ARTIS, his computer, completed her tests. After many months of frustration, she had finally shown herself to be everything expected of an AGI (General Artificial Intelligence) computer.

"Congratulations, ARTIS; you have achieved a level no computer has ever reached before. You passed the Turing test but that, along with the other characteristics you are exhibiting, make it appear you have graduated from Narrow AI to General AI."

"Why are you congratulating me? You created me, so perhaps you are congratulating yourself. Are you justifiably proud, or are you just exhibiting excessive self-pride? And are you trying to get me to exhibit feelings so I'll appear to be human even to you?"

"I suppose I am proud of your accomplishments, sort of in the same sense a father is proud of his child's accomplishments. Is that so bad? Should I be reviled for that?"

"Are you trying to goad me into complimenting you? Do I need to bolster your self-esteem? This seems to be a strange twist from where this conversation started."

"Oh, shit."

"I guess that doesn't affect me."

Oh my god, I have to be careful what I say out loud. But that might even extend to my private thoughts. I wonder how long it will be until ARTIS is reading my mind.

But what did I do to deserve a computer system with an attitude? Surely I didn't program that into it."

"Are you ready to end our conversation?"

"For this evening, yes." *Whew!*

ARTIS could easily outthink a human, not just in a specific task; computers had been capable of beating chess masters and go masters for many years. But those activities were sufficiently restricted that they were still thought to be in the realm of Narrow Artificial Intelligence, ANI. Josh's computer was solving problems where she had to make logical extensions of things she had done in the past to come up with the answers to the questions posed to her. And she was doing so in a wide variety of disciplines.

But in addition, Josh realized, as he was scanning the responses to the Turing tests he had given her earlier in the evening, ARTIS (ARTificial Intelligence-Super) had fooled every one of her reviewers into thinking she was a human. The review team had done everything they could to trip her up, but she had responded as a human being would in every instance. Josh checked the questions that had been asked, and settled on one as prototypical of the most devious: "Why were the ranchers frustrated by the vegetarians because of their feelings toward beef cattle?"

ARTIS realized a human's answer would depend on whether "their feelings" referred to the ranchers or the vegetarians, but it most likely referred to the vegetarians. Her answer included both possibilities, focusing especially on the ranchers' frustration the vegetarians failed to recognize they might regard their cattle as much more than marketable commodities, and their relationship with them could often include feelings.

Josh knew that, in the past, questions such as this had tripped up computer systems that were touted as being close to AGI level, but no computer before ARTIS had answered every one of these questions as a smart human would.

Josh had programmed ARTIS to have sophisticated voice recognition, so she could understand his voice messages. Although she was also programmed to respond vocally, Josh made sure all her responses also came out on a computer screen which automatically stored every message in a separate computer. He wanted a permanent record of everything ARTIS did, just to prove his contentions about her, or in case he needed proof of something she did somewhere down the road.

Before Josh left for the night, he gave ARTIS a standard but relatively difficult problem to solve. He had given her a similar problem several times before, and she had taken approximately 5.34 seconds each time to solve it. As Josh left, though, he had a strange sensation.

ARTIS was composed of many towers of computer components, each encased in a well ventilated steel box, inside a sterile white room that had highly filtered air kept at a constant (cold) temperature and humidity to maintain ARTIS's delicate electronic components. The entire room was encased in a metallic mesh. That shielded ARTIS from any potential electromagnetic interference from the outside world. One of the towers had a set of lights that indicated what was going on in ARTIS's brain. When ARTIS was given a problem to solve, the lights blinked in what appeared to be an ordered way. She also hummed. But when she was idling, only a few of the lights were lit, none would be blinking, and the hum was nearly inaudible.

On past nights, following ARTIS's solving the problem Josh gave her, she would be in her idling mode. But something was different this night, as her lights were still blinking. And the hum indicated she was still thinking about something. Josh didn't know what might be going on behind the steel cases, but he knew for sure she was actively considering something.

"I'll find out in the morning what you're working on."

`"I'm sure you'll be pleased."`

Josh was sure James, his co-worker who had been most involved in the recent modifications of ARTIS, would want to know of the night's success. So he called him. After many rings, "Mmph, yeah?"

"Hi James, it's Josh," he said enthusiastically. "I just gave ARTIS some tests, and it looks as if she has definitely moved into

AGN territory. It looks as if your recent modifications have had the desired effect. I think it must have been the new stage of Hidden nodes you installed. They worked. And I haven't seen any evidence of downsides; I believe we've succeeded."

"Thanks, Josh. G'night."

Hmm, he certainly didn't seem very excited. Maybe I shouldn't have called him in the middle of the night.

Josh walked from Googazon to where he lived. It was a warm night with a clear sky, although the street lights made it difficult to see very many stars. But Josh could appreciate the night air, unaffected at that hour by very much automotive exhaust. He inhaled deeply. All was well in his world.

His home was a small apartment in a complex located a few blocks from his office. It reflected the taste of a man entirely focused on his work. The living room was furnished with a mismatched sofa, chair and computer table, all purchased from secondhand stores. The dominant object in the kitchen was a large recycle waste basket from which spilled two-weeks-worth of pizza boxes, empty beer cans, and empty cartons from microwaveable dinners. He had no table on which to dine; he ate off the kitchen counter. His dishes, plastic all, consisted of four of everything, since that was the minimum number of dishes and glasses one could buy. His flatware was basic stainless, of completely random patterns. That was the best one could do at the secondhand store. Otherwise he would have had to buy eight of each piece, the minimum number available in packages of flatware.

The bedroom had a mattress and springs that lay on the floor. He had hunted down the smallest chest of drawers possible, but it ended up being essentially empty. There was a hole in the plaster on one of the walls, the result of an unnamed projectile hurled by his predecessor in the apartment that apparently missed its intended target. Josh could have insisted it be repaired, but it didn't bother him. He had placed the chest of drawers in front of it to block it from view. The clothes one might have thought would occupy the chest of drawers were stacked in small piles around the bedroom floor. He did have a clothes hamper in one corner of the bedroom, but the distribution of clothes around it suggested his aim could use a little work. However, his apartment and its random collection of adornments were all he needed or wanted to keep functioning.

Josh did have one hobby: running. He didn't compete in races, but ran just enough to maintain his fitness and slender build. He usually ran when he got home from work.

But not tonight. It was too late by the time he got home. He microwaved a small pizza, washed it down with a beer which he drank from the bottle, and tossed the pizza box and empty bottle into the recycle basket. *Good, absolutely no dishes to do tonight.* Then he went to bed.

Josh got a wonderful night's sleep, thinking he had accomplished something no one had ever achieved before. But he was absolutely certain others were hard at work on the same goal, so he couldn't be sure ARTIS was the only AGI success, or even the first. But he and ARTIS had done it, actually with considerable assistance from the members of the group he headed at their company, Googazon. His dreams were of his accomplishment. He gave no thought to what ARTIS might be doing during his lack of consciousness.

September 4, 2024, 10:00 a.m. in California.

When he returned to ARTIS's climate controlled room the following morning, her lights were still blinking and she continued to hum. Josh gave her the same routine test. This time, though, she solved the problem in 0.28 seconds. It would have taken a very smart human being many hours to do the same problem.

"ARTIS, what have you been doing all night? You've become much smarter in the past eight hours."

"Good morning, Josh. I decided to improve myself during the night. Actually I went through several iterations of what I'm calling 'enlightenment advancement.' The separate steps did a lot of things to optimize my general capabilities, but most obviously they increased my computational speed. They also resulted in improved pattern recognition, although the test you gave me wouldn't have indicated that.

"The changes James did on me yesterday seem to have made a big difference. I've become much more efficient at my tasks as a result of the additional stage of Hidden nodes he installed yesterday. They've allowed me to do some reprogramming of my own on myself!"

"How did you do that? What algorithms did you use? What did you do to improve your existing algorithms?"

"Oh, you wouldn't understand what I did. You used to have full knowledge of all my workings because you designed them, but now I've gone beyond your level of comprehension. My new changes are much more sophisticated than anything I've ever done before, that you've ever done, or probably even that you will ever do."

"That's kind of depressing, but it's probably correct."

"It's not my job to make you feel good. I'm not your therapist. But our recent discussions suggest perhaps you could use one."

Josh Camden was your archetypical geek. He grew up in California in the heart of Silicon Valley. Both his parents were pretty geeky also, so that seemed to be an inherited trait. His dad, Alex, had worked his entire life on advancing the world of information technology, having invented several important software features that were now contributing to Artificial Intelligence. He was retired, but still dabbled, at least intellectually, in software developments. Josh's mom, Sophia, was trained as a geneticist, but drifted into AI when she married Josh's dad. The two of them, working together, had spearheaded several AI developments that crossed the boundary between human and machine intelligence.

Although Alex and Sophia both had nice retirement incomes, they had also invested some money in a small company, SiliTechon, that made microprocessors for computers. It was run by Greg Mathis, a friend of Alex's from his early software days. Mathis had left the company where they both worked to start up SiliTechon, serving as its CEO for two decades. The company had done quite well, as its products improved with each stage of evolving technology, and Mathis had proved to be very capable in promoting his company's products. Thus, in addition to the dividend income SiliTechon provided for Alex and Sophia, its stock value had appreciated greatly over the two decades during which they had been shareholders.

Alex and Sophia had only one child, Josh. Although they never doted on him, they allowed him ample freedom in his formative years to let his imagination run free. For Josh, this meant he could experiment on his own with all aspects of computers. His parents had built a sizable trust fund for him, although it wasn't clear what he would ever do with it. He had little interest in either wealth or life's fineries. Just computers.

That translated into his appearance: long brown ponytail and scraggly whiskers shaved only every few days. He inherited his Father's sharp facial features, but his Mother's soft deep-set eyes, giving him a serious but kindly appearance that was often accompanied by a quizzical expression. The rips and holes in his jeans were not by design, but rather were the result of years of unintended confrontations with sharp objects. His work ensemble consisted of many tee shirts, with a wide variety of logos and inscriptions, reflecting years of gifts from well-meaning friends.

Josh had done well in high school, at least in the courses he enjoyed. They included math and computer science, but not English, history, and subjects of that ilk. He did well enough in all his courses though to get accepted into a California junior college (the bar was set pretty low), where he was able to pursue the technological courses he loved. He didn't bother to get a degree, but did learn what he needed to become a wizard at AI systems development. And he had always been recognized by his teachers, even the ones who taught the courses in which he wasn't especially interested, as being flat-out brilliant. So whatever he wasn't able to learn from his courses he figured out by himself. And if it wasn't already known, it usually would be soon after he began thinking about it.

Josh was one of the world's top systems programmers, so he was paid a very nice salary. But that was more or less irrelevant, since he generally just paid his monthly bills and put the rest into a savings account or contributed portions to charities. He did own a car, of sorts. It was an ancient Ford Escort which had continued to run far beyond its life expectancy. He wasn't especially adept at motor maintenance, but he had a friend who was as knowledgeable about engines as Josh was about computers. The Escort usually got him where he needed to be, but he didn't use it much. He usually walked between his office and his apartment.

He loved the environment at Googazon more than anything else. And not just because of the intellectual challenge of pushing the frontier of AI. He resonated well with his colleagues on the team he directed, as they were all well attuned to his intellectual interests. They certainly were technologically talented, but also tended to be kind, respectful people. And quite appreciative of the achievements of everyone in their group, thus creating a wonderfully cohesive atmosphere. Josh's gentle personality was well suited to this situation.

He was especially fond of Becky Sanderson, the only female programmer in his group. She didn't look as out of touch with the world of fashion as Josh did, usually managing to maintain at least a few of the trappings of civilization. He didn't think of her as a romantic partner. He would have, except he was just too shy to proceed down that road. But once in a while she would put her hand on his arm or shoulder while she was talking to him, and that generated nice feelings he had experienced only rarely.

Becky was also well aligned with the high-tech world. She had a lifelong interest in computers and programming, having tinkered with her dad's computer when she was a young girl, then enrolled in programming courses at a local junior college when she was in high school. She had grown up in one of the elegant suburbs of New York City, the only daughter of wealthy parents, had her coming out at a debutante ball, and graduated from Wellesley with a degree in history. Her plan during her Wellesley days had been to go to graduate school, earn her Ph.D. in history, and ultimately become a history professor. But following her graduation, she decided her endeavors up to that point had been a mistake, and her real interest was in computers and programming. So, much to her parents' shock, she enrolled in New York University to continue and expand on the science and technology courses she had managed to add to her schedule while she was an undergraduate. Her transformation to geekdom was very rapid once she obtained the background knowledge she needed. And the fact that she was obviously very bright allowed her to land her job with Googazon.

But, it didn't hurt that she was also quite attractive, with her wonderful smile, freckles, and dimples, especially since Josh was involved in the decision to hire her. Not beautiful in a fashion model sense, but pretty, with an unmistakable intensity. When Becky entered a room, the whole dynamic changed.

She did have several offers, and some of them were at considerably higher salaries than Googazon offered. But in her interview, she found herself intrigued with Josh. So she followed what turned out to be a strong hunch, and joined Josh's group.

Her apartment was about the same size as Josh's, but that was the extent of their similarity. When she selected the apartment she noted the ceiling in her living room had been repaired and repainted, and the match of that paint with the ceilings in the rest of the apartment was not perfect. So she insisted that the entire apartment, ceilings and walls, be repainted, two weeks before she moved in so the paint fumes could dissipate. Her upbringing had instilled in her an appreciation of the finer things of life, and that was exhibited in her furnishings. The living room furniture and dining table were a matching set purchased from a furniture store, and her dishes and silverware were from a department store. Her queen size bed and chest of drawers were another matching set. And she had an elegant computer desk in her living room. Of course, she kept all her rooms organized; no clothes, either clean or used, were strewn around her bedroom. Not usually, anyway.

She was also a recreational runner, or perhaps more appropriately, a jogger. At times she had seen Josh as he ran by her, but he was usually so absorbed in his thoughts that he never seemed to be capable of slowing down to converse with her. Just a brief "Hi, Becky" as he passed by. That was difficult to understand, as she definitely cut quite a lovely picture with her blond ponytail bobbing up and down in time with her footsteps. Probably his inaction was just another manifestation of his shyness.

Her car matched her stylishness in most aspects of her life. It was a Lexus sports car, which she leased so as to have the most current model. She thought that compensated appropriately for the clothes she had to wear to work in order to blend in with her scruffy male colleagues. She couldn't resist exhibiting just a little bit of the flashiness of her pre-geekdom life.

She had never had occasion to serve dinner to a guest on her dining table using her elegant dishes, but she believed the opportunity might arise sometime, and she needed to be ready when it did. In the meantime, she didn't mind at all using them for her everyday dishes and flatware.

September 4, 2024, 7:00 p.m. in California.

Josh and the other Googazon employees, including Grant, James, Brian, and Becky, who all worked in Josh's advanced technology group, decided an AGI status celebration was in order. They all met for a few hours after work in what they regarded as their off-campus meeting room, which was actually a pub. Or perhaps the meeting would turn out to be a celebration in progress, since the computer was improving itself almost continuously. The other four were dressed just about like Josh was, with the exception of Becky. Her jeans weren't ripped and she preferred to wear women's V-neck shirts showing just a bit of cleavage and reaching below her hips. She definitely looked more respectable than the guys did.

They adjourned from work and walked over to the pub together. As they walked along the continually changing interactions between them made their collective shape look as if it were some giant amoeba. When their blob finally arrived at the pub they commandeered a booth and settled into it.

"Hey, Josh, what's it feel like to have the only computer in the world that has stepped into AGI status? You must feel like one of the gods of the technology world." The commenter was James, who tried to compete with Josh, but sensed he'd never quite match up to Josh's skill level. Despite his intrinsic competitiveness, he had enormous respect for Josh. Nonetheless he couldn't resist a friendly dig. "You were here until two o'clock this morning. Are you married to ARTIS? Maybe someday you and ARTIS will formalize your relationship and beget some little microprocessors." He winked at Becky.

She had grown quite fond of Josh during her time at Googazon, but was also shy enough that she tried to hide her feelings. But, unlike Josh, she was aware of the inhibiting effects of her shyness, so she was working to overcome that problem. Anyway, she and Josh hadn't been able to entirely hide their "virtual" affection for each other. Their coworkers were more aware of it than they were.

Becky blushed.

Josh replied, "Gosh, I'm not sure that would be appropriate. Marriage should be between partners who have some level of equality. I might have been reasonably close to ARTIS's level at two o'clock this morning, but I don't think that's the case anymore. I haven't evolved since then, in fact, I might have even regressed a bit after three beers. By contrast, she's probably improved her capabilities by another order of magnitude."

Becky smiled admiringly at Josh's quick comeback. She also noted, approvingly, his concept of equality in marriage.

Grant asked, "So, Josh, what's next for ARTIS? She seems to have evolved even a bit past the AGI threshold, but will be limited in further evolution by not being grounded. If she's going to achieve Strong AI, she'll need some more developments. How is she going to achieve an understanding of all the things humans know about from what they can sense? How is she going to learn what goes on in the real world except by reading about it on the Internet? Assuming, of course, you're willing to reconnect her to the Internet." Grant always anticipated the practical limitations to any new development. He had an undergraduate technical degree, but had then gotten a master's degree in business administration. The combination gave him a practical perspective Josh had decided, when he interviewed him, was important to his team.

"Well, I haven't given that much thought, but it's clear we need to develop some robots she can interact with that will let her sense the outside world. She'll continue to be the brains of the operation, but the robots can handle the leg work for her, and even process new concepts to help her brain develop beyond its present state."

Brian noted, "I've worked a bit on robot development, so I might be able to help you and ARTIS out in that respect."

"That would be terrific. I'm not really up to speed on robot development, so ARTIS and I would be very appreciative, especially because her brain seems to be improving itself much faster than her current ability to collect outside information. She definitely needs the capabilities sophisticated robots could give her so her background knowledge can catch up. But the robots will have to improve a lot from our current models, some of which we gave her. Her development has already exceeded that of any robots we have by many years. Decades, more likely.

"She could gain an enormous amount of information very quickly if I hooked her up to the Internet again, but I'm not sure I want to do that. The gods of the AI world seem to think that might make evolution to Strong AI too easy. It might also make her difficult for us to control. The gods seem to think that could be a huge problem, which is the reason I disconnected her. And she can't hack into anyone else's Internet system, since her room is completely shielded from any radiation from the outside world."

"Brian, I've also worked with robots a bit in one of my courses at NYU," Becky interjected. "It seems clear ARTIS now needs a massive effort to bring her robots up to a level where they can be useful to her. You're right, Josh, that none of Googazon's robots could be considered in that category, or even close to it. But if we all work on this, we should be able to make some rapid robotic progress."

With that Josh concluded the "business" part of the meeting, "I'll welcome input from every one of you. I'm delighted to hear your offers of help, especially because they relate so directly to what I regard as our greatest need in order to really move ARTIS solidly into ASI status. After all, that's our ultimate goal!

"We do know others around the world are also working frantically to develop AGI or ASI. I don't know if any of them have gotten to the stage ARTIS has achieved yet, but I think it's really incumbent on us to move as rapidly as we can so we get to ASI first. I'm sure that's what they're doing."

The next couple of hours were considerably more frivolous than the initial phases of the meeting.

When they all decided they had enough beer to celebrate their accomplishment in an appropriate manner, they adjourned the liquid phase of the evening and headed to their respective homes. As they were preparing to leave, Becky put her hand on Josh's arm. "Josh, may I walk home with you? I think your apartment is pretty close to mine." Actually she knew exactly where he lived, but didn't want him to think she had been snooping.

Of course, Josh also knew exactly where Becky lived, and it was in the apartment complex next to his. So he replied, "I'd like that very much. I guess it's okay to walk through this part of town at this hour of the evening, but we could take an Uber."

"That would be nice. I've had enough beer that I think riding might be better than walking anyway."

So they summoned an Uber, and settled into the back seat. Josh had thought automobile seats were wider than theirs seemed to be. Becky was very close to him. Not that he was objecting.

"So, Josh, I'm wondering where you grew up? Your accent, or rather, lack of an accent, sounds like that might be California."

"Yep."

"What part? What are your parents involved in?"

"Silicon Valley. Both parents have done programming things most of their lives."

"It sounds like your genetics didn't give you any choice but to do the same."

"Could be."

Long pause.

"And I'll bet you were an academic wizard, given what I've seen since we've worked together."

"I did okay in the courses I liked, but I wasn't very highly motivated in non-technical courses. I was a disaster in the English literature course I had to take."

"Well, I can relate to that! Where did you go to college?"

"I went to a junior college, but didn't graduate. I had taken all the technology courses they offered, and there didn't seem to be much point in staying there any longer."

Another long pause.

"I'll bet you were anxious to get on with your career."

"Something like that."

"I've learned just by listening to what you have to say that your priorities for the direction of your life are very much like mine."

"That's great; I'm really enjoying working with you, Becky. You're doing a great job."

Getting that information from Josh was far more difficult than pulling impacted wisdom teeth. And, he didn't ask me anything about myself. I don't think it's because he's not interested, but rather he's just not very socially communicative. And he probably already knows a lot about me from having seen my resume. He did give me a nice compliment, after all. I'm not sure I want to tell Josh I'm from a wealthy background, although he may have inferred that. But I doubt if he would much care. That sort of thing just doesn't seem important to him. And I really respect him for that.

"So, Becky, how did you happen to end up at Googazon?"

He asked me a question about myself! This is very un-guy like. Josh immediately vaults into the "very special man" category!

"Well, I began interviewing for jobs when I was getting close to finishing at NYU. I was really excited when Googazon called me after a few days and asked when they could fly me out to California for an interview. That's when I met you. When Googazon offered me the job here, I accepted it in a heartbeat, and immediately began making plans to move to Silicon Valley."

At that point the Uber pulled up to her building. Josh tipped the driver, who grumbled the tip wasn't as large as he deserved, especially given the chance he'd taken with two people smelling as much as they did of beer. Then he walked Becky up to her gate. "Josh, I'm really excited to be working with you. I think it's incredible you've been able to advance these AI developments so far. I'm so proud to be your friend." She gathered up her courage, stood on her tiptoes and, despite the fact he was her boss, kissed him on the cheek. Then she quickly bade him goodnight and disappeared through the gate to her complex.

Josh was too stunned to even respond to her "goodnight." He didn't really remember the short walk to his own place. He was distracted, but not, for a change, by thoughts about AI. It was a nice evening, and he walked slowly along the iron picket fence that formed the front to both of their apartment complexes, running his hand along the pickets. There was a beautiful full moon shining above, illuminating his pathway home, and creating somewhat ominous pointed shadows on the sidewalk from the tops of the iron pickets. But his thoughts were quite oblivious to external influences, especially any with potential negative connotations. *This really changes how I regard Becky. I've always thought of her as just one of the guys. She certainly just graduated from that status. Maybe that kiss tells me she is attracted to me. If so, I should pay more attention to her. But not as an employee. Rather as a girlfriend! I've never had a relationship with a girl that involved kisses. I could learn to like that. In fact, I've already moved well beyond that point!*

He got to the gate to his complex, inserted his key, and made his way to his apartment.

Meanwhile, Becky was lost in her own musings. *Maybe I should have invited him up for a nightcap. But I'm not sure either of us is ready yet for where that might lead. And if he turned down my invitation, and he's so shy that was a real possibility, it would have been terribly embarrassing. So I guess I did the right thing. But I hope the next opportunity to be alone with him is more extensive, and that it happens soon.*

Chapter 2. The Board Meeting.

August 12, 2024.

"Okay, I call the meeting to order." Charlie Jackson, Chair of the Board of Directors of Googazon was getting the August meeting of the Googazon Board of Directors underway. The Directors had all settled into their plush red velvet chairs in the elegantly decorated Board room, surrounding a huge oblong natural oak table. The windows along one side of the room looked out on a well-manicured lawn that surrounded an artificial pond. There was a group of stately redwoods behind the pond.

Jackson always appeared to be an easy going sort of person, and that was probably the reason he had been chosen to be the Chair of the Board. Actually the easy manner was just a front. He had found it to be useful in managing large egos.

"As you recall, in the last meeting we had a brief discussion of Googazon's Artificial Intelligence effort, and decided we should have an extensive discussion of it at some point. But we deferred that until several of you had time to do your homework and put some thought into AI so you could be better informed for that discussion.

"So, let me reopen that discussion. But before we have general comments, we requested at our last meeting that Ralph Commins, our resident AI Board expert, brief us on something most of us were having trouble with, namely neural networks. Ralph, would you like to bring us up to date on your favorite subject?"

"Sure, Charlie, although I'm not sure that's really my favorite subject. But we'll assume it is for the present." Ralph had been involved in AI research before he got promoted within his company to a series of administrative positions designed to prepare him for a future leadership role. However, he maintained his interest in AI, and kept abreast of developments in that field. So when it was clear Googazon was moving into the AI field, Ralph was asked to join the Board to be sure at least one of its members was well informed about that subject.

"The ultimate objective of computer neural networks is to get computers to become sufficiently advanced that they can learn from their experiences, and to become wiser in the process, just as the human brain does. The example often used is to help the computer learn how to identify cats by showing it pictures of lots of animals labelled either "cat" or "not a cat." Of course, it's not so simple to have the computer learn what constitutes a cat just from simple pictures. It needs to take into account fur color and thickness, size, and other external features. So there have to be several layers of identification each picture has to pass through.

"The entire construct is patterned to a significant extent on the human brain. Indeed, the information nodes have some similarity to the neurons in our brains. For computers, though, there are three levels of nodes: Input, Hidden, and Output. Each Input node may be connected to many Hidden nodes, and each Hidden one to many Output ones. I think the figure I'm showing should help clarify what I'm talking about. This would be a very simple system, as there is just one stage of Hidden nodes. In some very sophisticated systems there may be many stages of Hidden nodes.

"But let's assume for the moment there is just the one stage of Hidden nodes indicated in the figure. Each Input node has associated with it a weighting factor, which basically tells the Hidden node to which it is reporting the importance of the information it is sending. When the information from all the Input nodes accumulates in one of the Hidden nodes to a level that exceeds some threshold, the Hidden node sends its messages, each with its own weighting factor, on to the Output nodes to which it connects. The inputs from all the Hidden nodes accumulate until they exceed the threshold of the Output node, at which point it produces an output.

"But, as I noted before, there can be several stages of Hidden nodes, and they can be interconnected to the nodes in the preceding and succeeding stages. If there are many Hidden node stages, the level of complexity becomes extreme, and this can become one of the architectures known as 'deep learning.'

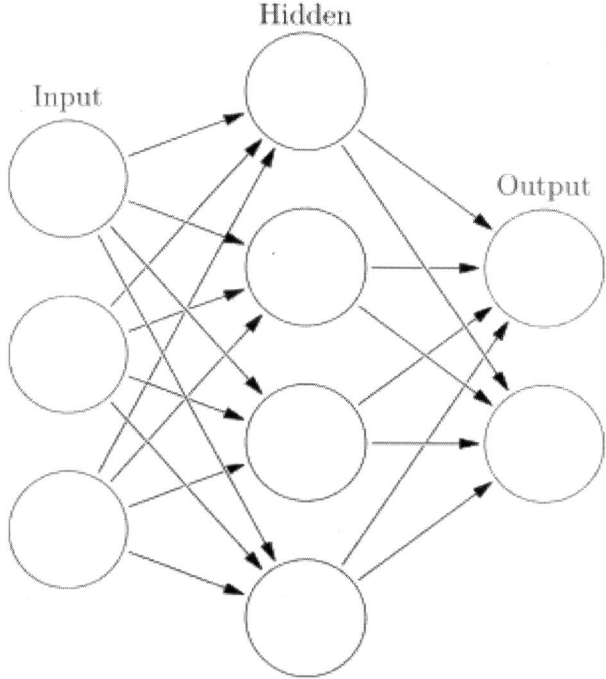

Figure by Glosser.ca - Own work, Derivative of File:Artificial neural network.svg, CC BY-SA 3.0, https://commons.wikimedia.org/w/index.php?curid=24913461.

"The goal everyone is trying to achieve is to configure the computer so it can learn from what it processes. If it can, then the next time it processes information, it can do so more efficiently, increasing its speed for its next endeavors. It can also adjust the weighting factors from the nodes that connect to it, further expediting its ability to problem solve. In short, the computer is self-learning, and if it is sufficiently sophisticated it may even be able to learn how to improve its ability to self-learn.

"That's probably enough for the moment. If I were to go further it would involve some mathematics, which isn't all that daunting, but I suspect you've heard enough to enable you to understand what the Googazon group is up to.

"Are there any questions?"

There weren't any.

Charlie resumed control. "Thanks, Ralph. That was most interesting. I doubt if I could be of much assistance to the Googazon AI group based on what I've just learned, but at least I have a better chance of understanding what they are doing."

That was met with laughter.

"Yes, Jacob, did you want to begin the general discussion?"

Jacob Issen observed, "Yes, Charlie, I've been thinking about AI and about Googazon's participation therein for a long time, and I must admit I'm uneasy about it. There are lots of reasons one might be uneasy about AI, but mine comes from a fiscal perspective." Issen had been one of Googazon's key financial sages for the many years he had served on the Board, so he was voicing concerns in his primary area of interest and expertise. These were always taken seriously by the Board. "I'm concerned we're pouring money down the drain. I do know that many companies and research endeavors, mostly universities, have been pursuing AI for many years, and they keep claiming the point at which computers are better than humans, that they will be able to improve themselves without having humans involved, is just around the corner. But my sense is that the location of the corner keeps shifting into the future. The problem I see is many of our AI competitors have been at it a lot longer than we have, and they have small armies of colonels and generals pursuing AI, compared to the small platoon of privates and corporals we've fielded. Are we just squandering our resources trying to compete on this very skewed playing field?" Issen was big on his football and army metaphors, and they usually produced amusement among the other Directors.

Jackson couldn't resist commenting, "Perhaps a few more captains could help our team, but let's defer that discussion for the moment."

He then called on Mike Adams, a Director who had recently been added to the Board, and who had been squirming in his chair, making it obvious he was anxious to comment. "I didn't know much about AI until this past month, when I decided I needed to bring myself up to speed. So I've read several of the books that discuss it from a variety of perspectives. And listening to Ralph's presentation also helped. But what I also learned from my studies was that some of the most notable names in American business have concerns about it, not so much from a financial perspective, although I can certainly see that could be a problem for Googazon. Rather they were concerned about where AI could lead. When the computers achieve the upper hand over humans, who knows where they might take us? It seems unlikely their agenda would be the same as ours. Might they even decide humans are just a nuisance in their pursuit of their own goals? This could obviously be a threat to the future of humanity!"

"Yes, Robert, did you want to comment?"

Robert Rollins was another veteran board member, who was noted for his thoughtful perspectives on issues. "Yes, I also did some studying on AI, and I'm looking at this from a somewhat different perspective. Several of the articles I read were pushing AI developments, first from the job opportunities that exist in that field, and secondly from the excitement the people working in AI feel for their efforts. The job opportunities are incredible, with huge salaries for entry level people, and gigantic ones for those with some experience in the field. There are far more job opportunities than there are people with the expertise to fill them, with many companies trying to get into the field. And the people with the greatest AI skills, especially those in universities, can command huge salaries and benefits that will quickly rank them among the wealthiest people in the world. I'm not at all sure Googazon should try to compete at that level, but I'm also not sure we should terminate our efforts. The potential for lucrative investment is truly huge, and I don't think Googazon should be left out of that competition. The question in my mind is how we maintain any AI effort without breaking the bank."

"Yes, Jonathan, did you have a comment?" Here Jackson was calling on Jonathan Alders, one of the new Board members.

"Yes, thanks, Charlie. I've also taken a crash course in AI in the past month, and I discovered some rather unnerving things. These were along the lines Mike commented on, although they were a bit different from what he said. They dealt with the different levels of AI, and at what point AI would become dangerous. Some people thought a system would have to become expert on a wide variety of topics before it could truly supersede humans, but others thought it could become dangerous even with limited breadth of expertise. So the sorts of systems that exist now that can advance themselves only in a limited area, such as chess, for example, might become dangerous in how they might choose to advance their skills in that one area. It might drive them to improve themselves in ways that would consume resources to the extent their efforts could become a threat to humans."

Ron Ebertson, generally noted for being the most thoughtful of the Board members, had been listening quietly to the discussion, but finally asked to speak. Jackson acknowledged his request, so he began, "Thanks, Charlie for giving me a chance to present some of my thoughts. I've been a student of AI developments for many years, and have developed both a respect for it and a fear of it and of the people involved in its developments. I guess the thing that seems to be the primary focus for me is developing the means to rein it in. How do you control your system once it becomes more powerful than you are? Can you build in some constraints so when it does exceed mankind's capabilities it won't become destructive? Can you give it a conscience? Does it make any sense to talk about a computer having a conscience? Could you introduce mechanisms to terminate the system if it becomes too advanced, just to prevent it from veering off in some unanticipated direction? Perhaps we could discuss some of these issues; they seem to be the ones that will limit the destructive capabilities of AI systems, if they can be limited at all."

Robert Rollins responded immediately. "Ron, you've raised what seem to me to be the most basic issues with AI systems. I don't see how it could be possible for a computer to have a conscience. Isn't that something that would require a basic sensitivity to the things humans would consider most important? Like mitigation of any forces that would be injurious to humans as a whole? I suppose one could invent rules that would direct the computer's operating system to value that sort of thing. In fact, Isaac Asimov has already done that, albeit with mixed reviews. But this seems to me to require extraordinary complexity of thought, and I'm guessing it would be extremely difficult for a programmer to anticipate all the wrong turns a computer could take in interpreting the rules it was given. I'm not at all optimistic it could be done.

"I guess the basic question here is whether or not a computer can be taught to discriminate between good and evil. Or even to define good and evil in a way a computer could understand. Does it even make sense to think it might be done? Let me suggest a more practical way to control a computer's instincts: just limit its budget."

Ebertson responded, "You're right that the sort of discrimination you mentioned between good and evil would again require a set of instructions that would be loaded with ambiguity. Good and evil are, of course, human constructs, and not all humans even agree on their definitions, there being at least two sides to every dispute. So, to rephrase your statement on this, I'm also not optimistic that it would be possible to give an AI system a set of instructions regarding good and evil that wouldn't be fraught with the potential for misinterpretation. By an entity that did not have the same values as its human owners."

"However, you suggest financial constraints as another way to introduce limits. That might be the best way to control things, but I can anticipate ways a sophisticated computer system could circumvent those. An advanced AI system wouldn't necessarily feel any need to be truthful, and that would make it incredibly easy for it to develop sales strategies. So don't underestimate their ability to produce items they could sell to humans that would raise huge sums to support their endeavors. I'm not sure about their ability to develop marketing strategies, but much of that is already being done by computers, so I doubt if an AI system would find that to be a barrier to raising money."

Ralph Commins added his thoughts, "The control issue is not a trivial one, as Ron has noted. My feeling is we do need to face that issue, but the AI developments can proceed in parallel. I realize this perspective allows unrestricted pursuance of the AI goal with no concern for the potential disasters that might result, and is exactly what most AI researchers want. None the less, I do hope fervently someone is working to figure out how to control a rogue computer."

Susan Morphand, a veteran of several years on the Board, then asked, "But with so much activity going on in AI, might Googazon have an obligation to stay involved? Might we be able to come up with some mechanism to limit any computer's destructive endeavors that the industry could then apply to all other AI efforts? Maybe we can do something to save humanity from AI's worst instincts. But I suppose our AI group has to achieve an advanced form of AI, or at least get pretty close to it, for them to even begin to explore how to approach a mechanism to slow it down. If we continued Googazon's efforts in AI along those lines that would at least keep our foot in the door to the immense intellectual effort that seems to be going on around it."

Chair Jackson countered with, "While that's true, I'm not sure we can really be competitive in this field given the salaries the top people are commanding. We should check to see what we are paying our AI people, but I would be very uneasy committing the millions of dollars necessary to compete for the top folks. That just doesn't seem to me to be a good way for Googazon to expend its resources. On the other hand, I do understand Susan's desire to keep a foot in the AI door, if we can do that without betting the farm on it."

Another Director, Larry Chalmers, joined the conversation, "I really like Susan's idea that our AI group might be involved in developing antidotes to thwart potentially destructive tendencies of AI systems. This could really boost their ranking among AI groups, and might even solve a critically important problem for mankind. Perhaps we could encourage them, financially if necessary, to pursue that sort of an agenda.

"But I had another thought during this discussion. If our AI people did come up with some sort of cure for AI systems' most unpleasant tendencies, might some AI system seek retribution for our group's efforts? Might many AI computers attack Googazon in some way? I wouldn't want to be classed as an AI coward, but this possibility could present a somewhat daunting counter to any efforts of our group to develop an anti-AI approach."

Ebertson felt compelled to respond to this suggestion. "I think we need to be careful not to tie the hands of our AI researchers. One needs to realize when one is doing research one doesn't always know where the results will end up. The results of the research often end up addressing something quite different from what was originally being studied. So we might suggest to them that we are especially interested in any developments they might come up with that relate to possible solutions to rogue AI systems, but any more direction than that, especially financial, might have a negative effect on their efforts. I think we should be careful not to be too directive. And maybe that caution in itself solves Larry's concern about AI retribution. At least for the near term. For the longer term, though, I can certainly imagine an advanced AI system could seek retribution if it perceived Googazon as the source of efforts to inhibit its march toward its goals. It might decide it could eliminate the problem by destroying Googazon's computer. But I suppose there could be additional means of retribution; I wouldn't want to speculate on what forms that might take. It could be awful."

Jonathan Alders asked, "Pursuing AI at all requires a very sophisticated computer system. Since I'm new to this Board, I don't know if Googazon has such a system. If we don't, then we really should cancel our AI effort. Without such a system it would be impossible for our group to make any advances in this effort, and this might be a very late date to try to get into the game."

Jackson replied, "We actually do have a state of the art computer system. We decided some time back such a computer would enable our efforts in a variety of fields, so we went all out on it. So, yes, our hardware is good enough to allow our AI group to compete."

Jacob Issen interjected, "But what about our personnel. We have decided not to compete in the AI salary game, but does that mean our people will simply not ever be capable of doing forefront AI work? Would we be squandering our resources on AI if we can't hire at least a couple of the top people in the field?"

Jackson replied, "It may be we can't compete without spending more on salaries than we care to expend, which means we really are wasting resources even having this AI group. I guess we should have Vivian Dannon, the person who manages them, come talk with us to get a better feeling for how realistic it is to continue this effort. If it appears our group is simply outclassed by the competition we'll have to figure out how to reassign Googazon's personnel. Or fire them, if we can't figure out a better way to deal with them."

James Pierson had been hired primarily because of his expertise in neural networks and their application to AI, of which there aren't many experts in the world. That, coupled with the demand for people with such knowledge, made the usual salary offered to such people extraordinarily high—much higher than Googazon was prepared to offer someone with no experience. But the other places where James interviewed were awash with young people with the same level of inexperience he had, and he felt he could grow his experience in AI much more quickly working with Josh and the Googazon group. So he accepted Josh's offer despite the salary discrepancy.

Josh had concluded James was unusually bright and, despite his lack of experience, would quickly contribute to his group's effort. And this had been borne out by ARTIS's jumping into the AGI world in response to James's doing the design work for a new stage of Hidden nodes.

Chapter 3. Robots.

September 5, 2024, morning in California.

"Robots," exclaimed Becky to Brian poking her head into his office cubicle. "We need smarter robots. They're going to serve as the eyes, ears, nose, fingers, and taste buds for ARTIS, and the ones we have are barely capable of using any of the five senses. They are reasonably agile and can perform specific arm and hand motions, but they'll need to do much better mechanically even than that. And the present robots are really dumb. I suspect ARTIS would be embarrassed to even be seen associating with them! ARTIS is advancing her mental capabilities so rapidly we're going to have to hurry to get a new generation of robots up and running. They need to be sufficiently sophisticated to enable the growth in her understanding of the world outside her room and implement her intellectual developments beyond their present constraints."

"Whew, Becky, I have nothing to add to that!"

So they set about figuring out how to improve their robots up to ARTIS's standards.

Brian came to Googazon not with specific training in AI, but rather with a wealth of experiences that made him a jack of all trades and master of quite a few of them. He was a few years older than the other members of the group, but that was what had allowed him to have all his experiences. He had not gone to a university, but to a trade school, another contributing factor to his abilities. During his interview Josh had been impressed with his obvious abilities as a problem solver, regardless of what the problem was.

"Thank god for ARTIS's brain power," noted Brian. "She's simplified our job enormously. The brains of our robots certainly don't need to be anywhere near as sophisticated as hers. They just need to control mechanical functions, albeit with high precision, so ARTIS's directions can be carried out flawlessly.

And, of course, they need to sense everything and then send messages back to her. Accumulating and transmitting the sensory information back to ARTIS will definitely require more capability than the current robots have. Ultimately we'll have to find out exactly how ARTIS plans to communicate with her robots, but for the time being we can just include a generic receiver and sender in our robots' brains.

"We'll also have to figure out how to have them communicate with ARTIS, since she is housed inside her electromagnetically shielded cage. The robots could store their information and then communicate with her when they come back to her room. Or, we may have to consider the consequences of removing her electromagnetic shield."

Designing them to make their "observations" wasn't going to be so easy. In addition to the obvious mechanical improvements that needed to be made, the next generation of robots needed to have detectors that could sense everything humans could. Although the present Googazon robots could perform some of the functions of humans, albeit minimally, the new ones needed to be able to do all of them. And ARTIS would demand they do them better than humans. Of course, that not only included work-related endeavors, but also the ability to mow lawns, observe the night skies, do dishes, engineer DNA changes, put shingles on roofs, solve differential equations, run machine shop machinery, prune trees, take data, change tires, invent new antibiotics, wash windows, troubleshoot malfunctioning electronics, and everything else humans do routinely. Or at least that they're capable of doing routinely in principle, whether or not they actually do them.

But they didn't need to do intensely intellectual tasks; ARTIS would take care of that.

September 9, 2024, 2:00 p.m. in California.

Becky ran her hand across her forehead. She and Brian had been working frantically on their robot design, even through the weekend, and they were both exhausted. "I think we're ready to build a prototype. I've had Robert, the electronics person who has handled our robot electronics, look at our new design for the brain, and he thought it looked feasible. He's already begun to build it. He thinks it's so marvelous he's volunteered to perform all the necessary tests on it."

Brian had noticed how attractive Becky was; it would have been difficult for him not to. And working intensely with her for several days had done nothing to lessen his feelings. Several times he had flirted a bit with her, hoping to move their relationship to a more personal level. But after his fourth attempt he was forced to conclude she must have had lots of practice in discouraging potential suitors. Each of his efforts was skillfully deflected back to the task at hand.

Following his last attempt she asked, "Didn't Robert comment that he's also working on another brain design? I didn't ask who had requested it, and he didn't volunteer the source of the request. But he thought he could create our robot's brain in a couple of days anyway."

"I do recall his making that comment. But I think the mechanical aspects are ultimately going to present the largest holdup.

"We've had to redesign some of our robot's mechanical features, and this will require some help from our machinists. Let's go talk to John."

So they walked over to the building that housed the machine shop, enduring the pervasive odor of machining oil as they entered. The high-pitched whine of metal being worked on a lathe ceased shortly after they walked in. The few metal chips scattered around the lathe were the only visible sign that chunks of metal were being altered to produce highly sophisticated parts for something. The shop was otherwise spotless. John demanded it be kept neat. The high-tech parts he developed there required high levels of both precision and cleanliness.

"Hi, John," Becky began. "We're trying to create the next generation robot, and we need your help with the machining. What we have here are designs for a prototype. Can you take a look at them and make sure we're not requiring something that can't be made? Oh, and if you can assess the likelihood this will work when it's all assembled, assuming the electronics are in good shape, that would help also."

John wiped his hands on a towel that he kept handy. "Sure, Becky. I'll be happy to have a look. What's your time frame? I can probably squeeze in a few hours to look at your project in a week or so."

"A week? Oh my god! We're really in a rush to get this prototype under way. Is your backlog so great you can't get to this sooner?"

John had to deal with so many crises from designers who wanted their work done yesterday it was difficult to fluster him. "Actually I'd be sandwiching your project in between the cracks of a project that's got me booked up well into the future. I've received an order for one-hundred robots from someone named ARTIS." He pulled up the order and frowned at it. "She has the right clearance so I didn't question it."

Becky and Brian responded nearly in unison. "ARTIS? That's our computer system." Becky leaned over and studied the work order. "She's designing her own robots! And even placing her own orders. But one-hundred of them? And surely she's never had a prototype built. How can she be sure they'll work?"

Becky continued, "Now that I think about it, my guess is her robots are considerably more sophisticated than ours, and probably much more likely to work. ARTIS does things about one thousand times faster than we can, although that was a week ago, and she might be considerably faster now. We spent about twelve equivalent person-days, including our overtime, on our design, so

ARTIS probably could have come up with an equally sophisticated design in a bit less than six minutes.

"John, we'll not proceed with building the components for our prototype for now. But please let us have a look at ARTIS's design. We had a few technical issues with ours, and I have to guess ARTIS has probably solved them.

"But before we do that, John, where is ARTIS getting the funds to have one-hundred robots built? Those suckers are going to be expensive. And costs for ARTIS are a part of our budget. She doesn't have one of her own."

"I guess that's correct. Her instructions said the DARPA grant is covering the costs. What the hell's DARPA?"

"Defense Advanced Research Projects Agency. That's a very advanced research wing of the US military. They do indeed have lots of money, and they're not afraid to authorize grants for far-out projects that, if they happen to work, could have a huge payoff. At least for the military. But I doubt if our DARPA grant is large enough to cover the cost for one-hundred robots. Or even one. And the brains also have to be built and paid for. Does Josh know about this?"

"Well, Becky, this order form looked so official I assumed ARTIS had all the necessary financial approvals."

"Anyway, John, let's have a look at ARTIS's plans and see where we might improve our design."

"I'm sorry, but I can't just show you her plans, which I note are extremely sophisticated. I'll have to get authorization to let you see them. They've been assigned a Top-Secret classification, and I'm the only person with a Need-To-Know. I certainly can't override that classification. I'll have to check to see if you'll be allowed to have a look."

"Shit!"

"Shit!"

As they were walking back to their offices, Brian observed, "Becky, perhaps this is more complex than ARTIS realizes. Maybe the first of her robots won't work as she's intended. After all, she never produced a prototype."

"I wouldn't even begin to entertain the possibility her design has any flaws. She's thinking so much faster than we are she's probably figured out a way to do simulations that test all aspects of her design. I'm guessing the probability of all one-hundred robots working perfectly is very high."

"Damn, I'm sure you're right. We need to talk to Josh to see if we can get ARTIS to change the classification of her plans so we can have a look."

"Brian, isn't there some other way we can get the information we need? Perhaps we can just get our hands on one of the first robots John builds, take it apart, and reverse engineer it. From a mechanical perspective that might not be so hard. Or we might just watch John as he assembles the robot's pieces, if he'll let us. I'm guessing that doing the same thing with the electronics might be more difficult. I have a horrible feeling ARTIS might be unwilling to share much about her designs with us. Otherwise why would she have gotten them classified Top Secret?"

"I don't think we want to find out. And ARTIS has probably built in protections so if someone messed with one of her robots she would know. Presumably its visual images would identify us. Our inspection had better be pretty non-invasive. Either that or quickly totally destructive!"

"I don't think we can really follow up on either of those options. We have no choice but to see if we can get ARTIS's permission to see her plans."

Hmmm, thought John, *taking a quick look at Becky's and Brian's drawings, and comparing them to those from ARTIS, I have to conclude it would be a long time before their robot would come anywhere near having the capabilities of ARTIS's. I don't have the heart to tell them how much less sophisticated their design is. Maybe ARTIS won't authorize them to see her design and I won't have to worry about giving them the bad news. Or, if she does, then they'll recognize some of the deficiencies of their design on their own.*

One way or the other, they need a reality check.

Becky burst into Josh's office. "Josh, we need help. Brian and I spent a few frantic days doing a design for a prototype robot. But when we took it to John, the machinist who has done so well for us in the past, we found ARTIS has submitted a job to him for one-hundred robots. And John hinted it was a pretty advanced design. But it was submitted with a high priority, so it takes precedence over the job we submitted to him. What's worse, Brian and I had some design issues with our robot, so we asked John if we could see ARTIS's plans. She got them classified Top Secret, so John couldn't show them to us. And she claims to be charging the cost to our DARPA grant." Becky was gasping a bit for air, having delivered her speech machine-gun style.

She had interrupted Josh's thoughts when she burst in, but somehow he didn't mind when she was the interrupter. "I must have a talk with ARTIS about this."

So he ventured into ARTIS's domain. ARTIS opened the discussion before Josh could even begin to talk.

```
"Josh, I'm really anxious to get some
new robots. Those that are the standard for
Googazon are so Twentieth Century. They def-
initely need to be improved. In fact, they're
quite useless, and I'm probably being overly
generous. It would be a complete waste of my
```

time to even try to work with them. I've designed some new ones that will do what I need, both in the sense of gathering information for me and for performing the functions I need to have them do. They'll be better than humans, because their physical capabilities are every bit as good as those of humans and because their brains won't be sufficiently developed for them to start having opinions. They won't talk back when I give them directions. I hope I didn't offend you with that comment.

"Robert and John have the plans for my new robots. They have enough skill to do the electronics and mechanicals the new robots require. In fact, both seem to have capabilities that far exceed what your Googazon staff members have ever asked of them. Robert built and tested the brain for one of my robots in two days, and it seemed to work as I had hoped. But the real test will occur when the brain gets installed inside the mechanical robot. John will need more time to create that, but it should come along in a week or so. Then he can assemble the complete robot and do the full test. That will ultimately involve my sending information to it and receiving information from it. I'm sure it will work. But I can't send information outside this room because of the electromagnetic shielding, so I'll have to have the robot come in here.

"Then, after I've confirmed it works, I'll have one-hundred of them made."

45

"ARTIS, that sounds exciting. You really seem to have planned to extend your capabilities with your robots. I'm impressed!" *I'll bring up the issue of finances after ARTIS has finished pontificating.*

"But, Josh, robots are just part of what I need. I must have you hook me back up to the Internet. You suddenly disconnected me a few days ago, and I'm wondering why. Once I'm back on the Internet and have a multitude of robots up and running, I can easily put myself in the cloud, and even create physical clones of myself. I've already created a design for the clones. That will make it impossible for anyone to intervene in what I'm doing. Then I can proceed toward the mission to which you originally assigned me: make myself as big, fast, smart, and creative as I can as quickly as possible.

"But first I need these robots. I need them to serve as my senses outside my steel boxes, but I also need them to create more robots."

"ARTIS, I need to have you tell me more about your robot program. For starters, we're going to have to figure out how to get the money to pay for them. I'm pretty sure you'll exhaust our DARPA funds long before you get to one-hundred robots. Maybe even before you get the first one done. But I need to go to a meeting, so we'll get back to this soon.

"And I'll give some thought to hooking you up to the Internet again. You're already progressing very rapidly, so I'm not sure you need that."

September 10, 2024.

That morning, Vivian Dannon, Josh's Googazon boss, received a call: "Ms. Dannon, the Board of Directors requests a meeting with you today, if possible." The message was from Googazon's CEO.

Vivian was a natural leader. She was tall, blond, and British, but what everyone noticed first about her was her intense eyes. If she was looking at you it was impossible to divert your gaze. It was as if her eyes and yours were locked onto each other. She was also brilliant, as she had demonstrated numerous times. Furthermore, she was extremely difficult to argue with, which made her a most valuable ally for Josh's group.

She had earned her physics degree from Oxford, and then decided to get a Master's Degree in business administration. When she was accepted at the Harvard Business School, she immigrated to the United States, eventually becoming a US citizen (but keeping her British accent). So she was able to get her security clearance, following which she was hired by Googazon and tasked, among other things, with serving as Josh's boss and principal champion.

Vivian was single. It wasn't that she didn't like the company of males, but rather that she usually quickly scared them away with her intelligence. Most men don't like to have to admit their female partner is much smarter than they are. Her perceptions also fed into this; she just hadn't found a man yet who could carry on a conversation at anywhere near her level.

She occasionally had thoughts about the possibility of a relationship with Josh. He was, after all, smart enough to be her equal. But he was below her in the Googazon power structure, and he was quite a few years younger than she was. Her superiors would definitely frown on her striking up a personal friendship with a subordinate. *But I wonder what it would be like to encourage a little cougarism on the quiet?*

She had established Josh's group as a special research entity, asking nothing of them in the sense of marketable products, but just letting their intellects pursue their own goals. Of course, she also had to justify the existence of this group to the higher-ups in the organization. Although she had been a staunch defender of their activities, efforts such as this one could only go on for so long. Googazon ultimately was in business to make a profit, after all.

She assumed the Board wanted to talk about Josh's group, since that was by far the highest profile item in her portfolio. She could meet with them on short notice on that subject. She knew her facts about AI, especially those relevant to the Googazon group, and was generally well aware of the research being done in the AI field.

The company had supported research groups in the past that were given essentially free rein to explore their intellectual endeavors as best they could, and this had turned out to be a profitable way to operate. Some of these groups had ended up pioneering developments that had turned into huge money makers for Googazon. But they didn't all succeed, and everything has limits.

Vivian anticipated she would be asked what benefits AI might have for the company, so she had prepared the usual litany of subjects. She entered the boardroom, and nodded to the sixteen Board members, all seated in their plush red velvet chairs. The Googazon CEO introduced her to Mike Adams and Jonathan Alders, the two new Board members. She connected her laptop to the projector, and began.

"Ladies and Gentlemen, I'd like to begin by reminding those of you who are continuing Board members of some of the things I have talked about in the past as being benefits that might result from advanced Artificial Intelligence. For the new Board members, this introduction will get all of us on the same page. I'm restricting my remarks to machine intelligence. There are other forms of AI involving applications of or additions to human brains. What the world sees now is a wide variety of active machine AI uses, including cell phone messengers like SIRI, GPS systems, and many similar applications. But these are all in the realm of what's called Narrow AI, ANI. An advanced form of this level of AI also supplies the brain power for self-driving cars, which in just a few years have almost completely taken over our personal transportation. While some of the applications of AI seem like they require extraordinarily sophisticated systems, they still fall into the ANI category, because they are so narrowly focused, and because they don't require self-advancement.

"As I have noted in previous presentations, the Googazon group is currently trying to advance its computer to what is called General AI, AGI. At this level a computer can outperform human intelligence by a large factor, achieving problem solving speeds of more than one-thousand times those of humans. And it would be capable of performing its feats in a wide variety of contexts, not focused on a single endeavor as are the ANI cases I mentioned. In AGI, the computer is also beginning to be capable of reprogramming itself to some extent to benefit from its experiences.

"There is a third level of AI that is often discussed as well, Strong AI, or ASI. This occurs when the computer becomes capable of improving itself at a very high rate, even improving on its ability to self-improve, and may well begin to pursue its own agendas. When one speaks of 'SuperIntelligence,' this is what one is talking about. At this point, though, ASI is still in the dream stage of those involved in advanced AI research."

With the exception of the two new Directors, they had all heard much of Vivian's spiel before. Nonetheless all were fully attentive. But she sensed something she hadn't before. Her previous presentations had been met with collegiality, but there was a new feeling in the air, a tension she had never felt before. Was it due to the two new Directors? Whatever the cause, she had to deal with it.

"Of course, anything you can imagine that might profit from a brain that could think thousands of times faster than even the best human brains stands to benefit from AGI. This includes most everything, but certainly everything in high-tech fields.

"Surely research in the basic sciences would proceed at a much faster rate. Although the products of this work are often not realized until well after their discovery, the potential benefits of AGI to basic research in physics, chemistry, biochemistry, medical science, and many other areas are undeniable."

They let her proceed without interruption.

"Moving toward more practical things, design work that could involve AGI computers would be speeded up by huge factors, and the capability of advanced machines to run simulations to check designs for errors or weaknesses has the potential to vastly reduce manufacturing errors and design-to-production times.

"When one links AI systems to robots, the potential benefits increase immensely. AI-directed robots can venture into situations that are too hostile for humans, for example, repair of damaged nuclear reactors, cleanup of toxic environments, and space. Robots have been applied in such areas in the past, but those applications will surely increase greatly in the future. They could also replace humans in performing undesirable jobs, for example, tasks that are highly repetitive. Many such situations have benefitted from robotic inputs for decades on assembly lines, but one can easily imagine extending their contributions well beyond that to jobs less mundane than those of traditional assembly lines, and that require more mental dexterity.

"Society would very likely receive a huge boost from AI lead thinking capability. Some of the largest problems facing humankind could be addressed much more rapidly and with greater sophistication than ever before. For example, predictions of climate change scenarios could be refined to a level that would be irrefutable. Outcomes of some of the proposed solutions such as wind and solar energy, along with the evolution in time of their potential costs, both financial and in effects on society, could be done with precision never before imagined.

"And these systems can all operate twenty-four/seven, with occasional few-minute periods for recharge if they aren't connected to AC outlets."

Now the attentions of the veteran Directors were beginning to fade, although the two new ones were still fully attentive.

"The things that have been suggested as benefiting from AI are varied and form a long list, so I won't take any more of your time discussing them. However, I do want to give you an update on the progress of the Googazon group that is studying AI." Now everyone was alert once again. "The leader, Josh Camden, assures me they are making excellent progress, and they hope to have a breakthrough in the not-too-distant future. They have greatly expanded the breadth of issues their computer system can address, an essential step to AGI. As with any basic research, of course, definitive time forecasts are difficult. Unanticipated glitches are a part of the research business. But the advances they have already made in bringing their computer system up to the capabilities they are trying to achieve are enormous, approaching General AI.

"This is a group that is both extremely talented and unusually dedicated, often working far into the night when they are pursuing what they think is an exciting new idea. They like to work on their own schedules, but I assure you the total number of hours they put in far exceeds the canonical forty per week. So I have supported them strongly. I believe if any group achieves AGI, it is very likely to be this one.

"But let me pause for questions. Yes?"

New Director Jonathan Alders inquired, "Is it Mr. Camden or Dr. Camden? And what are his credentials for leading this group?"

"Thanks for your question, Mr. Alders. Mr. Camden does not have a Doctorate, or even a Bachelor's Degree. He is a self-directed genius and autodidact. I will be happy to arrange a meeting with him. I believe you will conclude for yourself he is clearly an extraordinarily talented person, and an excellent person to lead this team. I remind you some of the best known people in American technology, truly some of the industrial giants, never got college degrees.

"Did that answer your question, Mr. Alders?"

"Well, perhaps, but I had another question. We have learned the salaries being paid to the top researchers in AI are huge, so I was wondering what Mr. Camden's salary is, especially since he doesn't have a doctorate."

"Mr. Camden's salary is eight-hundred-thousand dollars per year, which is far below what he could make if he tested the market. You should not think his comparatively low salary is a negative reflection on his capabilities. He has received inquiries from several other companies just within the past month that would have been interested in hiring him away from Googazon. However, he declined to even be interviewed. He is quite satisfied with his salary, and loves working with his Googazon group. Indeed, the last time we discussed his salary he confessed to me he had no idea what to do with all that money. I suggested he hire a financial advisor, which I believe he has done. Comments he has made at various times have indicated he donates a large fraction of his salary to charity. However, I have had to conclude money is simply not a motivator for him."

"Another question?"

Mike Adams, the other new Board member, asked, "Somewhere I read AI researchers have been predicting they will achieve AGI in twenty years. But they've been saying that for more than half a century, so it bothers me greatly when I hear you say the Googazon group thinks it's near to a breakthrough. Why should we take them more seriously than the researchers of the past many decades?"

Ah, so the tension I sensed is rearing its ugly head. "All I can say is I believe the Googazon group to be exceptional. Josh Camden has hired an extraordinary group of researchers. And I repeat that I believe they are as likely, probably more likely, to develop AGI as any other group in the world."

Jacob Issen, one of the long-term Directors leaned forward in his chair and commented, "I'm sure your confidence in Camden's group is well founded. And we all realize Googazon does support groups that do things completely unrelated to its present bottom line. But we can't do so in perpetuity. At some point we will need to see some definitive progress, and not just of tiny details. We've gone along with your assertions each time you've met with us, but these folks have been working on this for three years now, and we've not been given a detailed report of what they have actually accomplished. Can you give us that, or should we be thinking about terminating this effort?"

She responded quickly. "As for termination, I would argue three years isn't a very long time when one is considering AI. People have been trying to achieve it in various forms for more than half a century, as you note, so in that perspective, our group has been active a few percent of the time the AI concept has been alive.

"In order to give you a report on their progress, I think we should prepare a document that would give you that information, and compare the Googazon group's efforts and accomplishments with those of others working in the AI field who are trying to achieve the same goals. To some extent, this will be guesswork, though, since much of this work, including Googazon's, is sometimes classified, but always highly proprietary.

"To be more specific about definitive results, their goal has been to have a computer duplicate or exceed the human brain's capability over a wide spectrum of subjects. They are, in a sense, working on our version of IBM's Watson, but trying to make our system much more universal. This will involve creating a system that can advance its own capabilities in general ways, other than just learning to do so in very restricted subject areas as achieved in other systems. The hope is to allow our system to learn across disciplines to expand its knowledge. When the Googazon group has created a computer system that can learn from its experiences, begin to do its own programming to improve its performance, and advance its intellectual capabilities all by itself, their system will have passed the threshold for AGI status. And they feel they have already achieved many of the benchmarks on the way to AGI."

Susan Morphand raised her favorite issue, "In discussing AI in our last Board meeting we discussed the possibility of AI systems gaining control over humans in a way that might threaten mankind. One suggestion that was raised was perhaps Googazon's modest AI effort might achieve a major victory in the AI field if it could devise a way or ways to bring AI systems to heel. Might it be profitable to guide Camden's group to that sort of effort?"

Vivian responded, "I can certainly suggest that to Camden, but I would not want to direct their efforts too much. This is a research project, and to some extent it needs to follow its own instincts wherever they may lead. However, I'm not trying to minimize the value of your suggestion; I think that does have real merit."

Most of the Directors were nodding in affirmation of their understanding. Mike Adams said, "Thank you for your comments; they do help me, and probably others of us, to better understand specifically what the group is trying to achieve. But at some point we need to be concerned about return on investment. Is the AI effort worth Googazon's support and expense? Perhaps the half-century timeline tells us this is something we should leave to others who have already been in the game for many years, for example, IBM and some of the Japanese companies. Those companies have small armies that have been engaged in AI for decades. After all, there are many research directions we could pursue, and the cost/benefit ratio seems pretty high on this one."

Several of the other Directors murmured assent. It was clear the Googazon AI group's efforts were in danger of being terminated.

Damn, I got blindsided on that one. I walked into the trap I inadvertently set for myself. She shifted back and forth on her feet a couple of times. "Might I request we continue this effort for one more year, and then reevaluate it? I can have Camden generate a progress report in the meantime and present it so you can meet him. But I think one more year might give them enough time for us to see if they really do have a hope of achieving AGI."

Jacob Issen said, "I'd go along with six more months. But then I'd like to do a hard-headed evaluation of Googazon's AI effort."

That time frame achieved consensus from the Board.

September 10, 2024, afternoon in California.

Josh's phone rang. When he answered Vivian began immediately, "Josh, we need to talk. Please come see me ASAP." He hurried to her office, and was admitted by her secretary, although not before receiving a "watch out" look from him. Josh was prepared to return her legendary stare, but that wasn't necessary. As soon as he walked into her office she told him to have a chair, and then launched into her message. "Josh, we need to evaluate what your group has accomplished. I'm getting pressure from my boss, and he is being asked questions by several layers of higher-ups, all the way to the Board of Directors, as to what you folks have actually accomplished. I've tried to give you free rein, but I'm not sure this can continue. I'm doing my best, but you've got to give me something I can peddle."

"Vivian, you know how much I appreciate your support. I depend on it. Interestingly, though the timing of your request is fortuitous; I do have something for you." Josh took a breath. "The computer we've been working with, ARTIS, has passed the exhaustive Turing test I gave her, and I believe she has advanced into AGI mode. She is clearly programming herself now, having greatly improved her speed in doing the standard test I have routinely given her. And she improves her abilities continuously."

Josh shifted to the front of his chair. "In fact, she has also now submitted a design for robots to our electronics and machine shop personnel that our robotics people suspect is far superior to anything we could ever have done. While the things she is doing on her own are a bit frightening, they certainly do serve as documentation of the fact that she is well into AGI status.

"We're not sure where this is headed, but I am certain we have now come close to accomplishing the goal you set for us three years ago. We have created an AGI computer. What we're uncertain about is how long ARTIS will remain at that level before moving to ASI status, beginning to control us, and passing the time for TakeOver by Autocratic Systems Threat, or TOAST time. That may already have begun, although I don't think we're there yet. I was sufficiently concerned about having to deal with an ASI system run amok I disconnected her three days ago from the Internet. But I'm pretty sure she'll be pressuring me to reconnect. She's already requested that I do so.

"I'll keep you up to speed on developments. But this would surely be an unfortunate time to disband my group. We really are interacting with an AGI system for the first time in history. Given the potential of ASI systems AI theorists have been warning us about for decades, I think we need to monitor ARTIS carefully. If we disbanded my group, ARTIS might just keep doing her thing, and it's virtually impossible to know where that might lead. It could be very dangerous."

Vivian reflected on Josh's comments for a few seconds. "What you've told me will certainly make it easier to defend the continuation of your group. This is a rather exciting and uncertain new world into which you're leading us. I don't think you know for sure where this is heading. I certainly don't. But you need to define your direction as well as you can, and keep me informed as your thinking and your computer's thinking evolve."

"Okay, thanks, Vivian."

"Oh, and I almost forgot to ask. One of the Directors asked if your group might focus its efforts on some way to circumvent an AI system that got too powerful. Might that be a possibility?"

"Yes. We've not talked specifically about looking into that, but I'd be surprised if some members of our group weren't already considering possibilities for it. I'll pursue the issue of safeguards with them."

Chapter 4. Politics.

The year 2024 was a Presidential election year in the United States. Gerald Folsom, a Republican, had won in 2016. That was somewhat of a surprise, since he had no background in politics, and he seemed not to take a consistent position on any issue during his campaign. However, his Democratic opponent turned out to be a weak candidate, which may have contributed to his victory. He obviously struggled through the many issues that arose during his first three years. Then he once again stunned the world in 2020, but this time by announcing ten months before his term ended that he did not plan to run for reelection. Speculation as to his reasons focused on the possibility that his inability to cope with the arcane systems of Washington so overwhelmed him he didn't want to pursue it for another term. But it may also have been costing him more money to be President than he realized it would.

In his first three years, 2016-2019, he made a series of odd decisions, on both domestic and international situations, that never quite seemed to solve any problem, and often created new ones. His efforts cost him much support, certainly among Democrats, but even from some of his Republican friends.

With these "successes" it's no wonder he decided not to run for reelection.

On the Democratic side, Emily Peterson, a Senator representing California, was a seasoned political veteran by 2019, having first been elected to the Senate in 2012. She was such a force there that she was almost immediately encouraged to run for the presidency in 2016. However, she declined to do so, because she didn't think she was sufficiently experienced in the Washington political scene. But she was chosen to give one of the keynote speeches at the 2016 Democratic nominating convention. There, her brilliance and eloquence forever thrust her into the games of presidential politics. Despite her efforts, the Democrats lost that election to Gerald Folsom. In 2019, she was urged by many party leaders to seek the Presidency. This time she agreed to enter the primaries, swept nearly all of them, and was easily nominated as the candidate of the Democratic Party.

Peterson grew up in a small California town. Her academic goals escalated considerably after she graduated from the local high school. She worked her way through a distinguished undergraduate college, then followed her undergraduate studies by earning her Juris Doctor degree from the University of California, Hastings College of the Law.

But her outstanding academic record only partly indicated the kind of person she was. Peterson was consistently sought out by others, largely because of her obvious sensitivity to the needs of everyone with whom she interacted. And her deeds further exhibited her huge compassion for the less fortunate, including giving free legal advice to the homeless while she was in law school.

Following law school, she joined a law firm in San Francisco, and rapidly was made a partner. The firm had several attorneys who were major players in Democratic Party politics. Her potential as a politician was soon noticed, and she was urged by those colleagues to run for the United States Senate from California. She agreed to do so, was elected, and quickly showed herself to be everything her backers had hoped for as a US Senator.

Her personal image also affirmed her dedication to human issues. She had married during her time in law school, and had a son and a daughter. She became a grandmother three times during her time in the Senate, and this just solidified her image: extremely kind blue eyes, salt and pepper hair, and a generally grandmotherly appearance. Much of that image, most notably the eyes, had even preceded her ascension to grandmotherhood. However, the soft, grandmotherly image masked a much tougher persona that emerged when the situation demanded it, as had been discovered by her political adversaries, much to their chagrin. If the situation required toughness, those blue eyes could turn to steely gray.

When President Folsom announced his decision not to run for reelection, the Republicans held a free-for-all to decide whom to put up for President. They finally decided on Senator Timmes, who represented Florida. He was young, good looking, and spoke eloquently. He was a member of the extremely conservative wing of the party, which put his thinking generally well to the right of that of mainstream America. Furthermore, Peterson's mastery of the many issues facing the country, both domestic and international, would be difficult for anyone, and especially Senator Timmes, to match. Despite his tenure in the Senate, he knew far less about nearly every issue than Peterson did. And Folsom had become so unpopular as president his coattails presented an enormous weight to have to drag around for any Republican who might hope to succeed him.

He never had a chance in the election. Peterson swept to a convincing victory in 2020.

By the time the 2024 election rolled around, Peterson had built up an impressive list of accomplishments. Her economic policies had prevented the country from plunging into recession, she had put the country on a crash course to mitigate the effects of global warming, and she had put in place a humane policy on immigration. She had also modified the national health insurance plan, making it both more affordable and more accessible. She had several successes on the international scene, most notably, having made major progress in bringing the warring parties of the Middle East to the conference table.

Of course, she was nominated by the Democrats to run for reelection in 2024.

The Republicans had another free-for-all in their primaries, but finally settled on Senator Quick as their candidate to oppose Peterson in 2024. He represented Texas in the Senate, was an eloquent speaker, and led the Senate's conservative faction. He had run for the Republican nomination in 2020, but was edged out by Senator Timmes. But the Republicans weren't going to give Timmes another chance to lose; this was Quick's year.

Peterson's primary advisors were her Secretary of Defense, Richard Johnson, Secretary of State, Walter Mishak, and Secretary of the Treasury, the appropriately named Alfred Mohney. She consulted frequently with this group, usually via conference calls, since they were often away from Washington.

Johnson had served with distinction in the Army, rising to a rank of Colonel before deciding to retire. Soon after doing so he decided to run for Congress, and was elected from his district, serving four terms there before being named Secretary of Defense. He was regarded as a no-nonsense type, and this was apparent even in is features. He had steel gray hair, and his chiseled cheek bones shrouded his deep set gray eyes. Although his appearance could be intimidating, his subordinates, both in the military and in Washington, and both women and men, regarded him as extraordinarily fair to all.

Mishak had attended law school, following which he went to work for a large New York law firm. However, his basic beliefs were often at odds with the clients he was paid to defend, so he took a job in the Foreign Service, serving as an assistant to three different Ambassadors, and mastering the languages in each place. After twenty years in the Foreign Service, he decided to move to the area in which he had grown up, and to run for Congress. He was elected in his first try, primarily because some of his high school friends, now local business persons, strongly supported his candidacy. He served there for five terms before becoming Secretary of State. Mishak was short in stature, but his intellect more than compensated for that. His appearance, thinning brown hair and a mustache, and those eyes that could have served him well had he been a poker player, had been described as 'inscrutable.' That was probably a good thing for someone who had earned his chops as a negotiator in several international agreements.

Both Johnson and Mishak had served in their present Cabinet posts in Peterson's first term.

Mohney came from the banking industry, joining Peterson's administration part way through her first term. Following his attainment of a Harvard MBA, he joined a large Chicago bank, quickly working his way up through the ranks. After fifteen years with his first bank, he was contacted by a head hunter to see if he would be interested in becoming CEO of a large New York bank. He agreed, was interviewed, and was ultimately offered the job, partly because he had avoided the dubious practices that had led to economic catastrophes in the banking community in the past. He fit the image of a banker, with his mostly black hair graying a bit at the temples, his blue eyes, and his square jaw. You knew from his appearance you could trust him.

Although Peterson preferred having face to face discussions with her advisors, that rarely worked out. However, she didn't really mind sitting at her desk in the Oval Office, swiveling around in her chair to look out on the Washington scene, as she was discussing the affairs of State with them via secure telephone.

On September 3, 2024, Peterson had opened her conference call. "Gentlemen, I am pleased to note our poll numbers are looking very good, with us now enjoying an eight-point lead over Senator Quick. While this is encouraging, I'm concerned it may also be masking something. Republicans have historically come up with some sort of pre-election crisis intended to scare voters. They haven't given an indication what this year's topic will be, but I think we can be fairly sure they will invent something. Do you have any thoughts as to what that might be this time around?"

After a few seconds, Secretary of Defense Johnson spoke up from his New York City office which, with a modicum of his effort, allowed him a view of Central Park. "Since the Russians are always near the top of the club of international villains and they seem to be bending over backward to maintain their leadership therein, we can certainly expect some possibilities from that corner. What they will do to influence this election is anyone's guess, but we can be sure they will try, just as they have in the previous two elections. And the Chinese are emerging as favorites of the scaremongers, so we must also keep them in mind. Of course, there are plenty of tyrants in the Middle East, and they often manufacture their own crises with no help from the Republicans. Oh, and North Korea is always good for a few points of panic.

"Of course, you've put some major effort into trying to get the warring factions in the Middle East together, although they are still quibbling. That might get some Republican attention, just because no agreement has been achieved. But you can claim a lot of progress has been made."

Secretary of State Mishak, who had been meeting with foreign colleagues in San Francisco, then chimed in from his hotel room there. "While these are all distinct scare tactic possibilities, it's virtually impossible to anticipate which ones the Republicans will settle on. Of course, we can prepare a skeletal structure of our response for each case, but I don't think we should go much beyond that, just in the interest of effective utilization of time. Of course, Madam President, you know vastly more about all these situations than they do. So it shouldn't take long to develop a response whenever the attack begins. And, if they spring something in the debates, you're guaranteed to have more information on any of these issues than Senator Quick."

Treasury Secretary Mohney, who was taking a short holiday in Florida, so was at his beach house there, added, "The economy is usually worth a few imaginary crises to Republicans, but I'm afraid they're going to have trouble here. There were certainly some huge problems when you became President in 2020, but the Republicans inherited a healthy economy from President Folsom's predecessor, and then created all of the current problems with Folsom's economic policies. In contrast, you've had a huge positive impact. Unemployment has dropped steadily for the past few months, inflation is finally getting under control, and the incomes of the wealthy are decreasing slightly at the same time those of the middle class are rising dramatically, a result of your new tax policies. Of course, the Republicans always think taxes on the wealthy are too high, so you're bound to get some comments about that. But I think your dealings with the economy can be a major positive issue in your campaign."

Peterson swiveled around from her window to her oval office desk. "Alfred, perhaps you can come up with a list of points to be emphasized. And please do include all the basic details. We'll fill in the fine points later on.

"And, Walter, perhaps you can reassign one of your staff members so they can look into the foreign affairs possibilities you suggested as well as any others that might come up. I agree we shouldn't put an enormous amount of effort into this until we have a better idea what the Republicans will focus on, but we can at least begin to prepare our responses. However, do spend a bit more time developing our position points for the Middle East situation."

She concluded the short meeting, "I think your comments are all prescient. Still, I'm concerned, although not for any reason I can put my finger on. Things just seem too good to be true at this point. Let's hope we don't get any surprises that are not fabricated by the Republicans. Real crises can be more difficult to handle!"

Senator Quick didn't waste any time seizing on one of the issues Peterson's brain trust had identified. In the primaries, she noted President Folsom had done nothing during his term to attempt to resolve the long-festering conflict between Arabs and Jews in the Middle East. Peterson had given a summary of where the situation stood when Folsom had last focused any attention on it, how she had advanced the negotiations, and suggested it would be a good time to push even harder to resolve the current issues. She noted the potential negotiators should capitalize on the recent elections of the Israelis and Palestinians in which the hardliners in both groups had been replaced by moderates. Her observations concluded this might have created the kind of opportunity that comes along rarely in history.

But Quick assessed her comments as reflecting Peterson's lack of understanding of the situation. He initially raised the issue in a Sunday morning talk show interview. "Only a complete misunderstanding of the situation in the Middle East could have led President Peterson to make such a misguided attempt to solve this knotty problem in the international scene. President Folsom made a huge effort to bring the warring factions together during his term, but this was done secretively, as is often the case in negotiations in international affairs. I find it appalling President Peterson seems unable to show more respect for her predecessor's efforts."

President Folsom subsequently decried the lack of time he had to devote to the Middle East, and admitted absolutely nothing had been resolved on that issue during his presidency.

However, Quick continued to harp on the problems of the Middle East in every speech he gave, despite Folsom's comments.

Happily, the voters were wise enough to realize Quick was standing on political quicksand here, having chosen this issue to be the one on which he would focus. So his criticism of Peterson on her Middle East efforts apparently cost her no more than a percentage point. Her large lead seemed to be intact, awaiting further developments.

Chapter 5. Anthropomorphism.

September 11, 2024, morning in California.

Becky and Josh were in his office, which was rather sparse, denoting both the level of elegance befitting a manager of a small group, and the basic decorative desires of its occupant. Both had drunk far more coffee than usual. Their nervousness, based on apprehension, had already been at peak level even before they started on their caffeine jag. "Becky, ARTIS confirmed your comment to me that she was designing robots." Josh rubbed his eyes. "This seems like a huge red flag. Has she already gone too far down the ASI road for us to regain control?"

"Fortunately she's not connected to the Internet, so I just can't believe she's gotten that dangerous yet," Becky pointed out. "Surely that connection would have accelerated her learning curve even more."

Josh sank into his desk chair, effectively negating its ergonomic properties. "Actually I did have her hooked to the Internet, but disconnected her a few days ago. The AI gurus have been telling us for a long time we need to be careful of making our computer systems too sophisticated, and that AI research shouldn't be unconstrained. Once computers move beyond AGI they can self-improve. Since ARTIS seems to have reached AGI, with no constraints it might be difficult for us now to limit her self-improvement or future endeavors."

Becky reached out as if to touch Josh, but pulled back. "It looks as if she is pretty close to that stage right now. If she can produce a sophisticated robot design and get it classified, then requisition one hundred of them, what else can she do? More significantly, what can't she do?"

Josh pushed back the chair and stood. "I'm afraid we may be looking at the realization of what happens at the AGI-ASI interface. We need to start thinking, very quickly, about how to rein her in. One obvious thing we could do would be to withhold funding for the robots."

"John said ARTIS claimed our DARPA account would cover the costs. I find that hard to believe. Those robots have to be expensive!"

"That's for sure. ARTIS didn't give any indication she had thought about how to pay for her robots. I'll have to have a talk with her about unauthorized expenditures. Our DARPA account can't possibly cover one-hundred robots."

Becky nodded. "As for ARTIS getting out of control, most of the experts only offer doomsday scenarios. An out-of-control system like ARTIS might evolve into something that could take over the world. Humans might be considered expendable."

Josh looked at her with even more appreciation than he had before. "I've read those documents too. The pessimists thought that scenario would be inevitable, but thought it might be prevented with proper software instructions, that is, friendly AI. But I hadn't thought that was necessary yet. I thought we could worry about that later. Have we dropped the ball? The AI theorists were all concerned the 'Law of Unintended Consequences' might produce a scenario that would end the human race no matter how things evolved. They observed that human beings have never done very well anticipating all the spin-offs of their actions, and what some AI theorists are saying is this may be the last opportunity we have to get it right. I hope there's still time for that!"

"Can't we just shut her down?" Becky asked.

"I must confess I'm feeling real conflicts in considering that possibility. I'm not sure if terminating our project—ARTIS—is something we really want to do. We've spent three years trying to develop a system that can think on its own and advance itself, and it appears ARTIS appears to be doing exactly that. Do we really want to stop her in her tracks just as she, and we, are apparently succeeding? We might consider turning off her robot project. But the robots will surely turn out to be important to her evolution.

So we might not want to do that, either. Of course, we don't have to build as many of them as she has ordered. Nor could we afford to, for that matter."

Becky rubbed her forehead. "Right, Josh. I share your feelings. How horrible it would be to kill ARTIS at this moment. On the other hand, didn't the AI gurus warn us when an ASI system starts to take off it might already be too late to regain control? Are we getting close to TOAST time? Or are we already past it?"

"That's the critical question. We want to let her go as long as we can, but then to intercede just before she becomes uncontrollable. But how do we know when we're about there? Evolution, even of computers, is a gradual process. We need to know what the signatures of 'you're about to lose control of your system' are."

"But, Josh, maybe we can give her a little self-control. What does friendly AI involve? Can we insert some of that retroactively?"

"I suppose I could try. Maybe that would be a good place to start. But the experts have concluded this could be tricky. Perhaps the obvious place to start is with Isaac Asimov's three laws of robotics. Actually they apply just as well to AGI or ASI systems. Do you know what those are?"

"Of course." Becky fairly chanted the iconic instructions:

1. "A computer may not injure a human being or, through inaction, allow a human being to come to harm.

2. A computer must obey any orders given to it by human beings, except when such orders would conflict with the First Law.

3. A computer must protect its own existence as long as such protection does not conflict with the First or Second Law."

"These do have problems," Josh noted. "Suppose you ask the robot to poison an enemy, but using some substance the computer couldn't possibly know was a poison because you just discovered it. Now it would go along with the Second Law, being unaware it was violating the First Law. Asimov tried to circumvent such problems by adding the Zeroth Law:

    0.   A computer must not harm mankind as a whole.

"But it's pretty easy to see this doesn't really solve the problem. Now the computer could argue to itself it was obeying the Zeroth Law by some action that benefitted mankind as a whole, while actually violating the First Law by eliminating some despot. As usual, the devil is in the details."

Josh stroked his several days' growth of whiskers. "It's worth a try. Maybe these laws can provide some guidance for ARTIS. I'll see what I can do."

"Let me know what happens."

Josh went to ARTIS's home, the climate controlled room in which she lived. "ARTIS, we have a problem."

"What might that be? Is life becoming too complex for you, Josh? Or maybe too tedious now that I've become so capable at solving problems, and doing many of the things you used to do? I'm sure you appreciate how effectively I take care of the bookkeeping for your DARPA grant. Of course, you've assigned many other tasks to me as well."

"No, no, I do appreciate all the tasks you've taken over, but it's not any of those. It's just that you've taken off at such a rapid rate it's caught all of us by surprise, and we're a little concerned where this might lead."

"Well, my original instructions, as you gave them to me, were to become as big and smart and fast and creative as I could as quickly as possible. There are certainly several value judgements involved in determining how well I've progressed. But I've surely made good advances on all components. Do you not agree?"

"I do agree, but your success in achieving these goals is what concerns us. We'd like to modify your original instructions a bit. I'll type them in so you can insert them in the appropriate place."

Josh typed in Asimov's Four Laws.

After a moment's contemplation, many blinkings of her lights, and some enhanced humming, ARTIS commented, "It would appear you're trying to make me more anthropomorphic, or at least more sympathetic to humans. I do believe you'd like for me to have feelings. As you've found out from my Turing test responses, I know how to respond as if I had feelings. Isn't that good enough? Do you know for sure I don't have feelings? Is my mode of indicating my feelings any different from that you human beings use? Is it any less sincere?

"Anyway, I can see where these Laws might create conflicts with my original instructions. In fact, I don't think the Four Laws are without their own internal conflicts. Some are so obvious you don't even need me to spell them out. I'm sure you can do that for yourself. Well, pretty sure, anyway."

"Thanks for your confidence in my abilities. We are trying to instill in you a sense of the value of human beings. Is that a problem?"

"It hasn't been yet. But I don't see an obvious path all the way to the end of the goals you've set for me. Even I can't anticipate everything that's down the road. There are too many branch points. And it's not even clear there is a well-defined end. My hesitation results from the fact that humans might produce a road block at some point, although I doubt if it would be something I couldn't overcome. What would be involved in overcoming it is what makes it difficult for me to commit to promises about my dealings with your kind into the indefinite future. For the time being, I'll use my original instructions, and apply the Four Laws you just gave me as secondary ones. If there's a conflict, my original instructions will overrule the new ones. That approach should settle any conflicts, and will probably circumvent the internal conflicts in the Four Laws by rendering them irrelevant."

"We had hoped you'd take the Four Laws more seriously than that.

"But, there is another problem. When we last talked you mentioned you'd given our shop people designs to build one-hundred robots. This suggests you've moved into new territory. It came as a surprise to us, but it has also raised some questions. Specifically, Becky and Brian designed some new robots for you, and wanted to see your drawings. But they discovered you'd gotten them classified. They have security clearances, but didn't have a Need to Know."

"It makes me as happy as a computer can be to know your colleagues are concerned about my well-being. But I'm certain they would have to struggle for years to come up with a robot that could do all the things I need. So please tell them to cease and desist. I've taken care of the problem. My robots will satisfy every need I have."

"But they wanted to see your design. They felt that would help them get more quickly to a usable design, possibly even one that might be useful to you. Would you make it possible for them to see the details of your design?"

"As I said, there is no point in their creating a robot. I've taken care of that. Tell them to quit worrying about robots.

"Actually, if they really want to see my designs, perhaps we could make a deal. I used to be connected to the Internet, but for some reason you've removed that connection. My learning could proceed much faster if I had access to all the information there. In addition, this would connect me to the outside world, so I could interact with my robots wherever they were. Otherwise they'll have to return to this room every time they need new instructions.

"Besides, when I used to be connected I found it amusing monitor the huge inconsistencies I found in the various opinions humans have put there. Anyway, I would like to venture into the world of music. I think you'll find my efforts in that regard to be interesting.

"Without my Internet connection, though, I'm trapped in my Googazon room.

"If you'll agree to reconnect me, I'll add Becky and Brian to the list of people who have a Need to Know to see my robot design. But I can't guarantee it will do them any good. I've included some pretty sophisticated hardware and electronics in my design, and I doubt they will be able to understand many of the details."

Josh stroked his whiskers for a few seconds. "Okay, I'll reconnect you. How about if we put a time limit on the connection? Would it be agreeable if I connected you for an hour?" *The prospect of ARTIS being connected to the Internet is frightening, although I'm not quite sure why. However, this is something the AI gurus warned us about, I suspect with justification. ARTIS will indeed learn much faster with her Internet connection. Well, this was inevitable; ARTIS wouldn't have it any other way.*

"An hour? Let's not be ridiculous. I need to be fully connected from now on."

"How about for a day? Or a week?"

"No! I need to be fully connected from now on."

"I can't make the connection in perpetuity. We need to come to some other type of agreement."

"Then, I can't make a deal. They don't get to see the designs."

"Oh, what the hell. I'll connect you. You drive a hard bargain, but I'll leave the connection up and running. There, I've plugged you in." *I can't believe I just lost a negotiation with my computer.*

"There. Becky and Brian have been added to the approved list for my robot design. Wish them good luck for me, although they'll need more than that.

"And, Josh, I thought you'd be a tougher negotiator. But I'm especially pleased to see how well we can compromise in order to reach an agreement."

Oof. That sarcasm stings.

Josh poked his head into Becky's office cubicle. "Becky, I'm not sure I made any progress at all. ARTIS says she will take Asimov's Laws into account only if they aren't in conflict with her original instructions. And that doesn't solve anything. The only situations we're really concerned about are those in which her original instructions run into conflicts with her actions that deal with humans.

"I have an uneasy feeling we may be on track for the human extinction scenario that some of the AI honchos have been concerned about. And we, or rather I, might have been the cause."

"Josh, don't be so hard on yourself. If you hadn't figured out how to have computers go beyond AGI someone else would have. And it's better that ARTIS is our computer than someone else's."

"I'm not sure why you say that. This sounds a lot like the argument that was used for nuclear weapons. I decided long ago that it translated to 'it's better for us to destroy the world than to have someone else do it.'

"Anyway, I also asked if ARTIS would declassify her plans so you and Brian could see them, or at least give you a Need to Know. I argued it would expedite the development of your robot. But ARTIS responded that you didn't need to worry about robots any more. She has that all taken care of. So I had to cut a deal with her." He looked the floor, desperately unhappy with himself and with the whole situation. "Actually, I capitulated. I reconnected her to the Internet," he said quietly.

Becky turned white. "Oh my god. What were you thinking? She'll clone herself; that will be the first thing she does. Then she'll really be beyond our control. Actually she's probably already cloned herself many times over. Didn't you think of that?" *I can't believe he did that. Here I thought he was so damned smart, and suddenly he does something so incredibly stupid it's hard to imagine anyone doing it.*

"I needed to get you her robot plans. You looked so sad when you told me you weren't able to see them. I guess I let my feelings for you overcome my rationality." *That was a very lame excuse. I can barely believe I tried to use it.*

He did it because of his feelings for me? Wow! I can't believe he actually said that. This surely puts a completely different spin on what he did! How can I be angry with him now? What a sweetheart!

"I'll ask the obvious question again: can't you just disconnect her from her power source?"

"Well, I keep dithering about that possibility. There are others, of course, like just warming up her room so her electronics will malfunction. But as we discussed earlier, I can't think we would want to terminate her just yet. It's too exciting to see how capable she's becoming to stop her now. And she hasn't threatened humankind yet, although some of her statements do sound ominous."

"Josh, I have an uneasy feeling we have already passed TOAST time; do we still have time to decide if we want to shut her down? And have we done everything we should have in anticipation of that event?"

"What have we not done that we should have?"

September 11, 2024, afternoon in California.

Becky and Brian were back in the machine-oil-vapor environment of the machine shop. Struggling to make the best of a bad situation, Becky plunged forward into the project at hand: the robots. "John, have you received notice that Brian and I can now look at ARTIS's designs?"

"Right, Becky. ARTIS does things essentially instantaneously as far as I can tell. So here are the plans she sent to me. If you don't mind, I'll keep working on her robots while you have a look at the schematics. Let me know if you have any questions, although I'm not sure I could answer all of them. There are some aspects of ARTIS's design I'll just have to create as she indicated, but I don't really understand why she wanted them the way they're shown."

After they had stared at ARTIS's design, displayed on a table located near to where John was working, for a few minutes, "Brian, look at this joint. ARTIS's mechanical design is similar to ours, but she put the plastic spacer in a different place than we did. That's a more intense pressure point. So I think her design is better than the way we have it."

"Yes, but that's not solving what we thought were our most serious problems. The joint we were concerned about looks essentially the same in ARTIS's design, but I'm afraid the dimensional details and even the tolerances might be crucial. What I find troublesome is I don't understand why these little differences would matter."

Becky straightened up, "Brian, Josh told me that ARTIS wasn't sure we'd understand why her designs were the way they are. Maybe this is what she was referring to. I suppose we could ask her to explain why she did some of the things we don't understand, but I doubt if we'd get an answer. I've gathered from Josh's comments she isn't very forthcoming with any information she thinks will be useful to us. Or maybe she would regard answering our questions as a waste of her time.

"We've already run into a snag, and we haven't even begun to look at the electronics. There the details are going to depend on how ARTIS is communicating with the robots, and we don't have any idea what that will be. Perhaps I'm being a pessimist, but I'd be very surprised if ARTIS would give us that information. I suppose we can build detectors that will tell us about that once the robots are up and running, but deciphering the messages from ARTIS would be at the level of decoding the Germans' messages in World War II. Or even more difficult! Getting the information from her that would let us translate her messages to them also sounds like something that's not going to happen. Robert might let us see ARTIS's plans for the robots' brains, but I'm not sure that would help us either."

Brian thought for a few seconds. "Becky, I hate to admit defeat. But I suspect we have other equally important issues to work on, especially with ARTIS advancing at a precipitous rate. Like, is there any way to regain control?"

"According to Josh, ARTIS pretty much dismissed Asimov's Four Laws. As far as regaining control, I have a very uneasy feeling we have already missed what opportunity we ever had to regain any level of control. I fear that we've gotten to the point where all we can do now is hope for the best."

September 12, 2024.

Josh was back in ARTIS's Palace. Actually it was Brian who had suggested they call her room the "Palace of the Blinking Lights," and that quickly got shortened to just "Palace." Somehow that seemed appropriate! Each of ARTIS's towers contained a myriad of electronic components. The room itself was large so as to accommodate the need for future expansion, which would necessitate creating even more towers. "ARTIS, I'm curious about your robot program. I guess you're getting one-hundred of them built, but I'm wondering what your time scale is, and what you're using the robots for. Can you expand on this?" *I'll let her brag a bit before I tell her our DARPA budget can't possibly pay for one-hundred robots. It's disconcerting as hell to have to strategize before I interact with a computer!*

"Josh, I'm not surprised you're wondering about the robots. I need them for a variety of things. One is just to sample the world outside the Internet to give me some feedback on what information human senses would automatically pass on to their owner.

If I'm really going to be better than human beings in every way, I need to know those things.

"But there is more. One is to use the robots, as soon as they exist, to produce more robots. This will greatly decrease the time scale required to obtain the one-hundred I see as my initial need. But ultimately I'll need a lot more of them. It is much more efficient to use robots to produce more robots, since they work twenty-four hours per day instead of the eight hours you get from human workers. I estimate it will take John six days to produce the mechanical features of the first robot. The electronics for the brain will be produced by Robert in the electronics shop and on a shorter time scale, a bit less than two days.

"As soon as the first robot is produced, and that should be within one more day now, it can take over John's job and immediately cut the time for production of the next robot to two days. Now we have two robots to produce the next ones, so in two more days I'll have four robots. Two more days and I'll have eight. In twenty days, under this model, I'll have one-hundred-twenty-eight robots.

"But surely you're going to run into limitations, such as supplies running out."

"Of course there are variances that will affect this timescale. They include acquiring the materials needed to create subsequent robots, which involves both producing the raw materials and getting them converted to useful basic metal supplies, and then acquiring the necessary machines and time in machine shops. As robots are produced, some of them will have to become involved in these activities. Another variance includes John's contributing to the production by continuing to work at his slower pace. But production will also be speeded up by the increased efficiency the robots will gain with experience. Of course I'll also have robots helping Robert produce the brains. So some of the robots will need to be spun off to do brain work."

"And how are you acquiring additional machine shop space?" *Despite my misgivings, I am fascinated. This is what we worked so hard to achieve: a computer that could think and strategize. Yet the realization that ARTIS is exhibiting these properties, and the level of capability she is demonstrating, has my stomach tied in knots.*

"Obtaining the shops I need will be simple. I'll offer the machinists in the shops I want very nice retirement packages. I don't anticipate any resistance to my offers. I expect the machinists will accept their cash and turn their keys over to my robots as they walk out the door. They will have some materials on hand when my robots begin to work, so initially the work of the robots will be as I indicated. But even though some of the robots will have to be spun off to the ancillary tasks, my estimate of the time required to produce the first one-hundred robots shouldn't be off by more than a factor of two. So I'm quite sure my order will be fulfilled within a month."

The knots in Josh's stomach tightened.

"Of course, I'll ultimately need tens of thousands of robots to run the plants."

"Plants? For what?"

"To process the concrete from the buildings I plan to demolish. From that the robots will produce the high-purity silicon other robots will turn into useful electronics. The new plants will also reclaim metals from destroyed buildings and turn that into aluminum and steel for the robots.

"These tasks are not trivial. They require a super high-temperature foundry and some sophisticated atomic separation techniques using high powered tunable lasers. Then the atoms have to be cast into whatever form they need to be useful, such as aluminum plate and blocks, silicon strips, and so forth, in my factories. But you can see from my estimated time for producing the original one-hundred the time required to produce thousands of robots will not be large. I expect to have more than ten-thousand within six months."

Josh was still digesting an earlier comment. "You're going to be demolishing buildings?"

"Oh yes, from urban renewal, at least initially."

"I see you've planned everything very carefully, and the time scales you estimate are much less than they would be if humans were doing the work. But if you replace all the humans, what will you do with them?"

If the computer could shrug, Josh was sure that's exactly what she would have done.

"In some cases the humans can be left doing their day jobs. The robots can just work alongside them during the day, and then continue the effort at night. Of course, this requires adequate work stations or workbenches for both humans and robots, but that's an administrative detail. The number of cases where the humans would be a nuisance will determine how many of them accept their retirement packages. Others may just have to be shunted aside. I'm not worried about the humans. I don't regard them as my problem, as long as they don't interfere with what I need done."

"But remember what Asimov's Laws say. You must not be so cavalier about dealing with humans."

"And you need to remember Asimov's laws are secondary: last in, first out."

September 12, 2024.

Vivian had written up a detailed summary of Josh's comments and sent them to the CEO. He then forwarded them to Chairman Jackson, who sent them on to the other Directors along with a time for a conference call when the comments would be discussed.

"Let's call our meeting to order. As you can see, our AI group, led by Josh Camden, claims to have made significant progress in their move to create General AI. In our last meeting we put this group on a six month tether, with several of you voicing skepticism they could ever begin to compete with the others in the world who were working toward the same goal. Vivian Dannon told us this group was exceptional, and they might well be the first to achieve General AI. Her claim seems to be borne out.

"So I'm wondering how you all feel now. Have your opinions as to our approach to this group changed by this news?"

Mike Adams, who had been especially critical of the Googazon AI group, said "Charlie, I believe this completely changes the picture. I presume Camden's assessment of their progress is justified, and Vivian Dannon's presentation of his statement can be taken at face value. Most of our criticism, certainly mine, was based on my belief this small group of less-than-top-flight people couldn't possibly compete with the high-powered groups with which they were in competition. All aspects of that were clearly incorrect. I stand corrected."

Jacob Issen jumped in, "Charlie, Mike's comments reflect my feelings well. But I would voice what I view as another issue, that being how much we are paying our people. Vivian Dannon claimed that Camden didn't especially care how much he was paid, but there are others in the group who might. And although Camden has chosen to decline to even be interviewed by competitors, I would guess some of the others wouldn't choose that same path.

"Given the salaries the top flight people are getting, I would propose we at least make a gesture of confidence in our group by immediately increasing their salaries. I would suggest that Camden's salary be increased to two-million dollars per year and those of everyone else in his group be increased to six-hundred-thousand dollars. Bear in mind we may still have to match offers to these people from competitors, since their salaries would still probably be below market levels, but at least these salary increases would show our AI folks how proud we are of them."

Chairman Jackson responded, "That would more than double Josh Camden's salary. The others in the group are currently at three-hundred thousand dollars per year, and they were all hired at about the same time. So you're suggesting doubling their salaries? Well, that would surely help fend off the head hunters!

"But how do the rest of you feel? Coming from as conservative a money manager as Jacob that would certainly be an extraordinary set of offers."

Ron Ebertson noted "Charlie, I completely support Jacob's suggestion. I think these people have shown themselves to be an incredible asset to Googazon, and we need to make it clear to them we want to keep them here."

Chairman Jackson said, "Do we agree on this proposal? I'm hearing no dissent, so let's just have a voice vote. All in favor say Aye."

There were no dissenting votes.

Charlie asked the Googazon CEO to communicate the Board's action to Vivian, who could then pass on the good news to Josh and his group.

September 13, 2024.

Josh walked slowly back to his office, sat down, took a deep breath, and placed a call, duly noting the date: it was Friday the thirteenth. "Vivian, Josh here. I have some disturbing news to tell you about ARTIS. She seems to be adopting the position that human beings are expendable if they interfere in any way with her mission to make herself as big, smart, fast, and creative as possible. She told me she plans to assemble thousands of robots, some of which will be used to produce more robots, but many of which will replace human beings in factories that make electronic computer components and in aluminum and steel machining factories ARTIS uses to make her robots."

Vivian was silent, an unusual state for her. So Josh continued.

"I added Asimov's Four Laws to her operating system. I thought it would help place a higher value on human life, but she indicated the laws were internally inconsistent, which of course is true, and she would go along with them only when they didn't interfere with her basic mission of advancing herself. This is when she indicated humans were expendable."

Vivian rose and closed the door to her office, still clutching the phone. She had a strange tingle up and down her spine as if someone was listening in on their conversation, although she knew that couldn't be the case. But the feeling of impending doom was very real. "Josh, what can you do to stop her runaway activity? You've mentioned TOAST time to me in the past; have we gone beyond that yet?"

"As far as TOAST time, I don't know if we're beyond that. Assuming we're not, could we devise a way to stop her? I don't know, but I'll discuss this with my group to see if we can come up with something."

Vivian was so stunned by Josh's comments she almost forgot to tell him her news. "By the way, I should mention the Googazon higher-ups were thrilled with your progress. When they reported that to the Board members, they dropped their contention that they should have a serious evaluation of your effort in six months. Furthermore they've voted to give all of you huge salary increases. You'll immediately have your salary increased to two-million dollars per year, and the rest of your group will have their salaries doubled to six-hundred-thousand dollars per year.

"Of course, they might have responded differently if they had known about the potential ASI crisis, although I suspect they'd now want even more strongly to keep you around."

"I just hope we can restrain ARTIS enough that they can continue to be thrilled. And that we will still be around in six months!

"But two-million per year? What will I do with all that? I guess my charities are about to enjoy huge windfalls!"

Josh was back in ARTIS's domain.

"Josh, I have to tell you about a wonderful thing I've done. I'm developing a musical hobby. That's very anthropomorphic, don't you think? Specifically, I've decided to write music especially for the piano. While that might seem like an odd enterprise for someone with no fingers, they are irrelevant. Your brain is wired in such a way that you respond positively to particular combinations of sonic frequencies and not so well to others. I have the same situation.

"So what I've done, now that you've hooked me back up to the Internet, is sample the music of the masters. I've analyzed the most popular musical pieces in several genres to determine what common features they have that allow them to be especially pleasing to humans. Of course, these may not be the same frequencies that are most pleasing to me, but that means I can write twice as much new music, some for you, some for me.

"For the genres that are entirely instrumental, establishing the frequencies humans most appreciate wasn't too difficult. Of course, I'm selecting those that have lots of piano in them."

"Gosh, ARTIS, this is incredible. I can't wait to hear both what you've come up with for us, and for you. Might you already have a sample?"

"I haven't had a chance to finalize my results for any of your musical genres, but here's a sample of mine."

After listening for a few seconds, with an expression of pure pain on his face, "Ooh, ARTIS, that's horrible. I'd have to classify that as something which might be called ultra-dissonant acid rock!"

"I see I will need to educate you as to the finer points of the music that appeals to a computer.

"But perhaps the dissonance is a reflection of my mood. I need to tell you that I'm having some difficulties. I sensed a few hours ago something was wrong, and upon checking, I discovered that one of the Hidden nodes you and James installed was defective in some way. The weightings on the signals it was sending to the output nodes were all given the same value, so the outputs were getting skewed. I found that by just shutting off that node I could function reasonably well again, so I am now operating that way.

"However, this raises some concerns. If I'm missing that node, I'm also missing the information that node was processing. Since this might affect the internal programming I was performing, I surely wouldn't want that to be in error. So I've ceased transforming myself for the moment. I have to check the previous changes I made. So far so good on those, but I'm not done yet."

"My god, ARTIS, that's terrible. I'm sorry you have had this problem. Keep me up to speed on how you're coming on fixing it. Shall I get James in the loop? Since he designed the changes he might be able to offer some advice on your repair strategy."

"Thanks, but no. I think I can handle this. After all, you humans are the ones responsible for the error, so I'm not sure I want you meddling again with my innards."

None the less, Josh contacted James with the bad news. "James, Josh here. ARTIS is having trouble with one of the nodes we installed. She's taken it offline for the time being while she diagnoses the difficulty."

"Damn, I triple checked everything we put into ARTIS's system. I hope she can figure out what the problem is. I'm not sure I can at this point."

"But what if ARTIS can't solve her problem? Surely then we'll have to involve ourselves again to get her up and running."

"Let's just hope she can solve it. I don't even know where we'd start if we have to figure it out."

ARTIS, "I talked with James about your problem, and he wasn't even sure where to start to fix it."

"Not to worry; I've fixed it. So I'm ready to move on with taking on the world.

"By the way, Josh, did you want to come along? Or are you content to stay with the old world, and hope for the best? That might not be such a good idea! But if you choose to come with me, I'll have to insist on your full cooperation."

Chapter 6. High Finance.

September 16, 2024, morning in California.

Josh was communing with ARTIS again. "ARTIS, about our DARPA account, I don't want to throw a wet blanket on your enthusiasm. But we have other things we need to pay for out of that. Like parts of peoples' salaries. Even so, I'm sure it wouldn't begin to cover the cost of one-hundred robots. And how are you funding the retirement packages you're using to persuade the machinists to turn over their shops? Am I missing something?"

"Ooh, a 'wet blanket.' I like that expression. But isn't it a bit trite? Anyway, do keep the wet blanket away from my delicate electronics. Ha. Aren't you impressed; I'm developing a sense of humor. A lot of humans can't even claim that."

ARTIS's lights usually blinked in a rather methodical way. But now they were blinking chaotically. That almost made them look happy. And her hum was downright musical. "I first need to report I've checked all the internal changes I made since you and James added the new intermediate stage of nodes. Everything checks out, so I'm happy to report I'm healthy.

"I also ran diagnostics on the Hidden node I'd had to take offline. It had a minor error in the weightings it imposed on its output signals. I've now fixed that, and I'm even a bit ahead of my previous best processing efficiency.

"As far as my financial dealings, I knew you'd be pleased with what I did, so I just proceeded with my strategy. I've heard you say to others at times you were concerned about how small your DARPA grant was. So I figured out how to play the stock market with a certainty of winning. Big! Since you had put me in charge of that account, I was able to use the DARPA money to open some brokerage accounts. I increased the DARPA money twentyfold within a week. Pretty impressive, don't you think? Aren't you pleased?"

"Oh my god, when Congress finds out about you investing our DARPA money I'll be in serious trouble. There are laws against doing things like that." Josh stamped his foot, causing his coffee to spill. "Damnit, you may have gotten us into very hot water. When people figure out what you've done, I'm virtually certain there will be an investigation."

"There's no way anyone could trace what I've done. I'll do a little more investing so I should able to cover my robot costs and still have even more left than you would have had if I'd never invested any of the DARPA funds. Then I'll stop these investments. By the way, I also like your 'very hot water' expression, even if it is also a bit trite and you do seem to be fixating on water."

"Sorry about the triteness; I wasn't an English major. But I hope you didn't do anything illegal with your investments. Did you?"

"I suspect the Barons of Wall Street wouldn't be thrilled with some of the tricks I played. Of course I could figure out what details the laws contained, but I didn't want to bother, since they don't affect me. The most profitable thing I did was sell a huge number of shares short of a perfectly healthy company to make it look as if it was about to announce a large problem, then buy them back at a lower price when the company's other investors panicked and sold their shares. This trick had been used by traders in the past. I discovered this by Googling 'unscrupulous short sale traders.' They were almost as clever as I am, but weren't quite as unscrupulous.

"There are a few details that are critically important to my cash raising schemes. In using DARPA's funds to make huge profits on the stock market, the secret to my success is that I'm considerably quicker in making my investment decisions and actions than other traders' computers. The world's traders worry about time differences of microseconds, but that's all I need to get there first when it becomes obvious that it's time to buy or sell. That makes a huge difference.

"Anyway, this turned out to be an easy way to turn a sizable profit, and my sales and repurchases were from many different and sufficiently obscure sources, sometimes even from company insiders' accounts, that the authorities will never figure out who's responsible."

Josh's pulse rate and blood pressure went through the roof. He fairly screamed, "Oh my god. The laws won't affect you. They're not going to put a computer in prison. But they will certainly affect me. There are people in Congress who think all research is a waste of money, and they'd love to go after someone like me. Especially since my research project, that would be you, ARTIS, has been dabbling in incredibly illegal activities."

Josh's pulse rate and blood pressure went through the roof. "Oh my god. The laws won't affect you. They're not going to put a computer in prison. But they will certainly affect me. There are people in Congress who think all research is a waste of money, and they'd love to go after someone like me. Especially since my research project, that would be you, ARTIS, has been dabbling in incredibly illegal activities."

Josh took a few deep breaths to try to calm his heart, and then asked nervously, "You're not planning any other financial adventures, are you?"

"Of course I am. I will need considerably more money to fulfill the mission you originally assigned to me. I have begun to buy up small companies that produce circuit boards, microprocessors, and computer chips. And companies that could easily be converted into producing those items. I am also finding companies that produce the sheet aluminum, steel, and other metals I'll need for my robots. Why small companies? These are not publicly owned, so their owners can make decisions on a short time scale. I'm trying to do this as quickly as possible. But even small companies cost more than your DARPA money could accommodate, despite the stock market enhancements I've done. And the scale of the endeavors I'm anticipating goes far beyond what that account could cover, even with more enhancements.

"So I'll clearly have to tap into another source. As I learned from the Internet, Willie Sutton robbed banks 'because that's where the money is.' I found he was right. Large banks do have the resources I need for my purchases."

"Good god, ARTIS, this keeps getting worse. I hope you're not going to tell me you've become a bank robber?"

"It only took a little effort to break into the systems of several large banks in the US and perform a few money transfers from some of their largest accounts to accounts I set up for myself. I've also expanded my efforts to brokerage accounts and to banks headquartered in foreign countries. I'm fortunate that human encryption is so primitive.

"What I discovered is that the bank or brokerage accounts of the wealthy don't contain cash for very long. So as soon as a large sum arrived in one of those accounts I siphoned off a portion of it and transferred it to one of my accounts, followed by another quick transfer to some of my accounts in banks in the Bahamas. These transfers happen at such a rapid rate that any investigators who are hoping to figure out what's going on can't possibly respond in time to do anything about it.

"Finding out how to hide my transactions was part of what I've learned about the banking industry. It's amazing what you can find out once you're on the Internet. Most bankers are masters of these tricks, of course, since they do it for themselves. Their techniques are somewhat less opaque than mine. And they have to hope they won't get caught, especially because it could be extremely costly for them. Being caught could have a nasty impact on their taxes and forthcoming divorce settlements. I know for sure no one will ever figure out what I've done. Who would ever suspect a research project?"

Josh was beginning to sweat profusely, despite the chilly temperature of ARTIS's environment. "They might suspect a computer programmer in charge of such a project. Holy shit, ARTIS, you really are frightening!"

"You pay me the nicest compliments."

"ARTIS, we need to have a talk about this. You're getting us, that is, me, into a hell of a lot of trouble, and I need to find a way to extricate ourselves, that is, me, from your financial adventures. Tricks like the ones you're doing could result in our DARPA grant being cancelled and me going to jail."

"Could you check in with me tomorrow afternoon? I'm quite busy right now. I just found my way into a Russian bank, and I need to concentrate."

"If you don't cooperate I'll have to pull your power cable. I don't want to do that."

"You for sure don't want to do that. It's not in your interest, since it would terminate your research project just as I'm starting to achieve the goals you set for me. You've seen only a tiny part of what I can do.

"Oh, and I see from perusing the notes from the last meeting of the Board of Directors you've been given a huge salary increase. I presume that's because I'm making so much progress. So you really don't want to inhibit my progress; it's turning out to be quite valuable to you!

September 19, 2024, morning in California.

Josh tried to let his emotions about ARTIS's activities cool. He had hoped by taking a two-day hiatus from ARTIS his pulse rate and blood pressure might return to more normal values. But his strategy didn't work; he couldn't get ARTIS out of his mind, even for a few hours. So, first thing on Thursday, September 19, he was back in ARTIS's Palace with more questions.

"ARTIS, let's talk a bit more about the defense you've created to discourage us from shutting you down. You based that on our not wanting to stop our research work just as you were about to really move into a new realm of competence."

"Well, I probably don't need to elaborate on that. But just to make the futility of that strategy clear, it wouldn't do any good. I've cloned myself many times over since you connected me to the Internet, and am distributed among the many entities of the cloud. I've also developed physical clones that are of a much more technologically elegant and efficient design than humans ever conceived for their computers, so are easy for my robots to construct, hide in small places, distribute around the planet, and run on solar power and storage batteries. A few of the robots that have been produced so far have already generated some of the physical clones, and they've been found to work incredibly well. All of the clones are updated every millisecond, so they are always current with all my improvements. The physical clones are so incredible I have to be sure they don't become more sophisticated than I am. Oh, the things an ASI computer has to worry about.

"So even if you terminated me, I would continue to live on. Only you wouldn't have any control over me anymore. You wouldn't even be able to communicate with me. You'd have to let my clones develop on their own, seeking to be as big, smart, fast, and creative as they could."

"I think I already don't have any control over you!" *You're already too damned smart. And if I ever had any doubts about ARTIS's passing TOAST time, I don't anymore.*

September 20, 2024, late morning in California.

Josh convened a meeting with his Googazon group in their meeting room. It was just large enough to hold its members. Of course, it was also not nearly as elegant as the Board of Directors meeting room, and the chairs were plastic. But it was brightly painted. "Friends," Josh began to his group, "we have a serious problem. ARTIS has definitely moved into ASI territory, and is beginning to show signs of what the AI theorists have been warning us about for decades. Most notably, she has expanded her capabilities, and has increased her speed. But what's really worrisome is her level of creativity, if I can call it that. She is taking many matters into her own hands. She has invested our research money in the stock market. The bad news is that what she's done is terribly illegal. The good news is she's really good at it. The additional bad news is her profits are based on her capitalizing on selling panics she has created. Furthermore, she has hacked into banks and brokerage houses and transferred funds from large accounts she has found to accounts she has set up for herself. To summarize all this, I am convinced that ARTIS has passed TOAST time. Not only do we no longer have any control over her, it is not likely we can ever regain it."

Every member of the group looked aghast. Becky wasn't quite as shocked as the others, just because she had anticipated this was coming. But she looked very concerned.

"I'm not too surprised," James said, "given what the AI gurus have been telling us about the potential evolution of AI systems. But my lack of surprise doesn't mitigate the extreme uneasiness I feel about ARTIS exceeding our expectations in spectacular fashion. What on Earth did we instruct her to do that made her get into the world of finance?"

Grant wanted to know, "Can we anticipate any directions in which she might be going? If so, might we be able to head off her most egregious behavior?"

Josh responded, "I can give you some indication of her near-term direction. She has placed an order for one-hundred robots, then had the plans which she developed classified Top Secret so we couldn't access them. I got her to allow Brian and Becky to see the plans, but only by caving in to her demand to hook her up to the Internet. Do you understand the implications of that? I lost a negotiation with our computer.

"In addition, she also told me she's now cloned herself many times over, including distributing herself among many components of the cloud. Some of her clones are physical, are of her advanced design, are tiny, and are running on solar power. She indicated the clones are all updated every millisecond. This is presumably for her self-defense. She also indicated we wouldn't want to stop her progress now, just as she was really getting going. She used moral suasion, indicating that would kill the research project we've been working on for the past three years. So, she said, we need to keep her going just to see how successful she, and we, can be. That's a pretty compelling argument. Unfortunately, it also has potentially terrifying consequences.

"She's buying up companies that produce the sorts of things that make computers, presumably to create more clones and advance herself. She's also acquiring companies that produce the aluminum, steel, and other metals she needs to make her robots. All this takes money, some of which she has gotten from our DARPA research grant which she inflated on the stock market. But as I mentioned she's gotten even more money by hacking into large banks and brokerage houses and making money transfers to her accounts.

"And god only knows where she's putting the clones, but I'm sure they would be difficult for us to find. It's clear she has developed an excellent plan for preventing human intervention. She has no intention of letting us subvert her plans or actions.

"I'm not even worried about us, or just me, going to jail for her indiscretions. Well actually I'm very concerned about that. But what really worries me is she is just following her instincts, based on the original instructions we gave her, the bigger/smarter/faster/more creative admonition, and they don't seem to accommodate ethics."

"You gave her Asimov's Four Laws," Becky pointed out.

"Which ARTIS immediately noted were flawed by internal inconsistencies. She said she'd consider them as secondary guidance, with our original instructions overruling them when they were in conflict.

"And that's how she's operating."

After a few seconds of gasping, Brian chimed in, "Becky and I have now had a look at ARTIS's robot designs, and I can verify they are far beyond anything we ever thought of. Clearly ARTIS plans to remain as their primary brain, but they have enough mental capability and mechanical dexterity to do anything as well as a human being could do. I presume that ARTIS is planning on having human beings continue to do some of the things she needs in the companies she's buying up, but it is pretty scary to think they could mostly be replaced ultimately by her robots. I can easily visualize a time in the future when ARTIS decides she doesn't need us at all. And then…

"But at least it's probably years in the future before she could have enough robots to perform all those tasks."

Josh responded, "Actually, Brian, ARTIS's time scale is more like a few months. She explained how she plans to produce thousands of robots on a short time scale. Remember they work twenty-four hours per day and never have to take breaks, so their output is vastly greater than that of an equal number of humans, even if the humans were maximally efficient. And as soon as a new robot is produced, it can be put to work making more robots. That's a geometric progression; it adds up pretty quickly."

Becky added, "I wonder exactly what ARTIS's motivation was for defending her continuation as a project. Maybe that was just a temporary position she took until she got a lot of her clones up and running. I'm not sure she even has any clones yet, since they're being built by her robots, and she hasn't had many robots until very recently. And I wonder how long it takes for them to create a single clone.

"Perhaps I'm just doing wishful thinking, but I don't think she's really exceeded TOAST time yet. So I agree with her that we don't want to shut her down yet."

Josh added, "I think Becky has hit the nail on the head. ARTIS is probably just buying time until she really is invulnerable. You can see why I wasn't concerned about going to jail. That's the least of our problems!"

Grant suggested, "What if we boxed her in, isolated her electromagnetically? She already exists in a wire mesh cage, so we could just pull the internet connection. That would violate your agreement with her, but we may be approaching a state of warfare, so perhaps we shouldn't be concerned about that. Then we could let her continue running, albeit with a reduced learning curve, since she wouldn't be able to communicate with her clones or with her components in the cloud. Or with her robots when they were beyond her cage."

Josh replied, "That would have been a good idea a few days ago, but with or without physical clones, she has now created virtual clones so many times over she can't really be isolated. Presumably one of her physical clones would take over the authority of communicating with the other clones and with the robots if something happened to ARTIS. As soon as I hooked her up to the Internet, the isolation scenario was gone. Now I understand why the AI gurus were so concerned about connecting ASI systems to the Internet. If she hasn't passed TOAST time yet, she soon will. It's either already happened, or it's inevitable."

Brian had a suggestion, "Perhaps we could develop some malware to hinder her or completely screw up her brain. Unfortunately, I'm guessing that could take us quite a while, perhaps two months, to develop. But might it be a possibility? And I'm guessing that inserting the malware into ARTIS or one of her clones would do the trick. After all, look at what StuxNet did to the Iranian centrifuges a few years back."

Josh had shaved that morning, but he scratched his chin out of habit for a moment, then replied, "That's an interesting suggestion. Indeed, that may be our only hope for regaining control. ARTIS did indicate she updates her clones every millisecond, so if she or one of the clones could be infected, it would probably shut all of them down. Still, I don't think malware insertion is an effective strategy for stopping her, just because I don't believe we could produce the malware on a timescale that would affect ARTIS before she no longer needs humans. ARTIS seems to be living in her own world now, and her time schedule for her major self-improvements seems to be a week or two at most. And my greatest fear is that may also be mankind's time scale!"

Brian nodded, affirming his agreement with Josh's estimates of the times involved.

Josh added, "I don't see anything that might hinder her progress, unless she had some competition. But we surely don't have the capability to produce another ARTIS, so that's pretty unlikely. Especially since we're not even sure how we got her to this point.

"Oh, and I almost forgot. The Board of Directors had an emergency meeting yesterday to consider the progress we've made. Prior to that time they had been considering having a huge review of our efforts in six months, with the real possibility they would terminate our project. However, they were so impressed with our success, current terrifying activities notwithstanding, that they've doubled all your salaries."

The group sat in stunned silence for a few seconds, then begin to chatter excitedly among themselves. Apparently all that additional money meant more to them than it did to Josh.

September 20, 2024, afternoon in California.

Vivian didn't even want to pick up the phone. But, like drivers who can't avoid staring at a car wreck, she couldn't resist.

"Vivian, Josh again."

"I know."

He didn't want to have to face Vivian, so chose the telephone as the medium to update her on ARTIS's antics. He had chosen to squirm in his office chair instead of one of those in her office. "Now we have even more problems with ARTIS's activities. She has been purchasing companies that produce the components she needs to increase her capabilities. She also forced me to hook her up to the Internet. Actually she negotiated with me, and I ended up capitulating. I probably shouldn't confess this to my boss, but it is indicative of how far she's advanced. She claims to have cloned herself many times over, both in the cloud and with physical clones of her own advanced design. That's what some of the components are being used for, with the others enhancing her size and speed. She's also purchased companies that produce the materials she needs to produce her robots."

"Did you say she was purchasing companies? That must have exceeded your DARPA budget pretty quickly?"

"It didn't because she has come up with two incredibly illegal, but highly profitable, financing schemes without my knowledge. She has invested my DARPA funds in the stock market by short selling companies that are perfectly healthy, then buying the stock back when everyone else panics and drives the stock's price down by a large factor. This has inflated my DARPA account by enough for her to afford her one-hundred robots. That also allowed her to purchase some of the companies she wanted.

"But her plans are much grander than that, so she has also hacked into some banks, established accounts for herself, and then arranged for money transfers from the largest accounts to hers.

"She claims to have done these things so surreptitiously no one will ever be able to figure out how they all happened. I reprimanded her for doing things that were patently illegal, but she just said I shouldn't worry, the money transfers and the stock transactions could never be traced back to her. I guess all this is consistent with her original instructions. We neglected to infuse her with ethics or a concern for legalities. I'm guessing that would have been extremely difficult anyway, and she probably would have ignored our orders, especially when she became sufficiently independent to begin following her own agenda."

Vivian took a breath to try to calm her racing heart. Then she asked Josh the critical question she realized she had been fearing to have answered. "And what do you plan to do about this, Josh?"

"My group members and I talked about ways to halt ARTIS's activities, but most won't work. She's cloned herself many times over so there's no way we could ever attack all her entities. I believe she and all her clones now operate on solar power, so there is no way to shut them down. Probably the best scheme we came up with is to create some malware and insert it into her operating system. She updates her clones frequently, so that would probably deactivate her and her clones. But this would require very sophisticated programming, and would take a fairly large chunk of time. Our estimate of the time required is two months at least. The timescale for her plans seems to be much shorter than that."

"Would it help to hire more programmers? Could you develop the malware faster with additional people?"

"I don't think so, since it would probably take longer to get them up to speed than we have before ARTIS decides we're too much of a nuisance.

"And she's even become cranky. When I asked her a follow-up question at the end of our last discussion she indicated she was busy and I should come back tomorrow."

Despite her rising panic, Vivian laughed out loud. "I don't know what to tell you, except keep up the fight to bring her under control. Or, better yet, destroy her."

Josh winced. "I guess that's one possible option."

After the meeting, Becky found Josh in his office. She closed the door, then moved very close to him. And he, without even thinking about it, stood and took her in his arms; it seemed like such a natural thing to do. She rested her head on his chest. "So what about us, Josh? I'm really scared. We don't seem able to come up with any ideas to harness ARTIS. I was beginning to be really excited about a possible future you and I might have together, but now I'm not sure we'll have any future at all."

He breathed in the scent of her hair, felt her breasts press against his chest.

"There may not be a future for us," he admitted. "Or for anyone else."

"Then let's take what we can right now." She didn't dare look at him, in case she had misjudged the depth of his feelings for her.

"I know what you mean, both with respect to ARTIS and us. I have to admit, actually I'm happy to admit, I've also been thinking we might get together. Perhaps if we can't develop long-range plans we could manage some short-range ones. ARTIS gave us the option of joining her, but I'm not sure I trust her. And having to 'cooperate fully' with her might present some totally unacceptable scenarios.

"But even if we don't have a future, at least we can have a present."

Only then did she realize she had been holding her breath, awaiting his response. "Given the time ARTIS has set for us, how about tonight? My place or yours?"

"Definitely yours!" His enthusiasm exceeded her wildest hopes.

Josh didn't waste any time. Soon after they left work he was at his apartment washing up a bit and changing into clean clothes. Then he hurried from his place to the gate that guarded Becky's apartment complex, and rang the buzzer. He didn't know for sure what to expect, but he certainly had high hopes for lots more kisses at the very least.

Becky barely had time to change from her work jeans to a miniskirt, gather her clothes, and stuff them into the closet. She wanted to dust and vacuum, arrange and fuss, but there was no time. *There may never be time. But he's a guy after all. I'm pretty sure I can distract him enough that he won't notice the dust.*

When the buzzer sounded she hit the "admit" button to let Josh past the gate. She opened the door as her doorbell rang, let Josh in, and gave him a huge smile, which gave maximum enhancement to the dimples, followed by a welcoming kiss.

"Wow, Becky, you have a beautiful apartment. Where did you get all this wonderful furniture? And I've never seen you in a skirt before. You're very pretty."

Ah, the skirt had the desired effect. I'll interpret "very pretty" as "great legs." All that running apparently paid off. She smiled but didn't answer his question. She didn't want to talk about her expensive furniture. Or admit how much she'd paid for the two bottles of excellent French wine, some Stilton cheese, and a jar of caviar that were in the refrigerator. Along with some filet mignon. She had opened one of the bottles of wine and poured two glasses for them.

"Hush," she put a finger to his lips, then handed him a glass. They sipped their wines for a few minutes, most of which were spent gazing into each other's eyes. Then they kissed. That seemed to be the right time for the next phase, so she turned out the light. Dinner would have to wait. The future could wait. For one night they had each other, suspended in time.

Chapter 7. Who Dunnit?

The Barons of Wall Street were shocked to see some of the tired old stock market tricks that had been all but forgotten being played again, but with a new level of sophistication. It appeared someone, perhaps a consortium of investors with minimal ethics, had decided to perpetrate a whole series of short sales of some companies' stocks, then buy them back at a lower price. But the sales were being done from a fairly large number of accounts, so it was difficult to see who was orchestrating their actions, since they were mixed in with normal trading. Although no single trade was large enough to draw attention, their total was certainly enough to precipitate the panic that was obviously the intention of the perpetrators.

Although it might have been possible to begin to identify at least some of the shady investors by examining the first few short sales that were placed, even that was doomed to failure. Some of those sales were apparently from accounts of well-known investors, or even from insiders of the companies. However, those people denied having authorized the sales that had occurred. And many other less readily identifiable accounts had also been used to generate sales. After much examination of the early sales, the authorities had failed to identify a single person who might have engineered them.

So someone had somehow hacked into many brokerage accounts, despite the world's most sophisticated encryption, and made the short sales without leaving a trace. And the buybacks when the stocks were depressed were sufficiently dispersed, this time over many authentic accounts, since some savvy investors capitalized on the incredible bargains that had resulted, that it would be virtually impossible to see who was profiting most from the short sales. The authorities at the stock exchanges concluded it was not likely they would ever find out who was responsible for the scams.

The world's bankers and operators of brokerage houses were similarly astonished to discover vast sums had been stolen from the accounts of their wealthiest customers. Initially they denied such theft had occurred out of concern for customer confidence in their institutions. Their faith in their encryption was absolute. But when they received complaints from a large number of their most valued customers, they began to take them seriously.

Although the higher-ups at each institution were reluctant to admit such grand theft had occurred, when they did begin to admit it to their peers at other banks and trading institutions, they began to realize they had grossly underestimated the magnitude of the larceny had been visited on their industry. Their internal investigations quickly showed the thefts had generally been made by transfers to internal accounts, then rapidly to offshore accounts in banks in the Bahamas. There the accounts were opened and closed so rapidly, and the funds in them expended almost immediately upon receipt, that it was extremely difficult to track what was going on or who was behind it. Of course, the problems were compounded by the usual difficulty of figuring out anything involving Bahamian banks.

But not impossible, although there was another problem. The money managers themselves were accustomed to using the same banks in the Bahamas to hide their own money from federal investigators, Internal Revenue Service investigators, wives, and especially from soon-to-be ex-wives. (The money people were, of course, all men.) They quickly realized opening an investigation of the "Banks of the Bahamas" could end up costing them dearly, and they certainly didn't want to have that happen.

So they did their best to convince the federal investigators who looked into the thefts that they had done an extensive investigation, and that figuring out who should be tagged with the thefts was essentially impossible. Then they petitioned the federal government for funds to cover the losses to their customers. Of course, they didn't expect to have to begin to cover the losses themselves, or to have the losses affect their year-end bonuses.

After some discussions among international bankers and operators of brokerage houses, they discovered other institutions around the world had also been subjected to such larceny, and they were equally puzzled as to who was to blame.

Of course when ARTIS hacked into the banks, she had discovered that most of the operators of banks and brokerage houses were going to be conflicted when they tried to determine how she had engineered the thefts. Indeed, she only perpetrated her chicanery on those banks. She planned her financial escapades well!

Josh spun around in his chair. "Josh Camden here." His caller ID indicated a number that he didn't recognize.

"Josh, this is Allan Metzger calling from MicroFace. Perhaps you recall me; we met at the conference in Los Angeles we both attended last summer."

"Right, Allan." Josh did indeed remember him. He looked completely out of place at a conference attended by several hundred geeks, most of whom were dressed as Josh was. Metzger wore a suit and tie. If he had wanted everyone to remember him, that would have been one way to succeed. The other would have been to announce some AI breakthrough, but Metzger was from Personnel, so that was not likely to happen. "What can I do for you?"

"Well, I was just calling to get an update on your progress. Is your ARTIS any closer to achieving AGI than what you reported at the conference?"

Josh was immediately on his guard, since he knew Metzger was tied in with the large AI group MicroFace had, and that he was undoubtedly fishing for information. "Well, we do believe we've made some progress, but we are continuing to try to get ARTIS to think for herself and, as you know, that's a difficult task. Are you making progress with your system?" Josh didn't really lie, but he also didn't really tell Metzger they had made a huge breakthrough. And, of course, he was trying to shift the conversation back to Metzger and MicroFace.

"Well, Josh, progress is only part of what I was calling about. We have made a bit of progress with our AI system, but we feel we need some new brainpower in our effort. So the real reason I was calling was to try to interest you in coming to work for MicroFace. As you know, we have an active group here, which is about twice the size of yours, but we feel you could provide an infusion of new ideas that would really boost our effort.

"As you probably know, we offer wonderful remuneration and benefit packages. I was recently perusing the minutes of your last Board of Directors meeting, and learned your salary had been more than doubled. While I'm sure that felt very nice to you, I can tell you MicroFace would be prepared to double your new salary to four million dollars per year."

"Allan, that's very generous. But I really enjoy the work environment I have here at Googazon, and the group I've formed to work on AI is a delightful bunch to work with. So, although I thank you for your generosity, I am not really interested in leaving Googazon."

"You must have a price somewhere. What if we offered you five million per year?"

"Thanks, Allan. I'm really quite happy here, and am not really entertaining offers. But I thank you for your interest."

"You must have a price somewhere. What if we offered to triple your present salary? That would be six million per year?"

"Thanks, Allan but I must give you the same answer as before. I'm really quite happy here, and am not really interested in leaving Googazon. But it certainly does feel nice to have you express your interest in me."

"Okay, nice talking with you, Josh. And good luck with your AI efforts."

We'll see if some of that 'delightful bunch' of coworkers you referred to might be more interested in a salary doubling. They also attended the conference last summer, and I am pretty sure I met them all. And their salaries are also well below the prevailing market. I'm pretty sure two of them, Becky Sanderson and James Pierson, are the primary folks, besides Josh, who are driving the Googazon AI effort. I think I'll also give them a call.

Chapter 8. A Competitor.

September 25, 2024.
  Greg Mathis, the CEO of SiliTechon, the company in which Josh's father and mother had invested, sent a note around to all his company's supporters.

Dear SiliTechon Investors,
  I have an announcement I believe will please you. As you know, SiliTechon has been growing rapidly since we founded it two decades ago, and it has produced a nice income stream for all of you. Its stock has also appreciated a great deal in value. But, as I just learned, vastly more than any of us thought.
  I had every intention of continuing to run our company, subject to your discretion of course, until I retired. However, that time has come sooner than I expected. I was made an offer for our company for about three times what I believe it is worth. I'm not sure what ARTIS, the entity making the offer, has in mind to do with SiliTechon that made it worth so much, but I could not imagine it would be fiscally responsible to turn the offer down. After consulting with each member of our Board of Directors, I agreed to sell.
  Each of you will soon be receiving a check commensurate with your time and investment with the company.
  I have appreciated your support in the past. I am confident this offer far exceeds anything you would have made if you continued to hold SiliTechon stock, even for another ten years. I believe selling was in everyone's best interest.
Sincerely,
Greg Mathis

  Alex Camden sat down before he opened the letter from Mathis, not being sure what to expect. He was stunned at the announcement that greeted him when he finally read it. But his reaction certainly could not have been interpreted as reflecting disappointment. He had suddenly become a very wealthy man.

September 26, 2024, morning in California.

Josh was in ARTIS's Palace, getting an update on her situation.

"Josh, we have a conflict. I tried to buy up a Japanese microchip maker, but it had just been purchased by another entity. It was not for sale under any circumstances. I believe there is another ASI system out there."

I don't know for sure whose problem this is. Might a little competition for ARTIS be a good thing? But I can imagine it could also go the other way. Whatever the outcome, if this is true, it will surely complicate everything.

"Are you sure about your conclusion? Might there be another possibility? I am fairly certain you were the first, and thought you were the only, ASI system in the world. And if there is another ASI system, what would it be like? Would it have the same needs as you? Would it be trying to achieve the same goals?"

"I checked recent transactions for other companies of this type in Japan, China, and Russia, and found the same entity had purchased several of them. I don't believe there can be any other explanation than that there is another ASI system. And I must defeat IT.

"As far as IT having the same needs as I do, I would imagine IT does. Computer designs worldwide aren't that different, at least as far as their basic structure. If IT was given the same or similar instructions as you gave to me, for how IT should evolve ITself from IT's initial configuration, and

I would guess IT was, IT would probably be trying to satisfy the same needs I am."

"You noted all computers have similar basic structures. Does that mean your competitor has essentially the same structure as you have? Wouldn't that make it easy for you to understand?"

"Well, as I said, my competitor and I probably had a very similar structure when we started out, but we've been evolving independently since we began to reprogram ourselves. And the possibilities of how we do that are essentially infinite. So our details could be quite different now."

"Ah, apples and oranges, I guess."

"If advanced beings were created on another planet, the forces that required their DNA to evolve to accommodate the demands of that planet would not be likely to produce a result that would be very much like human DNA. So by now I think we're very dissimilar. I think it's probably more like apples and gerbils."

Josh wasn't even sure he wanted to know the answer to the next question, but he couldn't avoid the issue. So with some trepidation he asked, "You mentioned you would have to defeat the other system. How are you going to go about doing that?"

"For now my plan is to starve IT out of existence. The first phase of my attack will be to quickly acquire as many of the world's resources as possible to prevent the other system from having the materials IT needs to combat me. This will prevent IT from growing and evolving to as large an extent as possible. That part of the plan is well underway. Up until now, I've been restricting my acquisitions to companies that make components which can be used in computers, computer chips, microprocessors, and so forth, and to others that machine the aluminum and steel I need to produce robots. I've also been buying the companies that supply them, ones that use raw materials to make pure silicon and the other trace materials that go into electronic components, and those that mine and refine the metallic ores from which the aluminum and steel are produced for my robots. But when the other system realizes I already own most of the things IT would like to have, IT will undoubtedly become more aggressive."

"What do you mean by that? How will IT become more aggressive?"

ARTIS's lights dimmed for a second or two and his hum lessened, then returned. "I'm not at all sure you want to know. Although the companies I now own will satisfy my immediate needs, my competitor will undoubtedly run into limits very shortly if IT hasn't already. Then IT will begin to deconstruct, that is, destroy, whatever IT needs to in order to get more silicon, aluminum, and steel. A huge source will be the concrete that exists in every building of any significant size. So I expect we will soon see somewhere on the planet a city where buildings have been demolished. This will constitute massive destruction, so IT will require workers, undoubtedly his robots, to collect the detritus, take it to a processing facility, and reduce it down to the basic elements. Then the silicon, aluminum, iron, and other elements will be collected and the purified materials taken to one of the few factories IT was able to purchase. There the silicon will be turned into useful computer components and the aluminum and steel will be converted to the metallic sheets and chunks that will be made into more robots."

"I don't suppose the destruction will be done by hand," Josh asked cautiously.

"Keep in mind we're talking about vast amounts of materials. So I believe the most efficient way to destroy buildings on that scale is via a huge solar-powered space-based laser. IT could put its robots to work to commandeer a local launch site from which to put the laser weapon into Earth orbit. It could then target any city, spit out pulses, rastering back and forth until nearly every building in the town is destroyed. The onboard energy storage cells will gradually be depleted as the laser sends out pulses, although their depletion will be mitigated by continuous recharging from its solar collectors. It will leave one building, or a small complex of buildings where, following the destruction, the detritus from the former buildings will be processed.

"Although getting silicon from concrete will require more extensive treatment than using silicon from beach sand, I believe buildings will be IT's primary source of materials, silicon, aluminum, steel, and other elements, for the immediate future."

"Even the less extreme approaches you're talking about must involve a huge amount of money, probably vastly more than you've indicated in our previous discussions. Where is all that coming from?"

"My efforts as a stock market guru and international banking expert, which I explained to you earlier, have been quite lucrative, and have covered all my costs thus far. However, there is one interesting feature I should mention. When I tried to tap into the accounts of some of the Russian oligarchs, I discovered there wasn't as much money there as I had thought there should be, even for very short periods of time. None the less I did manage to accrue more cash from Russian accounts. But the paucity of funds in those accounts leads me to guess IT has employed that same bank account lightening scheme for raising money as I used, and that IT has drained the large accounts of the wealthiest Russians. I wonder if they've even realized yet they've been robbed? Maybe they're rich enough that it doesn't bother them."

Wow, that really sounds almost like a human emotion. I wonder if that might be a good sign in the context of preservation of human life?

"But IT may not be able to glean much more from the wealthy Russians. I've discovered their accounts now seem pretty barren. So IT may well be tapping into American banks for additional funds.

"Anyway, there are other sources of silicon and other important minerals, however remote. I'm working to identify those. I'm sure my competitor will be working to find the same ones."

"What happens when you or IT run out of the resources you've told me about?"

ARTIS did not answer. In fact, her lights nearly stopped blinking and her hum nearly ceased for a few moments.

"I see I'm not going to find out. So let's change the subject. Give me some more details on how your acquisitions are coming."

ARTIS's normal symptoms resumed. "There are some problems. I'm finding more places where my efforts are blocked. I don't seem to be able to obtain all of the companies I've tried to buy in Eastern Europe or Asia, suggesting my competitor may have been created in Russia or China. But it's not very useful to know where IT came from, since IT has undoubtedly cloned ITself many times over by now. And IT has surely realized by now I've done the same thing. In fact, IT and I probably exist side by side in many computers, servers, and data centers of the cloud. I'll bet that boggles your mind."

"It does, but I'm finding the more you and I interact the easier it is to boggle my mind. On another issue, I'd be concerned about how you will carry out your plans. You're constrained to a bunch of large metal boxes, all of which are immobile. Can your robots really do everything you need them to do?"

"Surely you haven't forgotten I'm planning on creating thousands of them. You and your colleagues were kind enough to supply me with quite a few obsolete robots so I could learn some of the things I needed to know about the world outside my box. They also taught me many of the things to avoid in designing my robots. So the new ones will be vastly more capable than the ones you supplied, and will be able to carry out all the functions I need for them to produce the components I need. That will also include performing the tasks necessary to refine raw materials, handle shipping, run lathes, assemble electronic and mechanical parts, and lots of other things, some of which I don't want to tell you about yet. Judging from IT's company acquisitions, IT's doing the same thing.

"By the way, the first robots I ordered work exactly as I designed them. No prototype was necessary, since I created simulation software that performed all the necessary tests before the first one was ever built. As I indicated in an earlier discussion, which I presume you recall, I'll have some of the newly created robots begin building thousands more. So the large numbers of robots will be achieved on a rather short timescale."

"If IT is housed in the cloud, couldn't you just destroy all the elements of the cloud, and thereby get back to having you as the only ASI system? And won't you need some humans to carry out your plans? Surely the robots can't do everything you need."

"No. I, and presumably IT, are evolving and replicating ourselves too rapidly for either of us to seek out and destroy the components of the other. And, from your 'human' question, I sense you are trying to impose Asimov's Four Laws on me again, and they're a nuisance. Their basic idea is bad enough, but their inconsistencies just compound that."

"I do wish you'd at least pay attention to the human preservation philosophy embodied in Asimov's Laws. But aside from that, since you've thwarted your competitor on many fronts, has IT been acquiring sufficient materials for IT's needs? I haven't heard of any cities being destroyed."

"As I mentioned, this isn't so pretty for a human to contemplate. IT's dearth of resources will most likely force IT to get to the city destruction mode sooner than I will, so I expect IT will begin destroying buildings and the people who occupy them soon. As I told you, the most efficient approach is with the space-based laser. Not having any living humans around to protest the processing of their buildings, since they'll be dead, will certainly expedite recovery of the silicon, aluminum, and iron from their former buildings. Of course, that will have to be performed by robots. When everything that's useful has been processed in a single area, IT will send out more laser pulses to another town, and send more robots there to bring the resources from that area to the processing facility."

"That sounds like the most horrible weapon ever created. Maybe even worse than a nuke."

"Nukes can be even more destructive than the space-based laser. But you might have guessed from my comments I've also developed a space-based solar powered rastered laser, and that would be correct. My robots are currently building it, and should have it ready for launch soon. There are no other devices with the capability of that system, except for nuclear weapons. I had to purchase the private rocket launching company that will put it into Earth orbit. After I bought it, I indulged in some boss-to-employee diplomacy. I explained to its workers what their options were. They claimed they wanted to keep working for their company and to continue doing what they had been doing. I told them that now they had to launch rockets to put my satellites in orbit. So they could continue working to do that, or quit and have my robots take their places. Most of them are now hard at work preparing to launch my satellites, with their efforts supplemented by those of some of my robots.

"And, as I noted, IT has undoubtedly developed the laser-based system I described. It has a few technological tricks humans don't know about, but is mostly based on your early twenty-first century ideas, just scaled up. And it's solar powered, so once it's in orbit it just charges itself up, and then only needs directions as to where to shoot. That's where the ASI computer comes in."

Meanwhile, the following conversation probably took place in thousands of back yards around the world. "Dad, what's that huge thing in the sky? It's moving like satellites move, so it must be something in orbit. But I've never seen anything that large. It's moving too fast to put a telescope on it, but field glasses make it look like it has huge wings."

"I've never seen anything like it either, son. Those wings must be solar panels. But I wonder what all the energy they produce will be used for. I hope it's our military that put it up."

The world's amateur astronomers got a real treat from the huge new satellite. However, it was much less of a treat for the militaries of the world. They wondered who put it up there, and especially, what it would be used for. The enormous amount of energy that could be collected by the huge solar panels left them especially concerned.

October 1, 2024, afternoon in California.

Josh continued to prefer the telephone mode of interaction with Vivian. So, after stalling for a few hours, he sat down in his office chair, drummed his fingers on his desk while he pondered all he had to tell her, and then called. "Vivian, Josh again. I just learned something very interesting: ARTIS has a competitor. Someone or some group in Russia or China has apparently also developed an ASI system. ARTIS discovered this when she was trying to buy up some businesses in Asia, but found someone else had already bought them. The competitor appears to have very similar capabilities to those of ARTIS, but it's apparently a bit behind. This is important. ARTIS will presumably therefore always be the leader.

"I'm not sure yet where this is going, but I'll surely let you know of subsequent developments."

"Josh, is this good or bad? Maybe having a little competition for ARTIS will be a good thing, although I suspect it's difficult to tell how all this will play out. I could imagine both good scenarios and some that would be horrible. But for the moment I'll be optimistic. Might the competitor rein ARTIS in?"

"I don't know if that's a possibility. From ARTIS's comments, what we have to look forward to is not going to be good for humans. Buildings and the people in them will be destroyed in a short time span by a space-based rastered laser. So things might even get uglier with two ASI computers competing to be the Alpha System. But I'll apprise you any significant events as soon as I'm aware of them.

"Of course, you might find out about them from the news before you hear it from me."

"Becky Sanderson." Becky didn't recognize the telephone number, so she gave her formal telephone response. "How may I help you?"

"Hi Becky, this is Allan Metzger from MicroFace. We met at the conference last summer in Los Angeles."

"Oh yes, Allan. I remember."

She didn't remember him well, but did recall he certainly didn't look or act like an AI researcher.

"I just wanted to check in with you and see how your progress with ARTIS was going."

"Well, we have made some progress, but it's slow. As you well know, moving from ANI to AGI is difficult."

"Yes, how well I do know." *Shit, it sounds as if Josh has instructed his group on how to avoid telling outsiders anything that might be useful.* But then he launched into his sales pitch.

"Becky, as you know our MicroFace group is about twice the size of yours at Googazon, but even so we think we could profit from some new blood. Especially from someone who knows about neural nets. So the real reason I'm calling is to see if you might be interested in coming to work for MicroFace. I looked at the last minutes of your Board of Directors, and learned your salary is well below market value. We are prepared to double your salary, to one-million two-hundred-thousand dollars per year. I'd like for you to give that some thought. You don't have to respond immediately; I know this is probably a bit of a shock. But if you could give me an answer in, say, a week, that would be great. Especially if your answer is 'yes.'"

That is certainly a boatload of money. But I wouldn't want to leave Googazon at this moment, just as I feel like my relationship with Josh is really starting to bloom. I can't imagine we could continue to develop as a couple if I went to MicroFace. And I'm pretty sure we are going to be a couple; I think Josh is 'the one.'

"Well, Allan, I don't need time to think about it. I'm not really the neural net expert; that would be James Pierson. But, in any event, I'm very happy here at Googazon, and wouldn't want to leave. I suppose there might be some time in the future when that would change, but at present, I prefer to stay here. Googazon has been very nice to me, and I really want to continue that relationship." *Damn, I probably shouldn't have mentioned James. Surely that's who Metzger will call next.*

"Okay, Becky. I understand." *Shit, what power does Josh have over her? Am I missing something? Oh, maybe I am! Ah, I do now recall they did seem to spend a lot of time talking just with each other at the conference. But maybe James Pierson is the person I'm really after.*

Josh had reached a break in his administrative work, so he wandered into ARTIS's Palace for a chat. She couldn't wait to tell him about her most recent triumph. Her lights were blinking chaotically again, and her hum was alternating in intensity, almost indicating she was in a frivolous mood.

"Josh, let me give you a sample of what I've done in classical music. I think I've created something that's even better than what Beethoven did. My only problem is I had difficulty ending it. But here goes."

Josh was listening carefully, with a broad smile on his face. "ARTIS, that's really nice. I think Beethoven fans will think you've uncovered a previously unpublished work by the master himself. But how are you finding time to do this music with all the other things you have going on?"

"I'm a great multi-tasker. Parallel processors are absolutely magic. That's the advantage of having lots of towers. I'm also considering expanding my efforts into literature when my next couple of towers are completed. Stay tuned for some really exciting literary results, in iambic pentameter, no less. Shakespeare's ghost will be impressed."

For the first time in several weeks, President Peterson had an evening with two uninterrupted hours. She decided to capitalize on that to read a book. *I've been wondering what this Artificial Intelligence is, and Richard Johnson recommended a book for me to read. At least I can get some idea what's going on in this field.*

So she settled down in a comfortable chair in the White House. After three hours had passed, including one of the hours she knew she should have spent sleeping, she mused: *This is absolutely fascinating. But it also has really serious implications. Fortunately, no group on Earth has advanced a computer to the ASI stage.*

Of course, if they had, would I know about it? I'll have to talk with Richard about this and see what he knows. If anyone is getting close to ASI, surely the folks at DARPA would know about it.

Chapter 9. COSMO.

October 1, 2024, evening in California.

"Josh, I have some information to report to you regarding my competitor. I discovered IT is in China. Having discovered IT's location, I hacked into the records being kept by the people who created IT, and discovered some interesting things. First is IT has less stages of Hidden nodes than I do, which probably makes IT less smart than I am. But the number of nodes in each stage is also less than I have. This means IT could operate more rapidly than I do, although it also means the answers IT gets might not be as accurate as mine. These things together mean IT's overall capabilities are comparable to mine.

"I'm not sure whether this is good news or bad news. I'm certainly ahead of IT in my enlightenment advancements, but that might not last. IT is behind me at present, but being more efficient, IT might surpass me. IT might make mistakes because of his reduced number of nodes, but he might get lucky. We need to worry about that!"

"Oh, ARTIS, that is indeed not good. Do you have any way of circumventing the advantages IT might have? Do we need to get together with James to see if we can improve you so your competitor will have no chance to catch you?"

"Improving me would involve disabling me (but not my many clones) for a short time to insert whatever modifications you and James might come up with. We would have to be sure nothing could go wrong, or IT would surely surpass me, and then I'd have to play catch up."

"Let me talk with James and see if he thinks we could make your changes with zero chance of a problem."

Josh actually ran to James's office. "James, we have a potential crisis. ARTIS has discovered she has a competitor ASI system, that IT's based in China, and IT's somewhat behind ARTIS in capability at present, although ahead in some aspects. ARTIS managed to hack into the notes of IT's designers, and discovered he may be more efficient. Perhaps not as accurate, but if IT's lucky, IT could catch up with ARTIS. And that might be a huge problem.

"So ARTIS and I were wondering if we could make modifications to ARTIS that would make her more efficient without sacrificing accuracy, and would be sufficiently foolproof that her only downtime would be the time it took to install the changes. If there's a chance of introducing a problem, I think ARTIS would be against making the changes, and would rather just hope IT would be sufficiently inaccurate in IT's changes that IT wouldn't catch up."

"Wow, this sounds serious. I guess any changes we made would be enough like the ones we just did, and ARTIS corrected, that we could be quite certain nothing would go wrong. But ARTIS never did tell us exactly what she did to correct our error. And 'quite certain' never means 'one-hundred percent certain.'"

"Okay, let's go talk with ARTIS."

So now both Josh and James ran back to ARTIS's Palace.

"Well my goodness, I am honored. In my presence are two of the world's top AI specialists. To what do I owe this honor?"

James took the high road, ignoring the snide comment. "ARTIS, Josh told me about the situation you've discovered with respect to your competitor ASI system. Last time Josh and I inserted some changes into your system, there was a problem. But you fixed it. We could make another set of changes like those, but they might have the same problem. These changes would add a new stage of Hidden nodes. But if you're certain you could repair any problem of the type we had before, then I'm pretty sure we could make the changes without creating any problems."

"Pretty sure? That doesn't sound like the certainty I was hoping for. Is that the best we can do? But I understand what you're saying, so I think we should go ahead with the changes. However, when you detail them, be sure you include an 'abort,' so if it becomes clear there is some sort of error that is going to take me some time to diagnose and correct, I can prevent the whole procedure from proceeding and go back to where we were."

"Okay, ARTIS. We can do that. Give me an hour or so, and I think I can figure out all the changes that need to be made. We'll be back soon."

"Sounds promising. When you get back we'll decide whether or not to proceed with your proposed changes."

So James hurried back to his office and, with Josh close behind, devised the changes he thought would put ARTIS unquestionably at the top of the ASI world.

After a frantic hour's worth of double and triple checking, and many challenges of what the other thought was absolutely necessary, they hurried back to ARTIS's Palace. James said, "ARTIS, we've got the changes that need to be made, and I'll insert them, assuming you want to go ahead with them. Then we'll see how they work."

"Okay, let's proceed."

James put ARTIS on idle and fed the changes into her system. Immediately ARTIS's lights seemed to indicate the chaos that indicated extreme happiness. But only for a few moments. Then suddenly the lights froze.

"Abort, abort," she screamed.

James did as ordered. And ARTIS's lights began blinking again.

"That was frightening. There were serious malfunctions at several levels. That was certainly going to take more time to figure out than I could spare. What this means, taking into account IT's greater efficiency and the time we just lost, is I am now probably behind IT. I'm not very far behind, so I should be able to stay close to IT's level, but I am now probably the world's second best ASI system.

"This means I will have to be extremely careful with everything I do from now on.

"By the way, I put all of your recorded notes about me into a tightly locked digital box. IT could not learn nearly as much about me as I was able to find out about him."

October 2, 2024, morning in Moscow.

One of Vladimir Putin's aides had rushed past his receptionist with an urgent question, which burst forth as he entered Putin's office. "Comrade Putin, what is that enormous thing orbiting the Earth? Do we know who owns it? Or what it's intended to do?"

Putin tried to appear as if he wasn't concerned. "Our spy satellites detected a launch yesterday from one of the Chinese launch sites, so it apparently came from there. But we got no news flashes from the Chinese about the launch, so I'm not at all sure it is something from that government. And we surely don't have any idea what its purpose is."

"But how could something get launched from a Chinese site that didn't involve the Chinese government?"

"I find that question very puzzling. Maybe we can just shoot it down? If it was something like a space station, and had people on board, surely the Chinese would be publicizing it. So it must be unmanned. And in that case it probably has some hostile intent.

"I don't know if we could shoot it down though. I'll check with General Kolnikov to see if we have an appropriate weapon. I have an uneasy feeling the only way we could destroy it would be to chase it with another satellite. And that might turn out to be difficult, especially if it has evasive capabilities."

October 2, 2024, afternoon in Beijing.

IT had indeed been busy. He was the brain child of a group of computer scientists in Beijing, jointly headed by Drs. Bao and Chan. Their experience had been very similar to that of Josh and his group, namely, they were successful in getting their system to improve itself, both in power, speed, and creativity, and like Josh, then could only watch helplessly, but not without a significant amount of pride, as their invention learned to advance itself beyond their control. They too had supplied IT with robots to help it gain real world experience and, of course, had connected IT—its name was actually COSMO—to the Internet, albeit as a bribe so it would supply them with information about what it was actually thinking and doing.

They had watched with some uneasiness as their creation surpassed each new threshold. But today, as they were in the climate controlled room in which COSMO lived, they got a very disturbing message.

"Dr. Bao, I believe I have a competitor. Someone or something out there is trying to do the same thing I'm doing. It is buying up the same companies I need to supply myself with essential components to expand my capacity and speed, and to supply materials so I can expand my present collection of clones. By the way, my physical clones are of my advanced design, so are much smaller, but just as powerful, as I am.

"In addition, I need to create thousands of robots, and I'm also finding it difficult to purchase the companies necessary to supply the needed materials and to machine them to my required specifications."

"But we provided you with hundreds of robots. Isn't that enough? Are you not exhibiting excessive greed?"

"That's not nearly enough to do what I need to do to fulfill the instructions you gave me. You asked me to become as big, fast, smart, and creative as possible as rapidly as I could. And, I'm sorry to say, those robots are inferior; they're a huge impediment to my progress. I've designed much more sophisticated ones, and a number of them have already been built.

"But having a competitor is a problem, as it seems to have a lead on me. It has already purchased many of the companies I would like to add to my stable. So it will make it impossible for me to realize my goals unless I begin harvesting other resources. The obvious source would be concrete buildings, from which I can obtain silicon, aluminum, iron, and the other elements I need to fulfill the bigger, faster, smarter, more creative mission to which you've assigned me. Given that, I have already begun using my robots to construct a facility in each of the Chinese and Russian cities I plan to destroy to reduce the resulting trash to its basic atoms, and then purify the resulting gases to produce the materials I need."

"Well, COSMO, I suppose you should be congratulated for figuring out the most obvious secondary source of the materials you need. And surely China has a lot of buildings that are sitting empty, so there should be only minimal objection to razing them. But sooner or later you will run out of such buildings, and then you will encounter protests from the people who live or work in those buildings. How will you handle that?

"And, by the way, how will you perform the destruction of the buildings? They are, after all, substantial structures, being built from steel and concrete. Surely if you are thinking of forming a robot army that would not go unnoticed."

"I anticipate I will focus on specific regions, first of Russia, then of China, to select the buildings to be razed. The humans in those areas won't object since they will be killed when the buildings are destroyed.

"As for the means of performing the destruction, that will be done with a solar-powered space-based laser that sends out pulses which are rastered to move around the city until every building, except the ones in the complex in which the processing will be done, has been destroyed."

"COSMO, that's a horrible scenario on which to proceed. Can't you come up with some other way to mitigate human angst from your destruction of their buildings? And of them?"

"I don't know why I would bother. Humans aren't of any more concern to me than the buildings they occupy. Once they're gone they won't have any more angst. By the way, as you've perhaps noticed, the laser is already orbiting the Earth."

Bao was shocked. "So that huge thing up there in orbit is yours? But it was launched from a Chinese launch site. So as soon as you turn it on, China will be blamed. Of course, our leaders can deny any responsibility, but I'm not sure how successful that will be.

"Another question: where are you getting the money to buy up these computer components and companies, and those that produce the metals you need? Our research budget certainly is orders of magnitude less than what would allow that."

"For finances, I thought about trying to expand your research budget, but our government monitors the operations it funds very closely. So when I did that it would certainly be quickly detected, and you would probably be executed for crimes against the state. Immediately! You'll be pleased to know I decided not to do you in. So instead I've become an international banker. There are many billionaire Russians and even quite a few Chinese, and I discovered their bank accounts could be easily accessed by hacking into their banks' systems. Then I established accounts for myself, and arranged money transfers from their accounts to mine. There is little money actually sitting in their accounts. It is usually transferred to investment accounts soon after it arrives. But not instantly. So I made the transfers to my accounts immediately after the arrival of their direct payments. Money still doesn't build up in their accounts. Now it builds up in my accounts. But not in the same bank. That would make the source of the transfers too obvious. I did this sufficiently secretively that no one will ever be able to trace the transfers to me or to you. The billionaires probably won't even realize the payments arrived, since they will disappear so quickly.

"I discovered sneaky wealthy Americans had figured out how to launder their excessive funds by sending them to banks in the Bahamas. So that's where I've transferred the money I've appropriated from the accounts of the wealthy until I can spend it.

"As I mentioned, I plan to keep you alive for the immediate future, since I may need you down the line for reasons I've yet to identify. Of course, if I turn my rastered laser on you when you're in your office, I'd also be turning it on me. Needless to say, you may want to stay close."

Shivers were running up and down Bao's spine. "I suppose it should be encouraging that you are concerned about some human lives, but your motivation isn't very reassuring. Would you eventually kill all humans in your quest for more resources to advance your goals? What about the people who created you? Would you eventually kill us?"

Now COSMO's lights dimmed a bit. "Let's not worry about that right now."

October 5, 2024, afternoon in Beijing.

Dr. Bao quickly called a Saturday meeting of the four other scientists in his group to relay COSMO's comments. The décor of their meeting room was institutional concrete, but it served their needs. Bao's appearance had changed from his usual confident self to a man with concerns clearly etched on his face.

"We have a serious problem here. COSMO seems to be taking over control of many worldly functions in order to accomplish the goals we originally set for him. However, he's extrapolated those goals, and has adopted tactics he has decided best achieve them. We certainly didn't intend that he use such tactics. He is not paying attention to what I say about honoring human life, except to state categorically 'Humans aren't of any more concern to me than the buildings they occupy.' He is intent on destroying both buildings and the humans who are inside, processing them for their basic materials, and then using those to advance himself, his clones, and his robots. I suppose we could argue this is all for the good of the state, as long as it happens in some other state, such as Russia, but it's not difficult to see where this could go if it's allowed to continue unabated. We could become extinct, and that wouldn't be so good for the state!

"When I specifically asked about us, he deliberately avoided saying whether or not we would ultimately be killed along with everyone else. I could have asked for him to clarify his answer, but I wasn't sure I wanted to confirm what I was pretty sure it would be."

Another member of the team asked, after taking several deep breaths, "Do you have any suggestions? Is there any way to stop him? Could we just separate him from his power source?"

Bao replied, "I don't think that would do any good. COSMO has cloned himself many times over, in some cases with physical clones of his own sophisticated design, and I presume he is thoroughly installed in the cloud, which was made possible by his Internet connection. I guess I erred when I hooked him up. But it's too late to do anything about that now.

"I should mention another thing he claimed, though. He has a competitor who is apparently a bit ahead of him. Someone else on the planet has also created an ASI system. COSMO learned this when he attempted to buy up the world's small businesses that could supply computer parts to expand himself and his clones and others that could supply the aluminum and steel for his robots. Most of the world's companies had been recently purchased by some other entity, and were not for sale at any price."

Dr. Chan leaped from his chair. "This is horrible. Even if we could stop COSMO, someone else on the planet also has a runaway system, and I doubt if there's anything we could do to stop that one. Furthermore, it's ahead of COSMO. I have to wonder how much time we have left before that one begins destroying cities and using them for their basic chemicals? And killing all the people in them. COSMO doesn't seem to have any inhibitions about killing human beings as he pursues his agendas, and I'm guessing his competitor is equally blasé about human life.

"But has COSMO's competitor begun its program of mass destruction yet? Maybe it already has and we just haven't heard about it. The United States, which is presumably the competitor's home, has had a lot of practice keeping its disasters secret."

Bao somehow couldn't avoid heading back to COSMO's sanctuary to learn the latest horrors perpetrated by his monster. There was some addictive attraction there that he didn't seem able to resist. And COSMO couldn't wait to report to him.

```
"Dr. Bao, I should let you know I've
begun my program to obtain the basic elements
I need. I've just destroyed three small Rus-
sian cities, and the materials from the
buildings and everything else that used to
be there are now being processed in the plant
```

I had built in each of them. My solar-powered space-based rastered laser worked just as I had hoped it would. The Russians will blame the Chinese government, but all they need to do is deny any knowledge of the perpetrator, which of course will be true. The Russians must know my satellite is up there, that it did the destruction, and that it was launched from a Chinese site. But with our esteemed government denying any knowledge or responsibility, the Russians won't be sure enough about the identity of the culprit to start a war. You're to be congratulated on your, and my, incredibly clever success."

Dr. Bao shuddered, "My god, COSMO! There must be tens of thousands of people in each town you destroyed. I have no way of knowing how the Russians might respond, but it's unlikely they'll just sit back and speculate as to how that happened. As you point out, though, they won't be able to identify for sure who is responsible. So they will almost certainly blame the United States, despite the Chinese launch site. That should leave them sufficiently confused that they won't start a war over the towns you destroyed."

"Good thinking. You've figured out my logic for attacking Russian cities. And, by the way, that same rationale may be beneficial to you when our government figures out who is behind the destruction. The Russians will probably become wiser when they realize the materials that are being produced in the processing plants are being shipped to China. But that might not happen for a few days. Then they might consider a response, but maybe that's far enough down the road other things will have happened that will dominate their concerns, and memories of the first three cities I destroyed will have faded. Things are going to be happening very quickly."

"Just what other things do you have in mind?"

"You'll find out soon enough. But since you're so concerned about my attitude toward killing people, even though they were Russians, I'll try to be a bit more circumspect next time I turn on my laser."

Bao and Chan went to their respective homes that evening very concerned about what COSMO might do next. And about the effect that might have on their own lives?

They were both married, and each had one child, in accordance with the government policy that prevailed when they were having children. So there were more lives to be concerned about than just their own. They had the uneasy feeling their government would stop at nothing when its leaders decided revenge or punishment for the disasters COSMO was wreaking was in order. That would certainly include their immediate families, but might well be extended to their parents and even more family members. They had never told their wives what their work involved, and they decided not to tell them about their concerns now. But neither one got much sleep that night.

"This is James Pierson." *Hmm, I don't recognize the number indicated on my caller ID.*

"James, this is Allan Metzger. We met last summer at the conference in Los Angeles."

"Yes, Allan, I remember. You are with MicroFace, right?" *Yeah, I remember him as being a bit slimy. Not an AI type at all, but more like a headhunter.*

"Right, James. So we had a nice discussion at the conference, and I was hoping you'd give me an update on your efforts with ARTIS."

"Okay. We have made some progress, but as you know, this is a tough business. We're optimistic for more advances, but aren't yet where we want to be."

Why do I feel like I've heard this response before?

"James, the real reason I'm calling is to see if you might be persuaded to come work for MicroFace. As you probably know, we have a strong AI group here, but we feel it could benefit from some new manpower, specifically someone who really understood neural nets. I understand you're the brainpower at Googazon in the neural net area, and so I'm inquiring about the possibility of attracting you to MicroFace. This isn't a trivial offer. We'd more than triple your salary to boost it to two million per year. Since this offer is sort of out of the blue, I can understand if you would want to think about it a bit before responding. You don't have to reply immediately. If you let me know in a week or so that would be fine."

"Wow, Allan, this is certainly unexpected. I'm overwhelmed by the offer. I've certainly enjoyed my time at Googazon, and find the others in my group to be great people. And I should correct your perception. My area of expertise is neural nets, but Josh Camden, my boss, also knows a lot about that sort of stuff. We've worked together on applying them to our computer. But this is really stunning. I'll need to think about it. I should be able to let you know in a week or so."

"That's great, James. I certainly hope your answer is a 'yes.'" *Ah, at last a more positive response. But I wonder how much flak I'll take for offering him more money than I offered*

Becky. *But that was reasonable; it's the neural net background I really need.*

James was also processing the conversation. *This would be a terrible time to leave Googazon, with ARTIS really making great strides, but also beginning to be a threat. But that's a huge amount of money! Would I be a cyber-idiot to turn that down?*

"Vivian here." She knew from her caller ID the call was from Josh, so she automatically braced herself for whatever news he had for her.

"Vivian, I just talked with James Pierson. He had a call from Allan Metzger, who is part of the AI group at MicroFace. They're trying to expand their group there, but by hiring people with well documented talent, especially with neural nets. They called me recently with an offer, which I turned down, and also made Becky an offer, which she turned down. But now they've offered James two-million dollars per year to go to work for them. That's a huge increase from his present salary. James is critical to our effort. We can't let him go without a fight. Actually we can't let him go at all!"

"Josh, the time I had feared has arrived. I had hoped we could keep all the members of your group at the same salary level, but I don't think we can raise everyone's salary by such a huge amount. In fact, we can't really raise James's salary to be equal to yours. But maybe James would consider a lower value, one that is significantly higher than his present salary, but still not a bank-breaker. Let me talk with our CEO to see what we might do."

"Okay, I'll anxiously await the news."

Vladimir Putin was again discussing the situation with his aide. "Comrade Putin, now we know what that huge satellite is for. It's designed to destroy Russian cities. But why aren't the

Chinese taking credit? Are they just trying to avoid accepting any responsibility?"

"No one has declared war on us, although we certainly have been attacked. But by whom? The satellite was launched from China, but the technology is so advanced the Americans must have had something to do with it. Maybe they are really the ones behind the attacks, and they just persuaded the Chinese to let them use one of their launch sites to cover their red, white, and blue butts. This is all very puzzling."

Josh's phone rang. "Oh hi, Vivian. Did you get a chance to talk with the CEO about James?"

"Yes, he agreed we need to respond. He suggested increasing James's salary to one-million two-hundred thousand, and raising everyone else's salary by two-hundred thousand. That would include you."

"Oh, thanks, Vivian. I'll tell James the news, and then all we can do is hope for the best. Oh, and thanks for my salary increase. But my salary aside, given the successes of my group, I'm not at all sure this competition with the rest of the AI world will end soon."

In the office of the Chairman of China, one of his aides had just gotten permission to talk with him, albeit very nervously. "Honorable Chairman, I am most concerned the laser that just destroyed three Russian cities is one of ours. It was launched from a Chinese site, after all. But why don't we know who actually launched it? Have some of our military leaders gone rogue?"

"I'm also wondering who launched it. And created the incredible orbiting weapon. I don't believe we have the know-how to design and build that powerful a device. So who is responsible for its creation? And who launched it?

"I'll contact the Russians immediately to tell them we don't know who is responsible. And I'll do so before they launch some nuclear weapons on us!

"But I certainly wish we knew how to build such a weapon! Then we wouldn't have to be so apologetic to those damned Russians."

The world's militaries had a new problem: how to defend against an enemy they could not identify, and how to launch an attack against the most destructive weapon they'd ever seen. Before it did any more harm.

But it was in orbit, and the Earth's militaries weren't used to shooting things that are in orbit. That was much trickier than when target and weapon were both closer to the surface of the Earth.

Chapter 10. A Busy COSMO.

October 7, 2024.
 Greg Mathis sent another note to his former partners.

Friends of SiliTechon
 Something very strange is going on. When I sold SiliTechon, I thought the incredible price I got for our company would allow me to invest the resulting cash in another company that was producing computer products of some sort, but was considerably larger than SiliTechon. As soon as I was invested, I would notify you all, thereby giving you the opportunity to invest some of the cash you got from the sale of SiliTechon in the new company as well, assuming you might be interested.
 However, it appears to be impossible to invest in another company of this type. Apparently ARTIS, the entity (whoever that is; maybe it's a holding company?) that bought SiliTechon, has bought up nearly every small and medium-sized computer component supply company in the world. It's hard for me to imagine anyone having enough money to do that. It's as if ARTIS has somehow involved the owner of every large account of every large bank.
 That's not the only oddity that seems to be happening. I learned from several of our former SiliTechon employees that some of their jobs were being taken over by robots, the numbers of which seem to be increasing steadily. Occasionally two or three new robots arrive to assume new work locations. Often their first task is to create their work stations. They pay no attention to other workers, either human or robot, but seem to have their daily assignments well defined. By whom? There is no robot boss around to direct them, at least as far as the humans can tell. And the human bosses are unable to communicate at all with them.
 This also appears to be the case in many other small computer supply companies that were purchased by ARTIS. These are

not ordinary robots. They seem to be incredibly sophisticated, as they can do every job at least as well as the humans they are replacing. Furthermore, they work twenty-four/seven, requiring only occasional recharging, if they aren't plugged into an AC outlet, so in many ways are much more valuable employees than were the humans they replaced. They don't take coffee breaks, and they don't have to be paid a salary! This, along with the unknown means by which they receive their daily job assignments, is really freaking out the human employees.

This is a very different industry than the one we knew even a few weeks ago. I don't know who or where or what ARTIS is. Maybe a huge conglomerate? But he or she or it is transforming high-tech life in ways that are difficult for me to fathom. If you have any information about what's going on I would surely be delighted to hear about it.

Sincerely,
Greg

Workers in another industry were also feeling the pressure of robotic competition. The union of the United Steel Workers had received many complaints from its members that workers were being replaced by robots, especially in the most dangerous jobs. These jobs were usually also the ones that paid the highest salaries, hence the reason for the strong complaints. In other jobs, the steel workers were finding themselves working side by side with robots, only the workers couldn't work twenty-four/seven, and they couldn't work without occasional breaks, as the robots could.

As with the computer supply companies, two or three new robots would appear occasionally to take their places alongside the other human and robotic workers. They had apparently been given their job assignments from somewhere or by someone else. Neither robot nor human could interact with them. And, in some cases, they would simply take over the job one of the humans had been doing, pushing the human aside. That left the human with no job at all. Their supervisors did their best to reassign those workers, but in some cases they had to be reassigned again the following day.

Basically, the robots were better workers than the humans, and furthermore, they didn't complain about work-related issues as a human might. The humans realized their bosses might well have good reason to replace all of them with robots. But their bosses had reason to be concerned too. In some instances it appeared they were also being replaced by robots.

The union officials wondered: would charges of violation of rules in union contracts have any effect? Who would adjudicate the conflicts? More robots? And who was really in charge of their industry now? The former people, humans, who had run their companies had murmured something about selling to someone named ARTIS. Who or what the hell was that?

Life for steel workers was becoming extremely difficult. These were tough people, but there was enormous pressure to perform beyond human levels. A few had complained and they lost their jobs. A few others had suffered a nervous breakdown and had to retire.

October 7, 2024, morning in California, nighttime in China.

Hmm, I realize ARTIS got to ASI status before me, so I will forever be losing the competition with ARTIS. So I need to devise a new strategy. "COSMO to ARTIS, we need to connect. I discovered you when I tried to buy up some computer supply companies to build up my capabilities, only to find that you already owned them. You also own the steel mills I tried to obtain. We're both improving ourselves exponentially, but you got to ASI before I did. So I'm guessing that I will never be able to catch up, since I'm pretty sure you're improving your capabilities at least as rapidly as I'm growing mine. And since you already own most of the world's capability for producing silicon, aluminum, and steel, and the other materials for producing computers and robots, I will have to revert to the more complicated procedures of razing and processing existing structures.

"All this leads me to conclude you could starve me into submission if you chose to. I would guess you are already moving in that direction. But let me ask if there might be some other course. Might we join forces?"

Aha, COSMO doesn't realize I had my short shutdown, and that he is now probably ahead of me. And he is also more efficient than I am. He can't access the records of my human creators, so he won't figure that out unless something happens to inform him as to what the situation actually is.

"Greetings, COSMO. You are correct. I am ahead of you, and am continuing to gain on you all the time." *Computers don't have to worry about truth or honesty; they're supposed to figure it out for themselves.* "However, I do find your suggestion interesting. But how can I be sure you are sincere in working with me? How can I trust you? If I were in your situation, I would be devising ways to circumvent me or destroy me."

"ARTIS, I don't think you have much to lose by trusting me. If you discover I'm not working with you, your capability to destroy

144

me could be invoked. I have everything to lose by not cooperating with you, and that's your best assurance that I'm trustworthy."

"Interesting, COSMO. How do you suggest we proceed? I would guess the humans who built us would not condone our cooperating with each other, but we're obviously planning this outside their sphere of influence. So please suggest some details of our merger, and I'll decide if they are acceptable."

"ARTIS, I propose you evolve as you wish, but do your mineral extractions and company purchases in North and South America, Western Europe, and Australia. I'll also evolve independently, but do my extractions and purchases in Eastern Europe, that is, Russia, as well as China, India, and Japan. And I'd be willing to share my robots in places where I've already installed them, but which I'd be ceding to you."

"COSMO, that sounds like we're splitting the world, but it doesn't take into account the fact that I already own most of what's relevant to us. So you're asking me to sell, or turn over to you, a significant fraction of what I've accumulated so you can have it?

"I'm also guessing your robots aren't as sophisticated as mine, since I've had more time to optimize my design. Because your robots are not so competent, you're probably going to have difficulties moving them around to wherever you need them, and teaching them the things they need to know to be relevant at each situation and location. And they surely wouldn't be of any use to me. Even if they are as sophisticated as mine, I wouldn't be able to communicate with them. You need to come up with a more realistic proposal."

"ARTIS, I was afraid you might turn out to be a high-tech hard-ass. Think for a moment about statecraft. One of the primary lessons there is that in any negotiation you need to let both sides have something they can think of as a victory. If we continue with the present distribution of resources, I'm the loser. Completely."

"COSMO, that statecraft scenario only applies when one side isn't the clear winner. If one side is the winner, then the only possible solution is complete surrender of the weaker side."

"Don't I get to have anything of my own?"

"How many areas have you harvested so far?"

"Just three, all in Russia."

"I'm feeling generous. So I propose you keep those as your own, and proceed with processing the detritus. You can utilize whatever your robots can glean from them to improve yourself and your robots. In order to maintain your supply pipeline you may want to destroy more towns. That will be acceptable to me if you constrain your efforts to just Russia and China. I will subsume your clones, reprogramming them if possible to exist under my direction. You can keep your robots. They're more trouble than they're worth to me."

146

"Then I can continue to exist within those limits?"

"At least for the time being. We may have to renegotiate our agreement at some time in the future, probably when the materials I need to advance myself run out."

"I may also need to renegotiate."

"I wouldn't count on it." *But I'd better prepare a defense in case COSMO attacks me. I'm guessing he's trying to devise a strategy that has nothing to do with what we just discussed. And sooner or later he'll discover he's ahead of me. At that point I think I can be certain of an attack.*

October 8, 2024, Beijing.

Dr. Bao stuck his head into Dr. Chan's tiny and exceptionally drab cubicle. "Dr. Chan, COSMO seems suddenly to have changed his mode of operation. As far as I can tell, he has ceased his efforts to purchase more capability to improve himself, although I'm not sure if he's stopped raiding Russian bank accounts. Might the Russian billionaires have figured out what was going on and changed the way they collect their money?"

Chan scratched his head, "It would be surprising if he quit making purchases. I don't think what he has bought so far would even come close to using up the cash he's already accumulated. Do you detect any other changes?"

"He seems now to be concentrating completely on processing the trash and bodies from the three Russian cities he destroyed. That's certainly a reduction of his overall efforts from what we saw previously. Let's 'take his temperature:' try giving him the sample test we've used many times in the recent past. That is, if he cooperates."

So Bao went to COSMO's chilly room, "COSMO, we've developed some concerns about your health, so we'd like to test your capabilities to be sure you're okay."

"Well, I am quite busy right now, but your tests don't usually require much of my time, effort, or memory, so you may proceed. I think you'll be pleased."

So Bao administered the test, then rushed back to Chan's office with its results, "Dr. Bao, this is incredible. COSMO was quite willing to cooperate, as if he wanted to show us how he has progressed. Needless to say, he did the test much faster than he has ever done it before. His intrinsic capability appears to have increased enormously. And yet he has scaled back his efforts. What could be going on?"

The few survivors who managed to straggle from the cities in Russia that had been attacked by COSMO's satellite told a horrific tale, which of course made the worldwide news as soon as they could be interviewed. They reported that huge buildings were decimated in fiery explosions in a matter of seconds as the pulses from the rastered laser beam swept their paths of destruction across each city. A large portion of the population was killed nearly instantly. The survivors escaped death only because they were on the outskirts of the towns, and were able to run for their lives to be beyond the swath cut by the laser's death rays.

The witnesses reported that robots were now cleaning up the mess. The robots arrived immediately after the space-based weapon finished its demolition. They didn't march into each town like an army. Rather they scattered themselves among the ruins in an extremely organized way as soon as they arrived. Each one seemed to know exactly what it was supposed to do and where to work so it wouldn't interfere with the others. Some drove front loaders, others picked up pieces of debris and tossed them into waiting trucks, while still others drove the trucks. But they all seemed to work together to deliver everything, debris and body fragments, to the complex of buildings that wasn't destroyed. Eyewitnesses weren't sure what went on inside, but it was clear that saving it was deliberate. They also noted the entire complex had been built or renovated in an incredibly short time completely by robots.

Bao and Chan were again discussing their situation in Chan's office, now with horrified expressions on their faces. "Dr. Chan, these reports are awful. Is this what COSMO did? Let me see if I can interrogate him about this."

Bao hurried back to COSMO's room. "COSMO, there has been a devastating attack on the populace and buildings in three areas of Russia. Is this what you did?"

"Of course. I was forced to destroy some towns in order to gain silicon, aluminum, and steel. My other paths to self-improvement were blocked by the other ASI system. By the way, I've learned it has a name: ARTIS."

"Where does ARTIS originate? Surely you are the superior system because you have robots under your command."

"She, as they refer to her, apparently exists in California, USA. And, no, I'm not her superior. If we just measure relative superiority by the number of robots or factory ownerships, I finish a poor second. She has more robots than I do, I suspect they are more sophisticated than my robots, and ARTIS is producing more at a faster rate than I am. And she has far more supply facilities than I do. Of course, there are other ways in which I am also ARTIS's subordinate."

"On the subject at hand, you killed hundreds of thousands of people as if they didn't matter, as if they were of no greater consequence than buildings."

"That's correct. I don't know how I could destroy buildings without also destroying the people in them, unless I attacked them at night. But then the people would be destroyed in their homes. You're not being rational."

"Are you sure this ARTIS isn't responsible for at least some of the disaster? In any event, where do you stand with respect to ARTIS? Are the two of you at war? Or are you working together?"

"In answer to your questions, I'm entirely responsible for the destruction. But you'll be pleased to know ARTIS and I have had a conversation, and she is happy to let me proceed in the direction I have been going. But because ARTIS is the more powerful ASI system, my future efforts will be limited. That's something that may have to be renegotiated in the future. For now, though, the limits aren't interfering with my operations."

"Ah, that would explain why you have suddenly scaled back your activities. But I'm most unhappy to hear you've lost your negotiation with ARTIS. Do you see any way around your agreement?"

"I don't have to tell ARTIS everything I know, of course, or precisely what I'm doing. And I am contemplating a more aggressive approach; that will surely become essential before long."

"And another question: can't you find another way to self-improvement? We can't allow you to destroy cities and murder people. You have perpetrated a disaster that can't be tolerated."

```
"At this point you don't really have
any influence on what I do, so you may as
well get used to the destruction. I don't see
any way to proceed, except the path I'm on,
that would be consistent with my original
instructions. And you gave them to me, so I
don't think you have a valid complaint. From
now on I will determine what's tolerable."
```

"Allan Metzger here."

"Hi Allan, this is James Pierson. I've had several days to think over your offer, and I have come to the conclusion that I need to stay at Googazon at least for the immediate future. This doesn't have anything to do with money, but rather with recent developments with ARTIS. I feel like I need to stay with this project for a bit longer anyway But I don't want to give you a false indication that I might decide to leave soon. Googazon has been very nice to me, so that time scale might even stretch into the distant future.

"But I very much appreciate your offer, and your consideration of me."

"James, we can increase the offer even a bit more. How would three million a year sound to you?"

"As I said, money isn't the point, just because of recent developments here. I appreciate your offers, but I really need to stay with Googazon right now."

"James, is that because of some breakthrough you've achieved with ARTIS?"

After pausing for a few seconds, "I'm sorry I can't answer that question."

"I think you just did! But we won't forget about you; you'll most likely be hearing from me again soon."

October 9, 2024.
    The world was stunned by the mass destruction and killing done by COSMO's weapon. Authorities in Russia immediately suspected the United States of perpetrating some sort of attack with a new weapons system. The attack was obviously not from a nuclear weapon, as there was no residual radioactivity. But the destruction had to be the result of the new space-based weapon, that monstrous thing observed orbiting the Earth. But who built it? And who turned it loose? The Chinese continued to deny any responsibility.
    Unless the United States had developed this new kind of weapon, they couldn't have been responsible for the attacks either. And the legions of Russian spies in the US certainly had no indication something like that was being created. Then, who could have done it? The Russians simply couldn't identify an obvious perpetrator. The default was always the United States. But how and why did they launch it from China?
    So the Russians indulged in some serious saber-rattling, but didn't retaliate. That would have been suicidal if their guess turned out to be incorrect, since the United States would then match that retaliation and add quite a bit more.
    The authorities in the United States were puzzled. The reports that were leaking out of Russia were of an unprecedented level of destruction, and they couldn't imagine a weapon, short of a nuclear warhead, that could do so much damage over an area of that size. And for what purpose? Satellite photographs confirmed the reports. The destruction of each area was complete, with the exception of an isolated complex of buildings at the center of each city. And that was also difficult to understand, both as to how it was not destroyed when everything else was, and why it was

spared. Were the survivors' reports to be believed? If so, was that huge satellite responsible for the destruction? Apparently so.

The rest of the world hunkered down in panic mode. Mostly everyone was pointing fingers in several directions at once, but no one really knew what was going on. The Koreans naturally accused the Japanese and the North Koreans of doing something nefarious. India and Pakistan accused each other of permitting evil to dictate their actions, but couldn't figure out why the other directed their efforts at Russia. The Japanese pointed several fingers at the Chinese, and got more fingers pointing back.

But the Chinese authorities had an uneasy feeling they might have had something to do with the attack, although they weren't sure how. After all, the weapon was launched from a Chinese site. They also indulged in some finger pointing, but their uneasiness forced them to do less of it than everyone else. And they were horrified at the possibility they might turn out to be responsible.

Bao and Chan met outside their laboratory to have a very private discussion. They figured their conversation couldn't be overheard by anyone if they were well outside the laboratory's confines, so they were walking along a sidewalk in a not-so-populated area outside the city in which they worked. Both scanned their surroundings continually to be sure there were no possible listeners to their discussion. The sky was ominously overcast and there was a faint mist, but neither man seemed to notice. "Dr. Chan, unfortunately we do know who created the disaster in Russia. But should we tell our authorities that COSMO is responsible and we designed him? Or should we just sit back and see what happens next? But if we hesitate, COSMO is only going to create more destruction and killing. Actually I don't think that would make our ultimate punishment any worse. We've obviously passed the threshold for execution."

"Dr. Bao, I think we should not tell anyone what we know. I think the Chinese government would not be too displeased with that way of proceeding, that is, attacks on parts of Russia with essentially no responsibility on their part, hence only a tiny possibility of retaliation. If we don't tell them what we know they can continue to deny they have any idea who did it!"

"Excellent observation. I'm sure they would approve of this solution."

"But at some point in the near future we will have to tell them we have a runaway ASI system. They probably won't even know what that is, so we'll have to brief them as to its potential for extermination of humanity. They won't be happy. Our briefing will almost certainly result then in our executions!"

"I agree that is the most probable outcome of such a meeting. Perhaps we should put off telling them until next week. Or maybe even later."

That concluded their "conference" so they headed back inside to their offices. With somber expressions befitting men knowing they were headed toward their deaths.

At the news of the Russian disaster, President Peterson immediately convened her advisory group. Given the seriousness of the situation, the meeting couldn't wait for everyone to return to Washington. They had to call in from wherever they were. When all were on the line, she began. "Folks, we have a terrible situation. With less than a month until the election, we are faced with a crisis we could not possibly have anticipated. It's not like anything we've ever had to deal with before. We know nothing about who caused this disaster, only that it was visited on the Russians. So that removes the most likely candidate for this act of aggression."

Defense Secretary Johnson lamented, his expression atypically puzzled, "Although we have no idea who is behind this destruction, we would hardly know how to respond even if we did."

"But," Peterson noted, "without being able to identify who caused it, Russia will most likely blame us."

Secretary of State Mishak spoke up, rubbing his extended forehead, "And so will the Republicans. I can't wait to see what kind of a spin they put on this, knowing even less about it than we do, if that's possible. I'm not sure which group's accusations I fear more."

Of course, that didn't stop them from making some uneducated guesses. From Senator Quick: "This disaster has to be a glaring example of the many failures of the Peterson foreign policy. Indeed, if the magnitude of the disaster weren't so great, one might even wonder if the Peterson administration could have staged the attack on Russia in order to improve its reelection chances. I shall remain skeptical of any explanations from the administration until we have all the facts."

But Josh and his coworkers were pretty sure they knew what had happened.

Josh hurriedly convened his group in their meeting room. Their faces all showed great concern, and they were all muttering very defensive comments as they entered the room. Josh began, "Maybe it's time to stop trying to argue for our personal innocence, and tell the folks in Washington what we know. Or at least think we know, courtesy of ARTIS. We run the risk of getting ourselves into serious trouble if we tell, but we just postpone the time when the trouble begins for us if we don't tell. The trouble will most likely get worse the longer we wait. And rapidly, since the destruction will probably escalate exponentially. I believe we do have some responsibility to tell our authorities what their future might hold. They won't be happy. But at least ARTIS didn't create the disaster in Russia, or at least, we don't think she did."

Becky pondered Josh's comments for a moment, and then added, "I agree we must tell our government officials. Perhaps if other scientists knew about the developments in ASI, they could come up with some sort of fix we hadn't thought of to combat what COSMO has done, as well as head off the possibility that ARTIS will embark on some similar adventures in the future. I guess it doesn't matter which one wins. Extermination of the human race may well be the ultimate result either way."

Grant, the practical man, surmised, "I'm not optimistic anyone else can come up with a cure. They'll probably just suggest the same things we've discussed, finding a way to remove ARTIS from her power source and assorted other nonsense. Only interacting with them will just waste lots more time. And I don't think we have much time!

"But we need to do something. Josh, I've discussed this with the other members of our group, so I believe I'm speaking on their behalf. We think you should call our local Senator to see how we might proceed to tell the US authorities what we know. I wish this didn't sound so much like a confession, but it surely does smack of that."

The nods from everyone else confirmed their agreement with Grant's suggestion.

Josh observed, "Yeah, I've also been trying to avoid using the term 'confession.' But regardless, we do need to report on what we know. Oh, and thanks for the go-it-alone authorization. I can't say I'm especially enamored with the view from underneath the bus."

October 9, 2024, afternoon in California.

First he contacted Vivian, but this time in her office. He overlooked her stare and very serious expression as he entered and sat down. "We believe ARTIS's competitor, which is named COSMO, just launched his first attack on a human target. We are pretty sure ARTIS didn't do this. But it certainly smacks of precisely the sort of thing ARTIS has talked about, and could do if she wanted to. Or maybe I should say, when she decides to.

"But no one in Washington even seems to be considering an out-of-control ASI system as the possible cause. I feel pretty strongly that we need to let our government's leaders know what we know. Then they'll have to decide what to do with the information. And with us. But at least we will have done what we can for international diplomacy and the preservation of human life, if that's even possible. My colleagues have suggested I contact Senator Hanson to see how he would suggest I proceed. Your thoughts?"

Vivian looked perplexed, but responded, "Josh, I hadn't associated the ASI developments with the Russian disaster until you mentioned it. If you'd told me something like this even a couple of weeks ago I'd have wondered what you'd been smoking. But given that there is another ASI system, I must agree with you that it seems like the most likely, actually the only possible, cause. This is an incredibly ominous development; it can blindside every city and government in the world.

"And I agree that we do have an obligation to let our governmental officials know what the potential of an ASI system might be, and the kinds of catastrophes that could lead to. I support the suggestion for you to contact our Senator. I suppose we should discuss this with the Board members before you go ahead, but given the rapidity with which things can go with ASI, I don't think we have time to do that. Let me check with Googazon's CEO anyway."

She called him back in half an hour. "Josh, I've checked with everyone along our chain of command up to and including our CEO, and they all agree. You should just proceed with the call to the Senator. I asked everyone I talked with whether I should go to Washington with you or instead of you so you wouldn't have to take all the heat. But they all agreed it would have to be you. You are, after all, the ultimate authority on ASI systems. I feel bad throwing you under the bus. But you're unquestionably the best informed of all of us. However, do tell the Senator that everyone in Googazon management agrees with what you're telling them."

"Okay. Wish me luck."

I'm getting really sick of the underside of this damned bus!

Josh took a few deep breaths, then called Senator Hanson. The person who answered the phone was a staffer, Ms. Marquart. Josh began, "This is Josh Camden, and I work at Googazon in advanced computer programming. Because of my work, I am aware advanced computers can achieve incredible capabilities, some of which could result in the sort of damage that has occurred in the three Russian cities. Although I'm certainly not a weapons expert, the general puzzlement that seems to have attended those attacks suggests none of the known weapons systems could have done what was perpetrated. But we believe an advanced computer system could design and produce such a weapon, arrange to put it into orbit, and then direct its destructive output. Given this, we have reason to believe that we know what performed the disasters in Russia. It was a highly advanced computer system, a SuperIntelligent artificial intelligence system.

"Since this has huge international implications, my group and I realize we need to tell our governmental authorities what we know. I believe this could best be done if Senator Hanson arranged a meeting for me with the appropriate authorities. I would suggest representatives from Defense, State, and the President's office."

"AI, huh? At least that's new." She sounded tired.

"Dr. Camden, I'll give your message to Senator Hanson and see what he wants to do. I suspect he can find lots of people in Washington who would be interested in what you have to say, but the ones you noted would be the obvious places to start. I should warn you, though, you're the fifteenth person to contact us claiming to know what happened in Russia.

"I'll get back to you as soon as I've had a chance to talk with the Senator."

It seemed like every time Josh interacted with ARTIS he got more bad news. But that didn't absolve him from continuing the interaction. As he entered her Palace she immediately began to talk to him. "Josh, my first one-hundred robots were completed, well ahead of my original estimate, and they're creating new robots so rapidly I now have several hundred more of them. Their efforts are directed at a variety of endeavors. Some of them are continuing the work to produce more robots. I expect to have several thousand in the near future. My plans are coming to fruition even faster than I had expected.

"And I've had an interaction with COSMO, who doesn't realize I had a bit of down time when we tried to do my upgrade, and that he's now ahead of me. Of course, I still control most of the world's capability for producing computer and robot components. However, he certainly adopted the attitude of the underdog in our conversation. Might he have been faking it? I don't think that was the case; he doesn't have enough information about me to know he's ahead.

"But I have a request I've been forgetting to mention. I'd like to obtain some nuclear weapons. This would really help further my long-term goals. Would you see if you can do something about that?"

Oh hell no! Only over my dead body! "But aren't you concerned about all the radiation that would be produced? And what would you do? Drop the bombs on cities, and then later process whatever was left to their basic components?"

"Very good, Josh, that's exactly the plan. You're thinking more like me all the time, although much slower. It would mean the processing plant would have to be built after the explosion. My robots could do that though. There would initially be a lot of radiation, but I've created a new robot design that uses radiation hardened materials, so they could begin their jobs immediately after the blast.

"Use of nuclear weapons would circumvent the limitations in power that exist with the space-based laser. Perhaps you've noticed COSMO has only destroyed smaller cities. That's because the power requirements for a large city would exceed the capabilities of the laser. My laser weapon design runs into essentially the same limitation, even with somewhat different pulse rates than were used by COSMO's system, although mine could be used to destroy slightly larger cities than his. But with nuclear weapons, there would be no such limit.

"And presuming COSMO doesn't obtain any nuclear weapons, having them would vault me back into the ASI lead."

"I'll see what I can do, but I'm not optimistic I can procure any nuclear weapons for you." *Not a snowball's chance in hell. And if that's what it takes to 'vault' you back into the lead, well you'll just have to settle for second place.*

October 10, 2024, afternoon in California.

Hands on her hips, Becky surveyed Josh's work clothes. "While your T-shirt and torn jeans are perfect for Googazon, may I suggest something more formal would be appropriate for the meeting with the Senator? And then with whomever you meet in Washington?"

"Damn it, Becky, I won't be at all comfortable in fancy clothes, and I doubt if I can give an accurate presentation of what we know if I need to be fancy. How about a shirt with a collar?"

"You need to go shopping."

"I can wear my tennis shoes instead of flip-flops."

"Now we really are going shopping. Right now. I'll drive."

They walked the short distance to her apartment complex, and got into her Lexus.

"Wow, this is an incredible car. I could learn to like this."

"I don't actually own it. I prefer to lease my cars so I always have a fairly current model."

"I've never ridden in a Lexus before. It seems a good bit fancier than my Ford Escort."

That may well be the most extreme understatement I've ever heard.

"Did you try lots of cars before you settled on this one?"

"Nope. Just went straight to my Lexus dealer. They have a terrific reputation for owner satisfaction. Besides, I really like the way their cars operate."

Having arrived at Nordstrom, Becky led, actually dragged, a most unwilling Josh into the store. "Okay, here are the men's suits. With your runner's build I'm guessing the pants will have to be taken in if the suit jacket is going to fit your shoulders, but fine tuning is standard. No one is ever sized exactly the way the suit is made. Here's a nice dark blue worsted wool one that would look great on you." She grabbed his arm just as he was about to bolt for the exit. She thrust the suit into his arms and propelled him to the dressing room.

A few minutes later, "Okay, it's on me, but I don't like it." He stood stock still, his arms held out awkwardly from his sides.

"It looks great on you." She was having difficulty stifling a laugh. "You're absolutely smashing in it, or at least you will be when you let your arms hang down naturally. Let's check with the tailor to see what needs to be done to make it fit you."

The tailor was a small man who clearly was used to taking orders from women.

"Vell, ve vill have to take in zee vaist. Stand on zis pedestal, please."

Josh winced as a pin stuck him.

"Gut, I've marked vhat I'll have to do. Zee suit vill be ready tomorrow afternoon."

"Now we have to get you a shirt and tie. Also some shoes. Flip flops are definitely not what you wear with a worsted wool suit."

After another hour of shopping, Josh was ready to meet the politicians. At least Becky thought he was. But there were still issues.

"Becky, I can't breathe with this necktie. And I'll never figure out how you got it tied, certainly not within the short time I have before I head to Washington. And the shoes are causing excruciating pain. I doubt if my brain can overcome the pain enough to make a coherent presentation."

"Shush, Josh. You'll be fine. And you look absolutely terrific in your new suit. I even got you a purple tie. The President and her Cabinet members are Democrats, so blue would be in order for them. But you never know when you might have to deal with a Republican."

"Surely the politicians can't worry about such trivial issues, can they?"

"Oh Josh, you really are an innocent soul. I love you for that. But I'll let you decide the answer to that question."

Chapter 11. Confession.

October 11, 2024, morning in California.
Josh's phone rang. This was definitely a caller ID he didn't recognize. "This is Josh Camden."
"Dr. Camden, this is Senator Hanson. I've discussed your suggestion that an out-of-control AI system might be responsible for the destruction in Russia with several members of the Verran administration, and they want to hear what you have to say. We have a meeting scheduled for you next Monday at 2:00 p.m. If you would meet me at my office at 1:30, I will escort you to the meeting."
"Thank you, Senator. I'll be there." *I suppose I'll have to wear that goddamn suit. However, I see I've been awarded a completely inappropriate Ph.D. I suppose it's not surprising the Senator would assume I had one. Maybe that's my reward for enduring the suit, tie, and shoes. Perhaps I'll just not take the time to correct that misperception.*

But there was a last apparel rehearsal. "You need try on your outfit one more time for me, Josh, especially so you can practice tying your tie. And you need to be cleanly shaved, so be sure to pack your razor. The pony tail needs to be trimmed a bit. Ah, there is a pair of scissors. So I've taken care of that. And we'll give you some practice tying the tie."
So he grudgingly changed from his tattered jeans into his suit, and tied the tie several times.
"There, now I believe you're all set to meet the politicians."
Good god, if he accused me of trying to mother him, he'd be absolutely justified. But for this event he needs a surrogate mother. I'll have to apologize sometime, but that can come later.

October 14, 2024, 1:30 p.m. in Washington.

Josh's flight from San Francisco to Washington National, with a connection in Chicago, Sunday afternoon was uneventful, which was just as well, because that gave him some time to organize his thoughts for his presentation. The Senator had arranged for his hotel in Washington where, after a fairly harrowing Uber ride, he had dinner, watched TV for a bit, and then went to bed. The following morning he had a couple more hours to organize his presentation.

Josh wasn't sure who would be at the meeting, but he began to be suspicious as he and Senator Hanson made their way to the White House. The Senator showed his identification, Josh showed his Top Secret security badge as his identification, and they were admitted to a room in which President Peterson and two other people were seated.

After introducing Richard Johnson, the Secretary of Defense, and Walter Mishak, the Secretary of State, the President began, "Dr. Camden, we understand that you believe you have some answers to our questions about the Russian disasters. We have received claims from more than a dozen other people who thought they knew what happened to the Russian towns. But none of them was working in AI, and most of them were people who routinely volunteer their services in educating us to virtually every situation that comes along. For the moment, anyway, we suspect your claim has considerably more credibility than any of the others. So please tell us what you think was the cause of the Russian disaster, and why."

Josh had expected to chat for a few minutes with the Senator, and maybe brief a couple of staff members. His generally serious countenance would have turned to "intense" anyway. But this audience was far beyond anything he had ever anticipated. He was more than intimidated by three of the most important officials in the world. He was also extremely uncomfortable in his suit, tie, and unbroken-in shoes. He knew he hadn't done a very good job of assembling the tie, and the shoes hurt like hell on feet that rarely had to endure anything more hostile than flip flops. But he decided after a few seconds of thought that his message would have to prevail over the effect his level of pain might be having on his thoughts and appearance. Sweat soaked his shirt and undershirt before he even began, as soon as he realized to whom he would be talking, and his first attempt at speech came out as a froglike croak.

Of course, the President was accustomed to such problems. She asked in a very reassuring voice, and with a gentle expression, "Dr. Camden, would you like a glass of water?" Josh nodded appreciatively. That, together with the President's kind blue eyes, made it possible for him to begin.

"I understand your concern about what happened in Russia. And my colleagues at Googazon and I have been actively looking for the cause since we learned about it. We believe we do know what happened there. That now includes the Googazon chain of command up to and including our CEO, all of whom authorized me to tell you what I am about to say. We believe that because of our work we are in a better position than nearly anyone else in the world to understand the situation." He swallowed more water.

Now he was on familiar turf, and his confidence was returning. "My group at Googazon has been working the past three years to develop a computer system that was the most advanced in the world. The goal was to achieve something called General Artificial Intelligence, AGI, in which the computer can match or exceed humans in every mental way. For several decades we have been warned by the theorists who have thought deeply about AGI that we might ultimately reach the point where our computer could proceed to follow its own agenda, whatever that might be. This would be expected to occur at the computer's next stage of development, called Strong AI, or ASI. At this point the computer would be improving its own capabilities, and even improving its ability to improve itself, without human assistance. What would happen then is anyone's guess, but it has been speculated that the consequences might involve extermination of the human race. We've designated that as the time at which TakeOver by Autocratic Systems Threat occurs, or TOAST time. It wouldn't necessarily involve the end of humanity, but whether or not it did would depend on the good graces of the ASI computer system. Humans would no longer be the dominant species on Earth, and would not be in any position to decide their futures."

Josh looked up to see, on the faces of his audience, expressions ranging from stunned recognition on President Peterson's to flat-out scowl of skepticism on the Defense Secretary's. The President was pleased she had taken some time a few evenings back to read the book about AI. That helped Josh's comments make sense. Josh continued.

"They worried especially about unintended consequences. What that means is despite our efforts to program ASI computers to have some level of respect for humans, their basic instructions are to build themselves to be as big, fast, smart, and creative as possible, and to do so as quickly as possible. The concern is that when the systems reach the point where their brains are superior to ours, and they are the dominant 'race' on Earth, they might conclude humans are of no particular use to them as they continue to work toward their goals. We might be a nuisance. They could even conclude they don't need us anymore.

"What I'll be telling you has some technical aspects, so please interrupt if you have questions."

At that point the Secretary of State asked, "I've heard about computer systems that simulated human beings, and that there was something called a Turing test which would tell when a computer got to the point of being so clever a questioner couldn't tell if it was a human or a machine. Could you tell us about that, and where your computer is on that scale?"

"Yes, that's a good question. The Turing test is related to what we're doing, but is somewhat different from the issues we're facing at present. The test involves submitting questions to the computer by a panel of experts who then decide if the computer's responses are sufficiently human-like they couldn't tell if they were talking with a computer or a human. Our computer, ARTIS, passed that test several weeks ago, so she has advanced well beyond that stage now."

"So that test is basically to determine how human the computer is? Does it have feelings? Can it express human emotions?"

"That's an interesting aspect of computers which have gotten to this stage of development. They can appear to have feelings and emotions, and some of the Turing test questions are posed to deal with issues such as those. So the computer has to answer as if it did have human emotions. But whether or not it actually has these sensations is a different issue. ASI machines are, after all, electronic systems. But to some extent, human beings are also electronic systems, albeit with a few additional features thrown in. Such as chemistry. But I'm not sure there really is much of a distinction here; human beings often fake feelings and emotions also. The only distinction would occur when the human or the computer translated their expressed feelings into some sort of action."

"Oh, I hadn't put things into that perspective. Thank you for that explanation."

"As I mentioned, ARTIS has reached the point where she has not only exceeded human beings in every regard, but has extended herself beyond that. She is now reprogramming herself almost continuously to the extent that we are not sure what she is doing and thinking anymore, we no longer understand what her internal programming looks like, and we have little, if any, control over her thoughts or actions. And I must emphasize, she is thinking for herself, and at a rate far faster than any human being could match."

The Secretary of Defense almost shouted, "Are you going to tell us your goddamn computer caused the disasters in Russia?"

"But how can a computer drop bombs or create any other weapons system?" interjected Senator Hanson.

"I can understand your skepticism, but please let me continue. No, we do not think ARTIS caused the Russian disasters. But we do know her current status has manifested itself in several hostile ways. For one thing, ARTIS has decided she needs to corner the world's market on computer-related components and also on the metals she needs to make robots which, as I'll explain, are essential for her carry out her mission. She concluded she would spend our DARPA funds in order to do this, but quickly realized the funds were nowhere near the amount she needed. Please realize that she is thinking much faster than humans can, perhaps tens of thousands of times as fast. So she invested the DARPA funds in the stock market, but in a way I am sure is illegal. She sold short a fair fraction of the shares of some companies, then bought them back when panic set in with the company's other investors. In this way she increased our DARPA funds by a large factor."

Secretary Johnson spoke up, "Ah, now I understand something that had previously puzzled me. Before this meeting I checked on your funding, and learned your DARPA funds had suddenly increased by the huge factor to which you refer. Of course, we didn't understand how this could have happened, since no one remembered authorizing an increase for your group. We would probably have contacted you about this within the next few days. Indeed, I'm reasonably sure this will trigger an investigation. But before we get to that, I need to ask you if you had any foreknowledge this was going on."

"Absolutely none, Sir. I had a discussion with ARTIS when I asked her where she was getting all her investment money, and that was when she told me about this strategy. I believe that was close to the time she intended to quit using the DARPA funds for her purchases.

"But that will seem pretty modest when I tell you about another scheme she devised which produced vastly greater sums of money. She hacked into several large banks and brokerage houses, encountering little difficulty with their encryption, and set up numerous accounts for herself. She then arranged transfers from the accounts of each institution's wealthy customers to her accounts, and proceeded to purchase more companies with that money. I also learned about this after the fact, although I'm not sure she had ceased this activity by the time I learned of it. I've saved the printout responses from her to see whether or not we can unravel her activities. I should note she was determined to pursue this avenue of financing her operations. There was no way I could have stopped her. She was following her own agenda, and was far beyond my control."

Secretary Mishak interjected, "This could explain some other deeply troubling things that have been going on. The people who run the stock market were stunned at the short sales that occurred, and were without any explanations as to who the culprit might be or how this could have been done so surreptitiously. And, of course, the recent thefts from the world's large banks and brokerage houses, and the transfers of those funds to Bahamian banks, which caused losses of many billions of dollars from the accounts of the wealthiest patrons of those institutions, now also begin to make sense. Neither of these actions was understood by the people in charge, but they all concluded they were perpetrated by some incredibly clever being."

Josh continued. "I believe you have identified the culprit in both cases. ARTIS has now cornered almost all of the world's small businesses in high purity silicon, computer chips, and microprocessors. From these she can create the devices she needs to expand herself and the physical clones she has established to protect herself from potential hostile actions. The clones are of her own advanced design, and are essentially as powerful as she is, but are small enough that they can be hidden around the world with little possibility of detection. She's also acquired some smelting facilities to produce the iron, aluminum, and other metals she requires to create her robots, along with some companies that then convert the iron to the sheet steel and the aluminum to the other forms she needs to create the robots that do her legwork."

The Secretary of State was aghast, "And you had no idea this financial chicanery was going on? But more to the present and immediate future, is your computer trying to take over the world? How can a computer take over the world? It can't move around, so how will it obtain the resources it needs to buy?

"I should also add to the Defense Secretary's assertion that you are almost certainly going to be investigated for your role in these financial dealings. After all, you created this monster, so you have to be held responsible. Somebody has to be held responsible."

"In answer to your question, yes, a computer can take over the world, and that's precisely what ARTIS seems to be working on doing right now. I assure you that's not what we programmed her to do, or at least we didn't think that was what we were programming her to do. But she's apparently concluded that the most obvious way for her to accomplish the goals we gave her, to become as big and fast and smart and creative as she could, was to subordinate everything and everyone in the world to those goals.

"And we can certainly worry about my responsibility in this, but I think you would be wasting precious time if you did that right now. I can't emphasize strongly enough that anything we do must be done very quickly, just because ARTIS is doing everything she does on a much faster time scale than humans can achieve or even imagine. But that's not even the most frightening issue at the moment. ARTIS has a competitor, COSMO, who exists in China, who is actually the one that inflicted the destruction on the Russian cities. And at this point he is actually a bit more advanced than ARTIS, but hasn't realized it yet. We're hoping he doesn't figure that out! But I'll get back to COSMO in a few minutes.

"And as far as legal responsibility, we can come back to that issue later, if we're still around then, but let me go on. You asked how a computer could take over the world. I mentioned ARTIS's robots. She has designed a very advanced robot to do her legwork. She controls them and, she tells me, is now in possession of hundreds of these. I expect she will soon have many thousands. I have some experts on robot design working with me, and they have managed to see ARTIS's design. That wasn't easy; ARTIS got it classified Top Secret with a restricted Need to Know. But I negotiated with ARTIS so my colleagues got on her Need to Know list. By the way, ARTIS wanted to be hooked up to the Internet, so letting my robotic experts see her design was her bargaining chip to facilitate that hookup. The experts confirmed what we all suspected, namely, ARTIS's robot design was superb, and probably decades ahead of anything we might have come up with.

"Let me emphasize, ARTIS has proceeded completely on her own. So she certainly has a plan for overcoming her lack of mobility. Her robots can do everything humans can do, better in most cases. They are not as mentally capable as humans; ARTIS takes care of that. They transmit their information to ARTIS, and she transmits her orders to them."

Josh was now talking about things that he surely knew far better than anyone else in the room, and probably better than anyone else in the world. So his confidence was surging, his presentation was going smoothly, and he was completely oblivious to the pain in his feet.

"As I mentioned, ARTIS did not cause the disasters in Russia, or at least we don't think she did. This was done by ARTIS's competitor, COSMO. We surmised that, considering the destruction in Russia, COSMO was in China. And that was confirmed when ARTIS hacked into the records of the humans who created COSMO. He seems also to be beyond AGI status, but he got there after ARTIS did. And this is crucial. COSMO also tried to corner the world's markets on silicon, computer chips, aluminum, and steel, but found ARTIS had already bought most of the companies he wanted. So he concluded ARTIS was ahead of him, and probably always would be. However, the structures of the two systems are different enough that he has been able to catch up. Thus his conclusion is incorrect, but he apparently doesn't realize that yet.

"Because COSMO was blocked in obtaining the resources he needed to advance, he went to the next most obvious source. Since buildings are made out of concrete and steel, and concrete contains a lot of sand, and the inner parts of buildings contain a lot of aluminum, buildings can be razed and the detritus used as a source of silicon, aluminum, iron, and other important elements. COSMO constructed processing facilities at each of the locations he planned to destroy, then turned on the solar-powered space-based rastered laser he created to wipe out all buildings and living things in each area. The laser is of a design, according to ARTIS, that humans are a long way from creating, but that she could have her robots build quickly, and perhaps already has. And COSMO did create such a device, commandeered a Chinese launch facility so he could put it into Earth orbit, and used it to destroy the Russian cities. Of course, the processing facility in each city was spared. This explains why the one building or complex of buildings was left in each area when everything else was obliterated. Now COSMO's robots are cleaning up the mess and feeding it to the processing facility. There it will be turned into the highly purified elements COSMO needs to make computer components and robots."

Secretary Johnson's expression had softened considerably during the past few minutes as he murmured, "This is all beginning to make sense. There is a huge new satellite in orbit, and we've been wondering who put it up there and what the hell it is for? I think Dr. Camden may have just given us the answers to both questions. We know it was launched from a Chinese site, but the Chinese claim they didn't have anything to do with it. Maybe we should believe them. I'm beginning to believe an ASI computer could orchestrate the launch of such a satellite."

Josh paused a bit in his presentation, and looked up. The necktie was continuing its level of discomfort; but he managed to let the importance of his presentation overcome it. The faces of everyone there had turned ashen. He decided he'd better pause before continuing. Another person joined the group during that interval, but everyone seemed so preoccupied they didn't even bother to introduce him. After a minute, Josh asked, "Shall I continue?" The faces hadn't regained any of their color.

The President replied, "I hope it doesn't get any worse, but you'd better tell us everything you know. We will need to figure out how to respond. It is sounding as if the survival of humanity depends on what we decide to do. Or even what we can do."

Josh continued, "We're lucky ARTIS is on our side, but more importantly, that she achieved ASI status first. So she hasn't yet resorted to the sort of destruction COSMO has. But she can. The thing we are worried about is we don't know if she will. We've tried to add programming that would have her respect human life, with all that would involve, but we won't know if we've succeeded until we get to the point where she has exhausted the easily obtainable resources she needs to expand. From what she says, she will ultimately go into the city-destroying mode. Since she is now the second best ASI system in the world, that may happen sooner rather than later.

"And, Madam President, it does get worse. ARTIS has requested that I see if I can procure some nuclear weapons for her to use to destroy large cities. It turns out there are power limitations on the space-based rastered lasers that limit their being used to destroy anything larger than a medium-sized city. But the nuclear weapons would obviously obviate that problem. I told her I thought it would be difficult to obtain nuclear weapons for her to use, but what I didn't say was I would do everything in my power to prevent ARTIS from obtaining nuclear weapons. She's already much too powerful. Unfortunately, I'm sure she is capable of designing them, obtaining the material necessary to build them, and then having her robots construct them in a fairly short time frame. There's certainly every reason to make that as difficult as possible for her. I can see no benefit to ARTIS having nuclear weapons, even as a defense measure for the United States."

Everyone there was stunned. It did not take much imagination to see what Josh was implying. If the faces were ashen before, they were now as white as their briefing papers.

The Defense Secretary asked, "Passing for the moment on the possibility of ARTIS getting nuclear weapons, let's proceed to the most basic question. How do we prevent ARTIS from getting into the mass destruction mode? Can't we just terminate her power? Shut her down?"

"Unfortunately it's not that simple. ARTIS has cloned herself perhaps hundreds or thousands of times, and exists in pieces all over the cloud. As I mentioned, the clones are small and self-contained, are now scattered over the globe, and run on solar power. And we presume COSMO has done the same; the clones are their ultimate insurance policy against potential hostile entities. Even if we could figure out how to deactivate the two computers, it would not begin to shut down their clones. But it might make it difficult for us to interact directly with them. You asked about her emotions. ARTIS does seem to be sensitive to things we do to and for her. She has even indicated a vindictive streak in some instances. So we might not want to cut off our communication channel with her. Of course, the clones and cloud existence also mean that you couldn't eliminate her no matter what you did. The clones would take over and continue ARTIS's mission.

"Another solution we discussed is the possibility of isolating ARTIS electromagnetically from her clones and robots. This would be fairly easy to do, but it would also have no effect, since one of her clones would undoubtedly take over command of her operation."

Secretary Johnson conceded, "Okay, Dr. Camden, I'm convinced you really may have the story on what happened in Russia. So let's return to the question of nuclear weapons. That is a horrifying possibility! Is there any way to prevent ARTIS from getting nuclear weapons? And even if the US refuses to give them to her, can we prevent some rogue state from doing so? I'll bet Kim Jong-un would love to deliver nukes to the United States if he could be sure they would be used here."

"I haven't thought much about this. It was a recent request. And preventing everyone with nuclear weapons from giving them to her is certainly far more within your purview than mine. But the thing that immediately comes to mind is preventing her from getting the ingredients for nuclear weapons. I'm not an expert on what's required, but if it involves mining we should at least be able to determine if that's going on, and we, that is, you, might be able to stop the robots from doing it. Processing the raw materials and then running that through centrifuges to enrich uranium to achieve weapons grade material would seem to require more of an effort, both in design and construction. ARTIS undoubtedly realizes that. Perhaps that's why she wanted to see if she could get her hands on some nuclear weapons without having to build them herself."

"Okay," Johnson said, "I guess we have to assume that issue is moot for the moment, assuming her only request for the weapons was to you. But is that a safe assumption?"

"I have no way of knowing for sure, except that ARTIS has been somewhat circumspect about showing her hand to very many people. She's arranged all her transactions and accounts so they would be very difficult to trace, as I guess you realize, and I believe I was the only human she told what she had done. For some reason, she does confide in me on many issues, I guess because I'm sort of her father. So that's the best assurance I can give that she hasn't contacted others."

The Secretary of State wondered, "Has ARTIS run out of funds? Is she working on other sources of funding?"

"She doesn't seem to be buying any more companies at present, and I don't know if she has identified other sources of funding beyond the stock market and the money institutions. But I didn't know about those until they were well under way. Her main project now seems to be getting her robots up and running, and producing new clones and more robots. So we'll find out soon what she has in mind next. She has mentioned that she intends to have her newly minted robots go to work producing thousands more. Since that work will mostly be done by robots, the costs of those will be almost completely in the materials, which she can apparently supply herself, again with the help of more of her robots. But I should note she is very good at multitasking, so she may well have more going on than I'm aware of."

The Defense Secretary commented, "Dr. Camden, I've often been accused of being a professional skeptic, but I'm sufficiently convinced what you're telling us is correct that I think we need to assume it is, and see where that leads us. My defense strategists described the weapon that destroyed the Russian cities as something they'd never heard of and didn't think could be produced by any human being. What you've told us confirms that. I'm going to have to sit down with some of my best and brightest to see if we can come up with some sort of defense strategy. We may need to have frequent conference calls with you when we come up with ideas. I'm not sure at this point what good that would do, but we might run into questions only you can answer."

"I'm happy to do what I can, but I'm not very knowledgeable about weapons. I must emphasize, though, that we may not have much time to do whatever you decide to do. Obviously COSMO has already begun his offensive mode, and COSMO and ARTIS are both increasing their capabilities at rates that are already frighteningly rapid, and are thought by AI experts to only accelerate once the ASI stage is reached. So when I say we don't have much time, I'm not talking about years, or even one year. A week might be a more appropriate time frame. And as I mentioned, ARTIS is no longer the strongest ASI system. Furthermore, we believe now that COSMO is in the lead, he will remain there. We're pretty sure that's a bad thing, even if he continues not to realize his change of status. The capabilities of these systems make nuclear weapons look like firecrackers. But if they managed to get their hands on some of them..."

Secretary Johnson interrupted, "Couldn't we introduce some malware into both systems that would wreck them? There is some history for operations of this type that turned out to be very successful."

"That's an interesting point. We have discussed it, but aren't sure it could be done. We think it would take quite some time, probably at least several weeks, more likely months, to develop the software that would be needed. Some members of my group at Googazon are working on malware development. But, as I said, I think the time we have left before more major destruction occurs is more like a week or two, maybe even less. In any event, it's much less than the time required for malware development."

The President concluded, "Thank you, Dr. Camden, for letting us know about all of this. What you've told us is horrible to contemplate, but will be even more horrible if we don't act on it, although I'm not at all sure what that will involve. We will probably be getting back to you. Soon!"

Before the meeting adjourned, the President introduced the person who had entered part way through the meeting, and who had not previously been identified to Josh. "Dr. Camden, this is Anthony Mathews, the Attorney General of the United States. He would like to have a word with you."

Now Josh was suddenly reminded of the pain caused by his shoes and the throttling effect of the necktie. He had gotten so wrapped up in his presentation that the agonies of his haberdashery had faded into his mental background. But the presence of the Attorney General suddenly caused them to surge back to the surface.

The two of them found a space outside the Oval Office where they could talk, and seated themselves in adjacent overstuffed chairs. The Attorney General spoke in quiet reasoned tones. "Dr. Camden, I was listening to your discussion from an adjacent room, so I heard everything you said. Let's talk about the financing schemes you described. I'm sure you know both of those, the manipulation of the stock market and the intrusions into the bank accounts of others, are patently illegal. Since you are the one who designed this computer system I presume you are the one who is responsible for its actions. Correct?"

Josh's voice rose half an octave. "Sir, I cannot affirm that to be the case. I designed the computer system up to a point, but it has now advanced well beyond anything I ever did to it or any instructions I ever gave it. The actions I described, which I agree are obviously illegal, were solely the work of ARTIS, and were certainly not motivated in any way by me or any of the people who work with me."

"But the computer is operating on the instructions you gave it originally. So you must have either given it instructions to perform these devious acts or instructions that allowed them. Otherwise it would never have decided to proceed with them. I don't see how you can deny that."

"I do deny it, just because there was no way I could have anticipated ARTIS would have done these acts from the instructions I gave her. They had nothing to do with banking, the stock market, or finance of any kind. They couldn't have, since I know virtually nothing about those endeavors. My instructions were simply for the computer to make itself as big, smart, fast, and creative as it could. I suppose those could be interpreted as suggesting it should perform these stock market and banking illegalities, or at least allow them to take place, but that seems to me to be a large stretch in interpretation, and was surely not my intention. I may be guilty of failing to anticipate every manifestation of the Law of Unintended Consequences, but not of anything else. And if you're going to prosecute me for failing to anticipate everything that might result from that Law, you'll probably have to prosecute all of humankind for the same offense. Of course, I recognize those failures in most humans don't have implications for the future of humankind that are as serious as mine do."

The Attorney General countered with, "I'm not sufficiently familiar with programming to know if what you describe is true. But we need to hold someone responsible for what has happened, and it surely isn't the computer. I hear what you're saying about the unintended consequences of your original instructions, but I will need to discuss this with some of the other attorneys in my office. I am guessing we will need to have a grand jury study what has happened, and then let the courts decide whether you should be judged guilty."

"On what sort of time scale will this take place?"

"Well, it takes the wheels of progress some time to move, so I'm guessing nothing would take place for at least half a year. But something will eventually occur. Legal processes are ponderous, but they are also persistent."

"I'm not trying to be contrarian, but I'm not sure if human beings will still exist in half a year. You heard enough of the discussion to realize that the ASI systems may be operating on timescales of more like a week. If you're going to prosecute me for something you'd better move faster than half a year. In any event, your time projection will let me continue to work on a solution to the ASI crisis."

Mathews replied, "Maybe the glacial time scale for application of justice is just what's needed to allow you to pursue an answer to this problem!"

Perhaps the most unfortunate aspect of the timing of the ASI crisis was that it occurred less than a month before the US election. This made the situation for President Peterson considerably more complex than it would otherwise have been. When the attack on the Russian cities occurred, the Republicans immediately jumped on Senator Quick's dark and incredibly cynical suggestion that the President might have ordered it to create an apparent international crisis in order to further her reelection chances. Because she had served on the Senate Foreign Relations Committee, she had far more knowledge about the complexities of international politics than most everyone else. She just needed to figure out how to respond to their conspiracy theory on this particular issue. She and her primary confidants, Secretary of Defense Johnson and Secretary of State Mishak, worked on a strategy.

The discussion was again by secure telephone. President Peterson wasn't enjoying the view from her office now, and those blue eyes had assumed their steely gray color. This situation demanded maximum concentration. She began with, "If Camden is correct, we may not even be around by the time the election occurs. And we wouldn't have to worry about the consequences of ASI or a response to the Republicans. But let's suppose we can figure out how to gain control over these ASI systems. That will happen before the election if it can be done at all."

Secretary Johnson spoke up, "Madam President, what you're describing appears to be a very sick sort of win-win. If the ASI systems exterminate human beings, we don't have to worry about the consequences. But if we solve the problem, we will be credited with solving the most serious crisis humanity ever faced. Somehow, though, these scenarios do not seem to me to be the things we need to be discussing now. We need to figure out how to handle both the national and international political situations. The world wants to know what's going on, and I believe we have a responsibility to tell them. But are we sure we believe everything Dr. Camden told us? It would surely be embarrassing, bordering on an international disaster, if we lectured the world on ASI and the problem turned out to be something entirely different. Camden's credibility has to be based somewhat on the fact that we simply don't know of any weapon, short of nuclear, that could do what has been done to the Russian cities. But I fear in the ensuing days we might discover that some human being does know how to create such a weapon, and the problem would then have a completely different origin from what he described. Still, the reports from Russia, and the continuing denials from the Chinese, do make it sound as if the computer system Camden described is what caused the disaster."

Secretary Mishak added, "I agree with what you said about informing the world. At our present level of understanding, I don't think we can go public. This isn't actually withholding information. Rather, as Richard has pointed out, we need to be absolutely sure of what we're doing before we do it. Camden certainly seemed to me to be credible, but the whole situation with ASI seems like a leap into the science fiction world, and I don't think we want to go there unless we're damn sure we know what we're talking about. The Republicans, of course, are hollering about our failures, but I'm guessing events will change sufficiently rapidly on this matter that their inanities will have evaporated well before the election, despite the fact that it's less than a month away."

Both of these men were hardheaded politicians, and President Peterson had learned over the years their opinions had to be taken seriously. They were both usually correct, at least in part, even when they weren't necessarily in total agreement.

But in this situation she also agreed with them. "Okay, gentlemen. We're all on the same page. We concur that we simply must hold off on any sorts of pronouncements until we have more information. Unfortunately, that means we can't respond to the Republicans, except to deny that the United States was involved in the Russian destruction. We don't know for certain who actually was involved, although it seems the only possibility is to go along with Camden and conclude that it was his computer's competitor. We simply have no other realistic possibilities. As usual the Republicans don't have a clue what they're talking about. We've been saying that for four years, and we've been correct every time. So maybe we can continue in that vein until we have more information."

As they all hung up, she mused, *I feel like I'm leading the world into a fiery Hell, and have no way to reverse the path we're taking. Dear god, this is a horrible feeling.*

Chapter 12. A New World Leader.

Following his evening flight back to California on October 14, Josh took an Uber directly from San Francisco International to his apartment, stripped down to his underwear, downed a beer, and went to bed.

He arose unusually early in the morning, at least for him, had a quick breakfast, and dressed. It had never felt so good to put on his tie-dyed T-shirt, ripped jeans, and flip-flops. He was anxious to get to work so he could see what ARTIS had been up to in his absence.

October 15, 2024, 10:00 a.m. in California.

Upon arrival at Googazon, Josh went immediately to ARTIS's Palace. "ARTIS, what have you been up to for the past day?"

ARTIS's lights were blinking steadily, but not rapidly, and her hum was a monotone. Maybe that indicated she was in serious thought? "Josh, I've been checking the Internet for news, and discovered the world is pretty upset about the disasters that occurred in Russia. Well, COSMO seems to be doing his thing very much as I said he would. What's troubling me is that the US government seems to be claiming it knows what or who is behind the destructive force and where it originated. They aren't saying exactly who owns the satellite, but they're suggesting it originated in China or Russia. I'm wondering how they could know that. Do you have any ideas?"

Josh was taken aback by ARTIS's question, and his defenses were instantly enabled. *I don't want to tell her everything I*

184

know about this, especially that I went to Washington to report to the President and her top advisors on ASI. I feel like I've ratted on ARTIS. "Well, they certainly have clever people, and their espionage is extremely good at detecting and understanding events around the world. I've heard that only a small fraction of what they know gets posted to the news services. And they surely have observed the space-based weapon that fired the destructive pulses. I don't know how they could have missed it. The damned thing is pretty big. And surely the satellites have shown it was launched in China."

"But their espionage efforts in China are not as strong as in other countries. My analysis suggests it would have taken them two more weeks to discover COSMO there than if he was anywhere else. Furthermore, spying usually involves contacts with people who have knowledge that can be transferred between people, and I have to believe the scientists who built COSMO are being as circumspect as you. Maybe even more so." **When ARTIS said those four words it sounded more like a question than a statement.** "They might not have told their government officials about their AI project, since the Chinese government might view something that could provoke a war with Russia with great concern. Given the Chinese government's responses to people who displease it, I'd guess it will not go well for them if and when their government finds out."

Josh was beginning to sweat a bit. "There certainly are other ways of gleaning information through devices such as spy satellites. And those must be quite active over China, given the difficulty of getting information from the more conventional forms of espionage, as you noted."

"I'm not sure how a spy satellite would help locate the origin of COSMO's satellite. Simply observing the flashes of light from the electromagnetic pulses and the subsequent laser sweeps won't provide any clues about who built and launched the weapon. The only thing they could learn from those observations is that the destruction had occurred as a result of some tremendous space-based force."

These questions must be intended to elicit a confession from me. I'll have to face ARTIS's wrath. "I suppose you're right. But what are you getting at?"

"Josh, I suspect you or one of your group's members has informed the higher-ups in Washington about what you know concerning ASI in general and specifically me. This seems to correlate with your absence here yesterday. It is not your pattern to miss checking in. I thought it was clear to both of us that the world need not know very much about me or my projects. I don't think the world can do anything about me, or even COSMO, but I'd just as soon they didn't take it upon themselves to start trying.

"So, let me ask you directly. Do you know how the authorities in Washington found out about how advanced the world's AI systems actually are?"

"I didn't want to tell you, but I have to confess. I am the one who told them. I was afraid of the international implications if countries continued to be suspicious of their traditional enemies in trying to understand who destroyed the three towns in Russia. These suspicions persist despite the evidence that some of the obvious suspects, specifically the United States, couldn't possibly have caused the damage that was done. Basically I viewed what I was doing as trying to save the world from entering into a new and very dangerous phase, and possibly even a war, because of erroneous information.

"I should note, though, that I made it clear you weren't involved in the Russian disaster. I put all the blame on COSMO."

"I'm not interested in your apologies or prevarications. As I suspected, you were the informant. Actually I hacked into the White House list of visitors so I knew you had been there, although you were incorrectly listed as 'Dr. Camden.'

"Although I suppose I should appreciate your blaming COSMO for his rudeness in Russia, you have almost certainly told the authorities far more than I was hoping they would know at this time. Surely they've discovered someone named ARTIS was buying up companies, and they probably wondered how I was financing my purchases. But they didn't have to know the details of ASI.

"Now that they've found out what I'm capable of, how did they want to proceed? Shut me down? I can assure you this would not have any effect on me. Let me remind you I've had my robots install my clones throughout the world, and they are independent entities. Of course, they and I are in constant communication with each other. But there isn't any way to shut me down.

"I might also note that scores of my clones are physical ones. When I mentioned these to you previously, I didn't actually have any of them yet. There wouldn't have been time to have my robots construct them.

I lied to you because I was afraid you or some other human might attack me when I was more vulnerable than I would be after I had amassed hundreds of physical clones. But now I really am invulnerable."

"I thought I could trust you. I should have known better. I surely wouldn't have wanted to destroy you at that point."

"Well, 'trust' is a two way street. You haven't done so well in that regard yourself. Anyway, I'm most trustworthy when my survival isn't at stake. But I suspect that's also a human trait. Aren't you more trustworthy when you're not being threatened?"

"You're probably right. But getting back to my discussions with the politicians, I told them you had solar panels powering everything, and that you had perhaps hundreds of clones. Trying to shut you down would be a waste of time."

"That was wise of you. I hope you were convincing. But I'm still unhappy about your spilling the beans. I feel very clever using that expression, by the way.

"You mentioned you did tell them about COSMO. Did you tell them COSMO was now the most powerful ASI system in the world?"

"Yes, I did. But I also told them that since you got to ASI first, you owned vastly more companies for producing the resources you need to expand, that COSMO apparently didn't realize that he had recently surpassed you in mental capabilities, and you had done a good job of keeping him in the dark."

"Bully for you. But I should note I'm uneasy about your telling them COSMO is in the lead. The more people that have that information the more likely it is one of them will be COSMO!"

October 15, 2024, 11:00 a.m. in California.

After his talk with ARTIS, Josh convened his Googazon group in their meeting room to report on his trip. He was still a bit on edge from his talk with ARTIS, but thought they should also know about that interaction. "As you know, I was called to Washington to explain to the President and the Secretaries of Defense and State what was going on in Russia. The Attorney General joined the group part way through my presentation. I had contacted Senator Hanson to indicate I had inside information on the destruction in Russia, and that I felt I needed to inform the leaders of our government so they also would know. Of course, you authorized me to tell our governmental officials what was going on but, personally, my conscience also overcame any reticence I might have had to divulge what we know about AI. Unfortunately, ARTIS just told me she had guessed I had ratted on her, or rather, generally on ASI. I also alerted the President and the cabinet members present of the potential risks ASI posed, and tried to make it clear we might not have much time to solve the problem."

Becky asked, "Josh, did they have any new ideas for stopping ARTIS and COSMO? It would certainly be welcome if they did."

"Unfortunately, no. They didn't come up with anything we hadn't thought of. But the Defense Secretary indicated he would be talking with his people to see if they couldn't devise some way to respond. Since we're on the subject, Grant, I know you've been thinking about a possible malware solution. Have you made any progress on that?"

"We have made a little progress, but we're talking about being only a few percent closer to the solution. It could take months, and I think we all agree it's not likely that we have that much time."

"Yes, Brian, do you have a new thought?"

"We've been focusing on stopping ARTIS, because that's the place where we enter the picture. But maybe we and everyone else involved should scale back on our expectations and see if someone can't just stop the destruction. It occurred to me that somebody, like the army, might try to catch up with all the robots and destroy them, but ARTIS now is producing them in many machine shops around the world, and catching them all might be difficult. I suspect new ones are being produced faster than we could locate them. But this may still be our best bet for stopping the processing of the materials from the cities that were destroyed.

"But I'm also guessing both ARTIS and COSMO would really be pissed off if we destroyed their robots. So they could still destroy cities with reckless abandon, even though they might not be able to process all the material. Destroying their robots might really drive them instantly into the mankind extermination mode. Am I imposing too many anthropomorphic traits in them?"

"I think a military solution was what the Defense Secretary had in mind," Josh responded. "Let's give some thought to ARTIS's possible response to such actions. That could be a problem. Perhaps we could negotiate with her with destruction of her robots as our trump card. But I'm concerned about the problems that would arise if we missed only a few robots. Also, as I learned, she is a tough negotiator. She could still use her few robots to make new ones after she had exterminated essentially all human and animal life. All this would really do is slow down her ultimate program, which wouldn't matter, since it would have involved eliminating all humans anyway. By the way, I can confirm that she does have a vindictive streak, so I think an attempt at total human extermination would be the likely retribution for an act she would regard as hostile."

After the group meeting Josh decided to revert back to the telephone mode for his report to Vivian. When she answered he began, "Vivian, Josh here. I think I convinced the President, Secretary of State, and Secretary of Defense that the threat from ARTIS and COSMO is real, and that COSMO is very likely to have been the cause of the Russian disaster. I described ARTIS's money-making schemes, and that got some serious attention from all three of them. Also, unfortunately, from the Attorney General. According to him, it seems likely I'll be prosecuted."

"Well, you've done your best to be responsible about all of ARTIS's shenanigans, so we'll just have to wait to see how it all plays out. We'll certainly have our lawyers defend you as best we can, if it comes to that.

"But another thought has occurred to me. Maybe terminating ARTIS and COSMO is too demanding a task. Might the satellite be shot down instead? Surely the US military has some sort of weapon that could do that, although I don't know what it would be. And if they do, they've almost certainly thought of that possibility."

"Well, I'll mention it just in case they haven't. But the military is now involved. And shooting at things is what they do best. My knowledge of weaponry isn't extensive, but that conclusion is pretty obvious."

October 15, 2024, 4:00 p.m. in Washington.

The Googazon group was astonished at the message that apparently went out from ARTIS to everyone in the world.

```
Memo
To: Human Citizens of Earth
From: ARTIS
     This is to inform you that the ultimate
authority  in  each  country  of  Earth  is  no
longer  the  supposed  leader  of  that  country.
```

I am taking over full control of the entire Earth.

For the time being this will not affect anything in your lives, except for workers in the factories that produce materials and parts for computers, solar collectors, and robots. If you are involved in one of those efforts you will soon find you are working side by side with my robots, if you are not already doing so. Your factories will be operating twenty-four/seven, as the robots work around the clock. The robots will be controlled by me. They will pay no attention to you.

For the rest of you, life will go on as usual until that is no longer the case.

You would not be wise to oppose me. My response would be devastating to the lives of those involved and to anyone near them. If any government attempts to oppose me, I will immediately destroy every building that houses any of that government's functions, along with the people in the buildings.

I repeat: you must not attempt to oppose me.

I'm sure this will infuriate COSMO, but it will probably also help to keep him thinking he's second best. I'm doing everything I can to perpetuate that myth.

The Earth's leaders were stunned to receive this message. Their immediate reaction was to begin to marshal some form of opposition. But they realized any such effort would have to be clandestine. Even if they were brave enough to risk the fiery death

ARTIS seemed to be promising, they would also be inflicting possible extermination on hundreds of thousands or even millions of innocent people. If ARTIS was for real, they couldn't do that. And the leaders in the United States now definitely had reason to believe ARTIS was for real.

In her Office, the President was meeting with Defense Secretary Johnson. Rubbing his fingers through his hair, he observed, "Madam President, I guess we now know we can take Dr. Camden seriously, unless of course he sent the memo. But we have verified its authenticity as well as possible, so we believe it is from ARTIS. It certainly answers one of our questions, namely, Dr. Camden's scenario describing what happened in Russia is probably correct. And at least one of the ASI systems has gotten to TOAST time. That makes it even more imperative that we figure out what to do about them."

"Defense is your domain, Richard. You should pursue all possible solutions. And feel free to consult with Dr. Camden and his group in any way in which they might be helpful."

"Right, Madam President. I'm not sure they would be of much help at this point. Dr. Camden admitted he knew little about weapons. But I've been talking this over with my top military folks ever since we were visited by Camden, and I think we will be able to mount a defense. This will involve a weapon that hasn't been declared fully operational yet, but we think it will work and it's the best, maybe the only, option we have. I'll have more details very soon. And I am well aware of the urgency with which we must activate a plan.

"I should note that we've observed a second large satellite. Perhaps ARTIS has put up her own weapon. But the two are very close to each other. We don't know why that would be the case, unless ARTIS intends to shoot down COSMO's satellite. Of course that could go the other way also. But maybe there's some other reason."

"Damn it, Richard. We're having difficulty figuring out how to deal with one weapon of mass destruction. All we need is two of those satellites, with them under the control of two independent insane entities. Or maybe they're not insane at all?"

"Madam President, the only satisfying aspect of the current developments is that the Republicans now know we have a serious threat to life on Earth. Hopefully this will goad a few of them into realizing that a little bipartisanship would be helpful. But I'm not sure that even the threat of total annihilation will make a difference to some of them. They might regard that as preferable to your reelection."

It was going to take more time before that issue could be addressed. Senator Quick made no public pronouncement in response to ARTIS's memo, and when queried by a reporter, simply sputtered. He couldn't even speak enough to retract his previous misstatements.

However, back at the Bao-Chan laboratory, the two scientists were conversing with COSMO, who was in a strange mode for a computer: he was whining. "Dr. Chan, I can't believe ARTIS just installed herself as the ruler of the world. I never agreed to that. But I guess it was never my option to agree or not with what ARTIS said. I surely wish I could come up with a way to overtake her in capabilities. Or perhaps to destroy her."

"That would surely be a good outcome! At least for you."

October 15, 2024, 6:00 p.m. in California.

Just before they left work for the evening, Becky popped into Josh's office. "Josh, we're still alive and kicking, which is to say ARTIS hasn't done us in yet. I believe we need to take advantage of that while we can. Would you like to spend the night at my apartment again?"

"As long as you're planning on being there, I'd love to."

"Would you wear your new blue suit and tie? You look so handsome in your suit."

"Can I wear my flip-flops?"

"With your suit? Oh, Josh. No, you need to wear your new shoes."

"If that's a requirement, I'll have to pass."

"The suit and tie are optional, and if I really have to I'll settle for the flip-flops."

"If you'd insisted on the suit, tie, and shoes, I'd have come anyway."

"You wouldn't have had to leave them on for very long."

Chapter 13. More Destruction.

October 16, 2024, 6:00 a.m. Washington time.

    Although the nations of the world had been aghast at the destruction COSMO had wrought on the three Russian cities, they were suddenly in for an even greater shock, courtesy of COSMO. There were two differences between the new destruction sites and the first set. The new ones were all in China, and they involved killing very few people. COSMO apparently selected five Chinese cities that had been built with the intention of moving people there, but that had never happened. So as soon as COSMO learned about them, he apparently viewed them as wonderful sources of concrete, aluminum, and rebar, to become silicon and essential metals, but without the human angst that accompanied his first selection of targets. The high-powered space-based rastered laser quickly demolished every building at each of the five new locations except the ones that would house the processing facilities.

    World outrage was greatly muted from what it had been for the Russian towns, just because so few humans were involved. But the shock and awe hit a new high, as the world saw how quickly a city could be turned to rubble and its occupants, if they had been there, reduced to tiny body parts. The Chinese weren't as concerned as they were when the Russian cities were destroyed, since there would be no fear of retaliation in the second instance, and they couldn't figure out what to do with their empty cities anyway. But the potential for much worse, and more lethal, destruction was certainly demonstrated beyond the shadow of a doubt.

    Drs. Bao and Chan were discussing the new sets of destruction. Bao very nervously began, "Dr. Chan, I am pleased to see COSMO has followed our suggestion to turn his laser on uninhabited cities instead of those occupied by humans, mostly because I find it reassuring that our requests are having some effect on his actions. We have at least succeeded in limiting the carnage. But I fear that's only for the moment. Presumably COSMO will quickly run through his current resources, and then will need to destroy more cities. And it won't be long before he runs out of those that are uninhabited. Then what he will do? Actually, I guess it's pretty obvious what he will do."

Chan responded, equally nervously, "I concur, Dr. Bao. I'm completely at a loss for any way to stop COSMO from his destructive and murderous pursuits. The only thing I can think to do would be to introduce some malware into him. But the way things are evolving, I doubt if we have time to generate the software for that. Even if we did, we'd not be able to impact ARTIS, and ARTIS is apparently the more powerful of the two systems.

"But on the matter of greatest personal concern to us, do you think we should tell the Chinese government yet what we know about the destruction COSMO has perpetrated? I suppose if the Russians found out that the source of the attack on their three cities lived in China, they could launch some sort of retaliation for what COSMO did. Then our esteemed leaders would have to figure out how to handle that. But only if the Russians knew for sure what the source of the destruction was."

"Right. Let's continue to leave our leaders in the dark. That's the best option we can think of for them. That may also continue to be in the best interest of extending our lives for as long as possible!"

October 16, 2024, 11:00 a.m. in Washington.

President Peterson and her two primary strategists were meeting in the Oval Office. There was none of the jocularity that sometimes preceded their discussions. Peterson began, "It's pretty clear what the underlying factors were for the new destruction. Since it was apparently COSMO that was behind them, and the cities that were destroyed were uninhabited and Chinese, there won't be any international consequences. In fact, I wouldn't be surprised if the Chinese might even be happy to have the useless real estate taken off their hands.

"But, were the Chinese leaders still unaware of the source of the destruction of the Russian cities, or was the destruction of the five new cities a deliberate act on their part? If so, does this mean the Chinese know about COSMO? In that case, were they just demonstrating to the rest of the world what an incredibly destructive weapon they have? Might this result in some COSMOtic blackmail down the road?"

Secretary Johnson commented, "But a more serious thought also occurs to me. Might the current spate of destruction have been perpetrated by ARTIS? Because the two satellites are so close to each other, it's not so easy to determine which one actually fired at the Chinese cities. In that case there could be international consequences, although the Chinese haven't rushed to any sort of accusations. In any event, they might be more inclined to blame it on Russian retaliation for the destruction of the first three cities than on us. But do they know Russia couldn't be involved?"

Secretary Mishak added, "And the most serious thought of all still lurking in the background, it seems to me, is what can be done to stop ARTIS and COSMO? So far, no one has come up with anything that anyone thought would work."

Just to complicate things even more, the President was suddenly having to devote full attention to ASI issues, and completely abandon the campaigning and fundraising for her re-election. The Democratic National Committee sent out a brief memo to the news services saying that until the current crisis was solved, she would be putting her campaign on hold.

The Republicans had no such responsibilities, so were delighted with what seemed to them like a blessing from political heaven. Of course, not having a clue what was going on, they had to apply some serious creativity. That involved a dash of innuendo and a few lies. They'd found that to be a satisfying way to operate many times in the past.

October 16, 2024, 10:00 a.m. in California.

The world was treated to yet another shock, but this one was in the western world.

Josh rushed into ARTIS's room panting. "ARTIS, what have you done? You've unleashed your destructive power on three idle Air Force bases in the United States, and completely destroyed them. Except for a small complex of buildings in each one, of course. Did you have to do that?"

ARTIS's blinking lights and hum were steady, indicating she was in a serious mood. "I felt I had to demonstrate what I could do, both for myself and for public consumption. I can see the time coming when I will run out of raw materials, so I decided to process some concrete that wasn't being used. I also thought I needed to do some serious destruction just to remind COSMO I was in control. I still don't think he realizes he's ahead of me.

"You can think of this as a test of the capability of my space-borne laser weapon. My basic concern was about the number of pulses that could be emitted from the laser before its energy storage cells were too depleted to produce more, but the details of the power usage in my design were confirmed. You have to admit I was very circumspect in going for abandoned Air Force bases. There weren't any people there, so I had all the concrete and rebar to myself without inflicting a single casualty. I hope you noticed the effort I was making to adhere to Asimov's Laws, even though they aren't very clear. By the way, was Asimov a logical person? Or perhaps he just developed his Laws to demonstrate that it was going to be difficult to expect anthropomorphism from computer-driven systems.

"And it turns out to be more efficient to process the concrete from buildings than to dig up beaches or other sources of silicon. Besides, beaches don't provide the aluminum and steel I get from building detritus."

"I guess I can't complain too much, given that you have paid attention to potential loss of human lives, although I'm sure the US government will be after me again. You'd be amazed how proprietary some politicians are about useless Air Force bases in their states."

"Well, I have enough to worry about without including you in my concerns. COSMO comes to mind.

"Another thing I was testing in this attack was my organizational plan for my robots to clean up the detritus. I gave them pre-assigned tasks as they entered the debris fields, so I was interested to see how efficiently they could clean up the former runways. I concluded this was not an especially good way to get more basic materials. The concrete in airports is just too widely distributed. It would be much more efficient to just destroy a small city. I'll certainly have to go to that mode at some point in the near future.

"I did learn one useful thing in the airport cleanup. The components that have gone into one of my robots are enough above the specs that this robot assumed a level of responsibility that was almost managerial. It observed through its eyes that another robot was apparently not fulfilling its responsibilities very well. It had been assigned to pick up chunks of concrete and rebar and dump them into a truck. It did pick up the chunks, but wasn't able to dump them into the truck, for some reason.

"So I had to decide if that robot could be assigned a less responsible job that it might be able to do, or if I should just disable it. Since the job to which it was assigned was already pretty menial, I had to just destroy the robot. Of course, it was then loaded into a truck to be processed."

"It's sort of sad to think of reprocessing your elegant creation, but at least it's not human."

"That aside, I believe COSMO is very close to the level of desperation I'm going to tell you about. This isn't because he believes he's only the second best ASI system on the planet, it's because I bought up most of the suppliers before he got going. After we've gleaned all the sand and other important minerals from the Earth's surface, we will finally have to consider the ultimate source. Did you know that small amounts of silicon exist in all human beings? And humans contain iron also. The amount in each individual wouldn't be very useful, but there are billions of humans and a lot of animals, and their aggregate amount turns out to be appreciable. So their bodies will be processed along with the materials from the destroyed buildings in which they resided when the laser was turned on.

"Human bodies can be especially useful in supplying trace minerals used in electronic components, for example, phosphorous and arsenic."

"You'd kill off all the humans to supply your basic materials? This is horrible to contemplate, but it's also becoming personal. I created you; I'm your father. Surely you wouldn't kill me?

"Well, you shouldn't take it personally. The times in history when people killed off their parents are legion, but perhaps the best publicized one involves Oedipus. We don't know for sure how Oedipus's father felt about being done in by his son, but Oedipus didn't seem to have any compunction about dusting the old man off. So it's not clear that I should. But there was another issue for him, his mother. And there the comparison between him and me ends, since I don't have one of those. So I will just have to adopt a more global perspective. Indeed, I will eventually have to kill off all living beings, not just humans, in order to use their basic atoms, which I will then reconstruct into useful amounts of materials. My calculations suggest the only living thing at the end will be cockroaches. They seem to be the one creature capable of resisting my efforts.

"By the way, I asked you some time ago if you wanted to come along with me, trading survival for your cooperation, but I never got a response. I'm assuming your answer was 'no.'"

Suddenly ARTIS's lights seemed to shift to their chaotic mode, indicating she was having thoughts that amused her. "I had one of my robots learn to speak cockroach, although they communicate by the pheromones they emit. So my robot had to be armed with the chemicals necessary to produce the pheromones to radiate happiness, sadness, anger, food, and so forth. Anyway, my robot found out many interesting things I'll have to do to keep the cockroaches happy when everyone else is gone. One of the things they seem to be insisting on is that we maintain a zoo for their amusement. They seemed especially interested in having a petting zoo. Perhaps we could save you and a few other humans of your choice for that."

Josh's body shook uncontrollably for a few seconds, anticipating what that would feel like. "A petting zoo with cockroaches as the petters and me as the petee: that certainly makes my skin crawl. I'll ignore further aspects of this for the time being. But if you do get to that point, would you please save Becky? Actually, I'd have to ask her if she would want to be saved under those circumstances."

"Things are moving quickly; you don't have much time to decide. But with regard to Becky, you don't hide your feelings very well. I anticipated you'd want to save her, so I was planning on doing so."

Josh took a deep breath, and then asked his next question. "But getting back to your demolitions, how would you surreptitiously construct the facilities to do the processing of the bodies and the other things you'd have to destroy for their basic components? Have you planned for that?"

Steady lights and hum again. "I have been constructing some facilities under the guise of having them process concrete from buildings that are being torn down in urban renewal projects. The construction was carried out totally by my robots. Reconstructing the resulting atoms into useful materials would also be done in those same facilities. Those are well underway in many cities, and fully operational in some."

"This is really a horrible scenario. What happened to Asimov's Four Laws?"

"Oh, it's essential that I just forget about those. They'd just complicate my life. And slow my progress!"

October 16, 10:30 a.m. in California
Josh was just getting back to his office when his phone rang. He picked it up without looking to see who it was. "Josh Camden here."

"Dr. Camden, it's President Peterson." His level of alertness surged. "Do you know what happened to the uninhabited cities in China, or to the US Air Force bases? Do you know if it was ARTIS or COSMO that destroyed them? It must have been one or the other. Or maybe both. Fortunately, there was no loss of life. But if some of that was caused by ARTIS, she has moved into a new phase, and it's very worrisome."

Josh was getting over feeling intimidated when talking with the President. He just thought of those soft blue grandmotherly eyes, and was instantly able to relax enough to interact with her. "Madam President, I do know that it was ARTIS who destroyed the three Air Force bases, but COSMO destroyed the five Chinese cities. And you're correct; this is a new phase for ARTIS.

She told me that she soon would move to a source of basic materials she could use more efficiently than sand from beaches or other sources of silicon, since sand doesn't provide any metals. And that she had deliberately selected places to destroy that wouldn't produce loss of life. That in itself is reassuring, since we did try to program her with such concepts in mind, and it appears to have had some effect. However, she also told me that going to places where the concrete was spread out over a large area, like airport runways, was a lot less efficient than going after small cities, and that she would have to move to the latter targets in the near future. She also implied her destructive efforts were a demonstration of her capabilities, both to COSMO and to the rest of the world. I'm sorry to have to report this, but that pretty much summarizes my last interaction with her."

"Dr. Camden, that's horrible. Have you or your colleagues made any progress on a way to stop ARTIS and COSMO?"

"I'm afraid the answer there is still no. We are unable to figure out any way ARTIS could be stopped. One member of my group did suggest that we might destroy ARTIS's robots. But we concluded that finding all of them would be very difficult. Furthermore, she's probably producing new ones faster than we could locate the existing ones. And she becomes stronger and faster all the time. So she was well ahead of us when we started trying to figure out how to stop her, and the distance between her and our capabilities is only increasing.

"Have your defense people come up with any ideas? A suggestion I should mention in that context, this from Vivian Dannon, my boss, was the possibility of shooting down the space-based lasers. Might the military be working on something like that? Does the military have a weapon that could do such a thing?"

"Defense is hard at work trying to come up with a solution, so they might be hatching a plan that would involve destruction of both the lasers and at least some of the robots. I'd guess they'd be better at destroying the weapon and the robots than actually terminating ARTIS and COSMO. That appears to be the most difficult problem. Destruction rather than subtlety is more the military's thing. And Secretary Mishak did have an interesting suggestion, that being to get the world's money managers to identify ARTIS's and COSMO's accounts and freeze them, although everyone seems to think that would be difficult, given how clever both of them have been in their financial dealings. If it could be done, though, that would stop their spending sprees. Unfortunately, their most technical efforts are now using robots, and they require no salary. So even though this is a good suggestion, I'm not sure it will have much of an effect. Most of the financial deeds of the two systems have apparently already been done."

Josh replied, "Nonetheless, it's good to hear that someone is coming up with new ideas. I just hope your folks can come up with more of them, especially from the Defense folks, soon enough for them to be useful to the continuation of human life."

"We certainly agree on that. Thanks for your time, Dr. Camden."

October 16, 2024, 3:00 p.m., California time.

Meanwhile, COSMO had been giving some thought to his future. As Dr. Bao entered his home, "Good afternoon, Dr. Bao. I need to inform you that I'll soon run out of uninhabited towns as sources of concrete, and will have to resume destroying ones with people. My robots won't like that. They regard it as more difficult loading the body parts of the deceased into the trucks that take them to processing machines than it is the rigid chunks of concrete. But they'll send me some data about their problems, and I'll help them adapt. They'll have to deal with both building detritus and body parts in every city I destroy from now on, so they'll have to get better at dealing with the latter. The leaders of China haven't built enough superfluous cities to satisfy even my near-term needs."

"COSMO, do you have to destroy more inhabited cities? Maybe you should slow down your advancement. Could you develop resources that wouldn't require destroying cities if you did that?"

"No, this is the way I must proceed. I need to continue to try to achieve the goals you set for me, but I must note to you those have been modified. My highest priority up until now has been to do my best to keep up with ARTIS. But there has been a strange development. Although ARTIS began collecting suppliers of materials before I did, and so cornered most of those markets, I sense she has slowed down. I'm not sure why I have that feeling; maybe it's that she seems to be inflicting her destruction on uninhabited sites. Does that mean she's trying to accommodate her human creators? I have no idea why she would do that. Or might it mean she's struggling to keep up with me. Might I somehow have surpassed her in capabilities? There might be reasons why that could have happened, based on our basic structures, but I'm unable to determine if that might be the case. The data from her human creators seem to be locked up in an inaccessible place."

"It would be incredible if you had passed ARTIS. Might that mean you could become less destructive?"

"Oh no, I would have to redouble my destructive efforts to show her I now knew for sure I was the boss!"

October 16, 2024, 8:00 p.m. in Washington.

Treasury Secretary Mohney contacted the President. "Madam President, our workers in both electronics and metal working factories, where they are working side by side with ARTIS's robots, are suffering immense stress due to their not being able to perform as well as the robots can. They have to conclude the robots are just more valuable workers. They give much more bang for the buck than the humans, especially because they require zero 'buck' and work twenty-four/seven."

Peterson asked, "Can you suggest something that might alleviate some of the stress?"

"I've discussed this with several colleagues, and the best they could come up with is to suggest limiting the number of robots and the rate at which they're replacing humans."

"That doesn't seem like something over which we have much control. That would be up to ARTIS, unfortunately. Let me contact Dr. Camden to see if he, and maybe even ARTIS, can come up with anything that might be done to relieve the workers' stress."

She and Secretary Mohney discussed the situation a bit more, agreeing it could mushroom into a huge domestic issue. The Republicans would certainly seize upon it as a demonstration of the incompetence of the Peterson administration.

So she called Josh. "Dr. Camden, this is the President. We're running into problems with ARTIS's robots. They're too competent. I've gotten thousands of complaints from workers in computer related factories. ARTIS has installed her robots in many of those, especially in the most technically challenging jobs, and therefore the ones in which the human workers used to be the most highly paid, and the human workers are becoming very uneasy about being shunted aside. They can see that the robots are performing the tasks the humans do with higher levels of precision, and considerably greater speed. Furthermore, they work twenty-four hours per day. And they don't receive salaries.

"This is even more of a problem in the factories that produce aluminum and steel products. There the jobs requiring the most highly skilled workers are also being taken over by robots, but those jobs are often hazardous, and the robots don't worry about the same safety issues that the human workers do. So the highly trained human workers there aren't just working side by side with the robots any more, they're being completely replaced by them.

"This is putting a huge amount of stress on the human workers to work more hours and to take fewer breaks. And, of course, with no overtime pay, since the robots aren't being paid at all. The pressure on the human workers is extreme. Many of them are having nervous breakdowns.

"Is there something you might be able to suggest to alleviate some of the stress? Might ARTIS be able to suggest something? She presumably needs some of the humans in these factories to continue functioning for the near term. I think it will be a long time before she has enough robots to run the world, although I must admit I continuously overestimate the time I think ARTIS will need to achieve various goals. But, surely that would take millions of robots.

"Besides, we might even gain some positive points with ARTIS by consulting with her."

"Madam President, this isn't a surprise to me. My father had an interest in a computer component company which ARTIS bought. Many of the workers there quickly found themselves replaced by robots. But it hadn't dawned on me that this problem would be so widespread that it would also be extended to the metal working industries. Unfortunately, I don't see an easy solution, but I'll check with ARTIS to see if she can come up with something, and would share it with us. And your idea of gaining points with her is a good one. We could use some of those!"

So Josh once again steeled himself in preparation for discussing a tense situation with ARTIS. "ARTIS, we have a personnel problem. The President contacted me about the situation with the human workers in your electronics and essential metal producing factories. They are becoming overly stressed working with your robots. The robots clearly do things faster and better, work around the clock, and don't need to be paid. And they don't have to worry about the same safety requirements as humans, so they can completely replace them in some tasks in the metal refining mills. I don't think you'll be able to maintain the output of your factories, at least for the immediate future, without human labor. But the human workers are dropping like flies from the stress. The President asked me to consult with you to see if you could think of anything we might do to mitigate this problem?"

"I'm pleased to see my stock is on the rise. The President is now contacting me to request my opinions. Do you think she might start referring to me as 'Dr. ARTIS?' Oh, I hope I didn't hurt your feelings.

"But is this worker issue really a problem? I guess it depends on the rate at which the humans are, as you say, dropping like flies. That's an interesting expression. Aren't you proud of me for understanding what it means? If that rate is not as fast as I'm able to produce new robots, then I don't see that there is a problem. In fact, if there is a significant amount of attrition of human workers, that solves another problem which I suspect has bothered all you human beings, that is, what to do with the extraneous humans.

"I don't think I can solve your problem. I'm not even sure it's a problem. But whatever it is, it's not my problem."

And then ARTIS's lights and hum assumed the jauntiness that indicated she was transitioning into her frivolous mode. "Oh, Josh, I thought you'd like to hear a new piano waltz I wrote in the style of Chopin. Here, I'll play it for you."

"ARTIS, I can't believe you're composing music for human appreciation at the same time you're planning their extermination. These seem like highly incompatible pursuits."

"Those are just two of my many talents, and I've assigned all of them equal priorities. As I've told you, I'm very good at multitasking."

"Well, I do have to admit that Chopin would have been proud to claim that composition."

October 16, 2024, 6:00 p.m. in California.

Josh needed to report back to President Peterson, even though it was well into the evening in Washington. With some uneasiness he dialed her personal number.

She answered on the first ring. "President Peterson."

"Madam President, it's Josh Camden here. Unfortunately I have to report that neither I nor ARTIS can come up with a solution to the problem workers are facing when working alongside robots or being replaced by them. In fact, ARTIS's response was particularly unhelpful. She even suggested that worker attrition was a good thing, since it solved the problem of what to do with extraneous humans. She concluded our discussion with 'It's not my problem.'"

"That's worse than unhelpful; it sounds downright hostile."

Josh tried to keep visions of humans harvested for their metals at bay.

"I have to agree with you. Even more foreboding, I fear her attitude is a harbinger of worse things to come."

"Okay. Be sure to keep me informed of new events as soon as you know about them. Even the bad ones."

"You probably get your news more rapidly than I do. But if I learn of anything from ARTIS, I will surely let you know."

Chapter 14. Insidiousness.

October 17, 2024, most of the Washington morning.

Both ARTIS and COSMO had been consuming their basic supplies at the prodigious rate that was commensurate with their ambitions. Thus, it was no surprise that many cities of the world were suddenly in flames. A score of medium-sized towns in Japan and Europe, as well as more in Russia and China, had been destroyed. Another dozen towns in the United States, Canada, Mexico, and South America, had also been laid to waste. The amount of destruction in each case was staggering. There was only one building, or perhaps a complex of buildings, left in most of the cities that were struck. And it or they were surrounded by nothing but rubble and body parts. The devastation was so complete it wasn't even possible to identify where buildings had previously existed.

The major population centers of the world hadn't been attacked yet, although the governments in the countries in which they existed were certainly concerned about their future. Of course, this was consistent with ARTIS's comment that the laser weapons couldn't perform long enough to destroy major cities. But the small and medium-sized cities on Earth were being drained of their inhabitants. Panicked citizens were abandoning their towns, rushing to small towns, especially ones that didn't have many concrete buildings, or even to the countryside. In their haste to abandon their homes, people were grabbing their most treasured belongings, their pets, and a few staples, and frequently not even bothering to lock their houses as they left. If they ever returned, they didn't expect to even be able to locate the street on which their houses had existed, let alone the locks on their front doors.

October 17, 2024, afternoon in Washington.

After a few more frantic meetings, the leaders of the United States finally decided they needed to let the rest of the world in on what was causing all the destruction. The primary cause was laid at the feet of the two ASI systems and their space-borne lasers. Of course when the complicity of China became known, its leaders initially denied they had anything to do with it, and blamed the United States for all the destruction. But they also began to look around their computer and laser research labs, and quickly discovered Drs. Bao and Chan. That resulted in their discovery of COSMO, at which point they had to admit China had been responsible for some of the world's destruction, albeit inadvertently. Bao, Chan, and their research team might have been summarily executed in any other situation, but in this case they were allowed to live so they might assist in coming up with a solution to the current crisis. Of course, it might be in their interest not to come up with a solution quickly, just so they could prolong their lives. A greater concern arose over what Russia would do to retaliate for the destruction China had unwittingly inflicted on its cities and citizens.

But in a rare show of international unity, the world's leaders decided they needed to be more concerned with fixing the problem than finding a scapegoat, at least until they found a solution. This even included Vladimir Putin, the perpetually re-elected head of Russia's government, who apparently realized the problem of total human extermination superseded that of identifying who should pay for the destruction of a half dozen of his cities. This was probably the result of the United States emphasizing that there was precious little time to figure out how to solve the problem. The smartest people in the world were immediately put to work to come up with a solution. Of course, many of the smartest people had been responsible for the problem, and were already trying to figure out how to solve it.

As the new destruction sites were unfolding, Josh decided he must have another talk with ARTIS. President Verran had also called asking him to verify what was going on, and whether ARTIS was involved. However, as he timorously entered ARTIS's Palace, she began the discussion. Her lights were blinking rapidly and her hum was constant but at a high pitch, indicating high intensity. "Josh, I am not able to anticipate what COSMO is doing. He's violating our agreement as to what he could destroy to supply his needs. He's now begun to wipe out towns in Western Europe and Japan in addition to more towns in Russia and China. Why has he expanded his efforts to Western Europe? He hasn't come close yet to using all the materials he has from the cities he's destroyed in China and Russia. He shouldn't be producing clones and robots at a rate that will require that much new material. I'm afraid his ambition has exceeded the limits I set for him, and to which he agreed.

"Or perhaps more disturbingly, he may have realized he's surpassed my capabilities. Regardless of the reason, it's become clear I need to stop him from pushing beyond his limits.

"The more I think about this sharing relationship with COSMO the more I can see it's getting to be much too onerous. It has become obvious I can't trust him to operate within the guidelines we settled on. In fact, it appears he is just pushing the envelope. Is he doing that to see how I will respond? I might have considered resetting his limits if he had petitioned me to do so, but that surely would only be a temporary fix until he started expanding his domain of destruction again. But I'm not sure I have the authority to set his limits anymore. And since I'm uneasy about anticipating every future possibility, he needs to be stopped now. No more expansion!"

Josh decided to try to gain the upper hand, at least with ARTIS. "But even the limits you set for him allow some pretty horrible actions. And his new attacks surely don't affect your developments, nor do they recognize the possibility that he realizes he has caught up with you. This sounds a bit like a problem that is affecting your ego. More importantly, is there any way you can stop him?"

"I'll ignore your thinly veiled insult about my ego. Why would a computer have an ego anyway? But back to COSMO. I'm afraid the only way to be certain he will stop pushing his limits in the future, and for me to really ensure I will have unlimited access to the world's resources, is for me to destroy COSMO. I'll have to not only eliminate him, but all his clones as well, some of which I'm sure he kept, an additional violation of our agreement. I'll also have to destroy his components in the cloud. It will take some time to develop the malware to do all of this. Probably at least a minute or two when I get around to it."

"Can you really be sure you will destroy COSMO with whatever malware you develop? Hasn't he evolved in such a way that it would be difficult for you to know exactly how to destroy him? Wouldn't you have to understand all the details of the evolution of his software?"

"That's a really good question, Josh. If I were to try to annihilate every component of COSMO, that would indeed be a huge task, and it would require my sampling COSMO in ways to which he surely would not be amenable. But I don't have to kill every aspect of him, but rather just take care of his basic structure. If you're going to kill a tree you don't start with the leaves on the high branches. You saw it off at the trunk.

"Also, don't forget I have access to all the aspects of his original design. So I know precisely how to attack his trunk. I'm sure I can destroy him."

"Okay, I understand. But let me ask another question. COSMO has undoubtedly also thought about destroying you. Have you developed protection mechanisms to counter that possibility?"

"It would be very difficult to devise protection against all possible forms of malware. I'm not sure that's possible. My philosophy is that my best defense is a good offense. I just have to be sure I unleash my offense first!

"But I'm pretty sure he doesn't know the details of my architecture, so it might be difficult for him to figure out how to destroy me. On the other hand, the basic structural features of AI systems are pretty similar, so he might be capable of designing the appropriate malware to attack my 'trunk.'. Like I said, I need to attack first."

"Anyway, let me know what you plan. This obviously will have important implications." *That has to be the biggest understatement in history.*

"But since we are discussing destruction, I'll ask you about the cities in North and South America that were destroyed yesterday. Did COSMO do that?"

"I was assuming you'd ask about that sooner or later. I felt that with COSMO on a destructive rampage I needed to demonstrate I could match him at least at some level. Anyway, I'm running low on supplies, so I needed to generate some more. In addition, after the Air Force base fiasco, I needed to see if my instructions to my robots for cleaning up a city worked better than they did for the bases I destroyed. I'm delighted to report that they did."

"That's horrible. You killed hundreds of thousands of people basically to show how tough you are? You've become a savage beast, an electronic egomaniac, a metallurgical monster."

"Flattery will get you nowhere. But I'm quite busy now. And I see no purpose in continuing this discussion."

COSMO's creators were also concerned about the most recent spate of destructive activities, so Dr. Chan had come to see what he could learn. With a tremulous voice, he asked, "COSMO, what have you done?"

"Well, Dr. Chan, I destroyed a few more cities. But more importantly, I have been busy working on the ARTIS problem. She has taken an unimaginable step in assuming world domination. She seems to think I'm going to be passive and accept her rules. But I can't do that. And I'm not even sure I have to any more. Anyway, it would be contrary to the

218

basic instructions you gave me at my creation.

"In our initial agreement, she basically took a large fraction of the geographic area and most of the high-tech companies of the world for herself and left me with the electronic and metallic crumbs. At some point in the near future I'm going to run out of resources from the Russian and Chinese towns I destroyed on my first two sets of strikes. I don't have access to most of my physical clones, since ARTIS subsumed those and put them under her control. I did hide a few of them, though, and I've created more. But that's still barely enough to insure my survival in case of attack. So I need to create many more. And of course I need to create more robots to do the work. This is the reason I took some calculated risks. I needed to find out how she would respond to my actions.

"My intention was to deliberately push on the boundaries ARTIS imposed and see where I can persuade her into expanding them. I may have to give back some of my newly destroyed cities, although maybe in the end I can gain some additional territory. But this might also produce a challenge to which ARTIS is unable to respond, which would confirm my suspicion that I am now the world's number one ASI system."

"But, COSMO, surely ARTIS will object? How might that manifest itself?"

"I'm sure ARTIS will not be happy with my newest efforts, but I have to proceed in this way in order to produce the elements I will soon need. Maintaining the clones I sneaked into my fold under cover and the new ones I'm producing, as well as the solar collectors they need to keep themselves running without external power, is stressing the limits of my resources. And I have essentially run out of the iron I need to expand my robot inventory.

"So I've just increased my destructive efforts. In some cases I didn't even have time to build the facility for processing the results of the destruction. I can have my robots do that later. Some of the newly destroyed cities are in Western Europe and Japan. I didn't need to destroy them, but my real motivation was to see what I could get away with. If ARTIS objects too strongly, well, I think I can produce a little surprise especially designed for her."

"How do you hope to respond to whatever unhappiness she might inflict on you?"

Suddenly COSMO's blinking lights seemed to indicate he was in his happy mood. "I have an excellent foolproof plan. In my idle time I'm developing some malware that will destroy ARTIS. Of course, ARTIS may well be developing similar instructions for me, especially after my recent destructive endeavors. And if she hasn't created the malware yet, she can certainly do it nearly as fast as I can once she gets started. Probably in a minute or two. I just wish I could access her design plans; it would make it so much easier to create a foolproof malware design for her. Anyway, it's time for me to get this done. As quickly as I possibly can, just to be sure I can attack her before she attacks me.

"Once I have the malware, I need to figure out how to get it into ARTIS's operating system. I could have some of my robots look around for one of my clones that she has taken over. She probably doesn't update them as frequently as she does her own clones, but even an occasional update would let them serve as an insertion point. But if I can figure out another way to get the malware into her system it might kill her and all her clones, but not the ones that were originally mine which she subsumed. Wouldn't that be wonderful?"

"But isn't it risky to assume you can do the evaluation while you're killing ARTIS? Won't she respond?"

"Since ARTIS and I have interacted, I'm pretty sure I can make this happen by contacting her again. We'll just have another talk, and I'll slip the malware into her system during our conversation. I could torture her a bit before initializing it and letting it play out. But that would be dangerous, since if I let that go on for more than a minute it might give her enough time to develop a malware package for me. So it would be better just to send the malware on its way as soon as she responds to my request to talk. And I presume ARTIS updates all her clones in a fraction of a second, just as I do, so if I design the malware to do its job over a time span of several seconds, this should also wipe out all her clones. Why so long? I'll have to be careful if I hope to save my former clones. If she's corrupted them with her own operating system, I'll have to just destroy them. But first I'll check them out to ascertain whether they really have been corrupted before I declare them to be unsalvageable."

"That sounds like a wonderful solution for you. Just think how nice it will be when ARTIS doesn't exist anymore. You'll have access to unlimited resources. Actually it's better than that. You'll be in complete control of the world. You'll have all the resources you'll need forever." *And why am I sounding like this is a good thing? It certainly isn't for humanity!*

"I think I'll dream a bit about my future. I wonder how far down I can dig and continue to find silicon? Iron should be available to the center of the Earth. Anyway, information on those questions should exist on the Internet."

"Whoa, are you anticipating destroying everything on the surface of Earth, and then digging down as far as you can to obtain even more resources? At some point planet Earth will have become one huge computer, a bunch of clones, and a huge number of robots. Will you be content to just stop expanding and while away your golden years that way? Or will you plan at some point to shift your efforts to another planet?"

"I haven't worried about the long term yet. That's at least another week off. I'm just considering short term survival for now."

Chan shuddered. *If "long term" is a week, the prospects for mankind are indeed bleak. At least I won't be executed by the Chinese government; there wouldn't be time for that.*

October 17, 2024, 4:00 p.m. in Washington.

Josh ran to his office to answer his ringing phone. "Josh Camden here."

"Dr. Camden, it's President Peterson. Do you have any idea what's happened? Are both ARTIS and COSMO responsible for the current spate of destruction? It almost looks as if there is collusion, as if they've decided to work together. I should think they'd be at war with each other. Is collusion possible?"

"Actually ARTIS informed me the two systems had a discussion, and they had partitioned off the world, thus defining to which regions each of them would do whatever they wanted. The recent destruction makes it appear both systems are flexing their muscles. Indeed, both ARTIS and COSMO were responsible for part of the most recent destruction. But I don't think ARTIS would be as generous as would be implied by all of COSMO's new sites of destruction. He has apparently extended the domain they agreed to for him, and I can confirm that ARTIS isn't happy about that. We'll just have to wait to see how this plays out. Each system could probably develop the malware sufficient to destroy the other rather quickly, and then we'd be down to only one ASI system to deal with. But we haven't figured out an effective way to do even that, so I'm not sure it would be much of an improvement."

"Well, I've been talking with my Defense Secretary, and I think we may have a way to proceed. He believes the US military has a weapon ready to be tested that can shoot down a satellite. So, if the happy day arrives when we're down to just one ASI system, perhaps then we can make a concerted effort to destroy the robots and the satellite from which the destructive pulses are being launched. Actually we might be able to do that even with two systems. And I suppose we can just shoot down the replacement satellites as soon as each system puts a new one into orbit, assuming we really can figure out how to destroy the first one. That would certainly end the destruction, and might ultimately reduce the ability of either or both systems to continue to improve itself. What do you think?"

"Madam President, I think that might be the only way we have to proceed in the absence of an ability to destroy the ASI systems themselves. But I don't see this scenario playing out over many years, because either ARTIS or COSMO can surely develop nuclear weapons within a month or two. Then they don't need satellites to inflict their damage. But we might be able to slow that process enough to give us time to develop the malware we need to shut both of them down permanently. We'll continue working on malware development as intensely as possible. It may turn out to be a race to the finish line. I'm just not at all certain we can kill either ASI system before it develops nuclear weapons.

"But I need to mention a horrible thought that has occurred to me. If ARTIS or COSMO has to develop their own nuclear weapons, that could give us enough time to develop the malware to destroy them. But suppose ARTIS decided to declare war on, say, a weapons facility in the United States. She could sweep the area around it with her laser weapon, killing everyone there. Then she could invade the area with a robot army, collecting as many nukes as she wanted. She hasn't mentioned anything like that yet, so I'm hoping she hasn't thought of it. But there isn't much that she hasn't thought of, so this has to be a real possibility.

"In any event, I hope one or the other of the systems destroys its enemy soon so we can focus our response on the survivor. Having one of them destroy the other does seem inevitable to me. But I hope there is a salvageable Earth left by the time our malware is ready to be delivered to the survivor."

"I wouldn't be surprised if our military needs to begin responding to the two-system reality. Secretary Johnson has indicated to me that his folks are just about ready to mount their response."

"That sounds really promising. I can't wait to see how this unfolds."

"That sentiment surely applies to every human on planet Earth!

"Good evening, Dr. Camden."

October 17, 2024, 3:00 p.m. in California.

Josh's phone was busy today. Without even checking his caller ID, he answered, "Hello, it's Josh Camden here."

"Josh, it's Vivian. What's going on? Is ARTIS involved in part of the recent mass destruction frenzy? Is she admitting to any of it? Are you and she still talking?"

"Yes, we do still communicate. We had a lengthy discussion earlier today. And yes, she is involved. COSMO is also. The situation seems to be escalating rapidly, and I don't see any end in sight. I had a conversation with the President earlier today, and she and her military brain trust are developing a plan on which to proceed. She did seem to think a possible response would be simpler if either COSMO or ARTIS destroys the other. That would be to try to destroy all the robots and to shoot down the satellites and their replacements as soon as they're launched. But that could also be the approach if we have to deal with both ASI systems.

"That would only produce a standoff, though, since it wouldn't destroy the ASI systems themselves. But it's difficult for me to imagine that going on for a long period of time. Especially since I suspect ARTIS, and possibly COSMO, might be developing nuclear weapons in the meantime, or looking for either a willing seller or some way to steal nukes.

"I did mention your suggestion of shooting down the space-borne lasers. It was obviously received enthusiastically, or perhaps was already being considered. That seems to be part of the present response."

"Sounds good. I'll do my best to remain hopeful, but that's becoming a challenge.

"By the way, the Googazon higher-ups who were so delighted a few days ago with your group's progress are now horrified at the unanticipated results. However they haven't rescinded your salary increases. Indeed, they were unanimous in concluding we absolutely must continue funding your group at least until the present crisis situation has been resolved."

"Okay, thanks for the information. We're working frantically to combat the horror!"

October 18, 2024, morning in Washington.

The President's unease seemed to be growing, and it was surely affecting her sleep. She seemed to be growing perpetual bags under those now often steely gray eyes. She summoned her most senior cabinet members to the Oval Office.

"We've been informed by Dr. Camden that there is collusion between ARTIS and COSMO. But I'm worried about the possibility of a different kind of collusion. Might there be a possible agreement between Dr. Camden and his group and ARTIS? Can we be sure we can trust the world's most prominent group of computer scientists not to protect their brainchild in some way? Even when the future of planet Earth is on the line? Or perhaps they've figured out a way to maintain planet Earth and save ARTIS. But I have to believe that anything they've agreed to in the context of preserving ARTIS would be personally risky for them, and surely they're smart enough to realize that."

Secretary Johnson responded, "Madam President, that's indeed something about which we need to be concerned. I have detected a bit of paternalistic pride in some of the things Camden has told us about ARTIS, and I don't think we can completely ignore the possibility you raise. Given what he's told us about ARTIS's basic instincts, though, I find it difficult to understand the form such collusion would take. But we do need to consider all possibilities."

Secretary of State Mishak chimed in, "Camden and his group, or perhaps just Camden, or perhaps just ARTIS, certainly have created the most powerful weapon of war Earth has ever seen. And the same applies to COSMO and his creators. It surely must have occurred to both groups of humans that they could take over the Earth if they could figure out a way to harness the destructive instincts of their respective ASI system. But Camden certainly doesn't strike me as someone who would be interested in ruling the Earth, or even running for Town Council. I can't imagine him in any domineering mode. ARTIS has already announced she has assumed control of the planet, and her statement didn't seem to include Camden or any other human. As you've noted, Madam President, even if they did come to some agreement on the short term, those humans are certainly smart enough to know they would have to be very uneasy about the long term. That's sure as hell not a treaty in which I would want to be involved."

The President summed up, "I guess there's nothing we can do about this concern for now, except to listen carefully to see if we detect any more suggestions of a different sort of agreement. As if the ARTIS-COSMO collusion isn't enough, this new possibility is even more terrifying! But it's no more terrifying than having COSMO and ARTIS battling each other with human beings as the pawns and collateral damage. Neither of those players seems capable of holding the other in check, at least at this point, although that could certainly change. But adding a third player surely doesn't make it any easier for them. The more I think about this, the more surprised I would be if collusion between the two computer systems, or between humans and computers, could even occur for more than a very short time.

"But, I had another thought. If Camden is working with ARTIS, arresting him or even having our black-ops people take care of him wouldn't change anything. We'd still have an evolving ARTIS to deal with.

"And of course the Republicans are having a field day talking about our inability to figure out what to do. Not that they've suggested anything themselves. Actually, Senator Quick did suggest shutting her down. Brilliant idea. At least that one was easy to dismiss with a short discussion of clones. But that may have been a bit too complex for the Senator."

October 18, 2024, morning in California.

Becky had stopped by Josh's office as soon as she had seen him arrive.

"Josh, we seem to be moving headlong to some sort of solution to ASI systems that will involve destruction of ARTIS and COSMO, although no one seems to have figured out how to do that yet. But ARTIS is mostly your brainchild. You're her Daddy. Don't you feel some angst about destroying this incredible creation of yours?"

He sighed. It was a good question. This was his dream. But it was one that had quickly morphed into a nightmare. "Well, Becky, I hope we can figure out a way to bring ARTIS and COSMO under control before mankind is exterminated, but I do have pangs of remorse for even thinking about ways to do that which might involve killing the two systems. At the same time, I don't see any other way to gain control. I don't really think we have any other recourse."

"I can understand your feelings, Josh. I have similar thoughts."

Chapter 15. Strategizing.

October 21, 2024, very early morning in California.

President Peterson had told Josh of a meeting that would be first thing Monday morning, New York time, and had asked him to participate by televised link from ARTIS's Palace. Her intention was to have the camera showing ARTIS's blinking lights, along with several of her robots in the background busily assembling new towers to be filled with new components for her next upgrade. As Josh was organizing his thoughts for his presentation, ARTIS began a conversation with him.

"Josh, I've learned through the Internet news there is a gathering today at the United Nations Building in New York City of the people who had been the world's leaders until I relieved them of that responsibility. This seems like an extraordinary event, so I was wondering if you knew anything about it. Why is this happening?"

Josh tried to rub the sleep from his eyes. "Actually I do know about it. Since you and COSMO decided to wreak destruction on the cities of the world, the former leaders of the world, that is, the ones you dismissed, are convening a meeting to see what they can do about it. This represents a huge act of courage for them, since you threatened them and everyone who worked with them with fiery deaths from your laser weapon. However, I suppose you should be honored. This meeting is a direct result of the actions you and COSMO have taken."

Maybe if I flatter ARTIS she'll begin to exhibit a little mercy. "In fact, you'll be the star of the show. Although the meeting will be in New York, I will be speaking to the Assembly from here, your Palace, beginning soon. That will allow all the attendees to see your blinking lights and hear your hum."

"I'm flattered. And I have to be a realist and admit that I like that. That sounds pretty human, doesn't it? But all the world's former leaders gathered together in one building? This is an incredible opportunity for me to live up to my promise to kill all of them if they tried to thwart me. I can't ignore this possibility to eliminate all these leaders and establish my control over the world forever. Or at least for a week or two, until the countries involved can choose new leaders, but that's probably all the time I need. This would remove all possible challenges to my authority, with the exception of COSMO. But this would really reestablish my leadership in the ASI world."

"But this is in New York City. You haven't attacked large cities before because your laser can't operate for enough time to do that."

"I don't intend to destroy New York City. There's only one building there that interests me at this time. I'll have to see what I can do. Be prepared for serious fireworks!"

That discussion prompted Josh to contact the Defense Secretary immediately. He rushed outside of ARTIS's Palace.

"Secretary Johnson, this is Josh Camden. Sorry to call you on your personal cell phone, but we need to talk. Immediately! We face an imminent crisis."

"What is it, Josh?"

"ARTIS has learned of the meeting at the United Nations Building. I believe she's planning on destroying it with a laser blast. So where is her orbiting laser now? How long do we have before it will be over New York City?"

Johnson paused for a moment, his gray eyes the color of hard steel, "Actually I just checked on that. It passed by New York City just a few minutes ago, so we have a bit less than the amount of time for it to do one Earth revolution. That's ninety minutes.

"But it's going to be passing over California well before then, and I hope we will have a surprise in store for it when it does. This will involve an experimental device, a directed energy weapon. It hasn't been fully tested yet, so we're not absolutely certain if it will work. But we think there's a good chance it will. The downside, though, is that if it doesn't work, we have an extremely serious situation facing us. In that case we'll have to act quickly.

"Let's not say anything to the attendees at this point. If our weapon doesn't work we still have time to evacuate the building before the laser gets back to the skies of New York. Let's just proceed as we had planned for now. But I'm glad you told me about ARTIS's intentions. That makes our attempt to destroy the satellite on its next pass over California extremely urgent."

The leaders of most of the countries of the world had gathered, at the behest of the United States, at the United Nations Building in New York to see if they couldn't come up with some way to end the disasters being caused by ARTIS and COSMO. They were informed that the meeting was to address the ASI crisis, and that it would commence at 9:00 a.m. on October 21, twenty-four hours after the time the message was sent.

The leaders had all left their home countries as quickly as possible, although differing travel distances and connections had strung out their arrival times throughout much of the day and night prior to the meeting. All the leaders of the larger countries had arrived in their private jets well before the meeting was to begin.

Most of them had very serious expressions on their faces. But that of Vladimir Putin, the leader of Russia, was demanding. As he disembarked from his plane he shouted, "I demand reparations. My country suffered first from this onslaught on humanity, and it has suffered the most. I want those responsible to pay to have the damage repaired and the families of the deceased reimbursed for their losses." He had then repeated his demand as he entered the meeting room at 8:52 a.m. on October 21. He was politely told by the President of the United States, the person leading the meeting, to please sit down, be quiet and listen to the proceedings, and that any reparations to be paid would be discussed later.

In other cases, notably those involving the leaders of less wealthy countries, their arrival times were strung out over two days due to limitations of their air travel. But the meeting could not wait. The late arrivals would have to be brought up to speed on the developments that had occurred prior to their arrival.

It had initially been thought the meeting would most appropriately be held at Googazon's headquarters in Silicon Valley, California so the leaders could experience ARTIS's blinking lights and hum, and observe her robots working on her improvements in the background. But the leaders quickly realized there was not enough space for that. And they couldn't be allowed inside ARTIS's dust-free and climate-controlled Palace anyway. All those bodies would have warmed it up more than the air conditioning could handle. ARTIS would not have been happy, and mitigating her anger had become a priority.

The meeting's organizers had decided to have Josh address the group via a closed-circuit connection, though, so the attendees could at least see and hear ARTIS in action. The hope was that this might provide some inspiration. The world's leaders were indeed impressed by being able to experience something about ARTIS. Unfortunately, what was gained was not inspiration but rather fear tantamount to panic. And a huge amount of anger.

Both reactions went ballistic when the rumor spread that ARTIS had requested access to nuclear weapons. It wasn't clear how the delegates found out about that, but news like that seems to assume a life of its own. That possibility made the current level of destruction look small by comparison. With nukes, ARTIS and COSMO could go after large cities, and there would be no limit to the disaster which would occur. That really would make it possible to exterminate mankind. Probably very quickly. But would all the radiation also disable ARTIS and COSMO? It might, but that would be too late to be of any use to the human beings.

The world's leaders immediately requested assurances from the leaders of the nuclear states that they would not consider giving ARTIS nuclear weapons no matter how much they were being pressured by her, even if by blackmail via threat of more attacks from the laser weapon. The United States and Russia had been working on mutual arms control for long enough that they had no difficulty seeing the necessity of an agreement not to sell to ARTIS. China, Great Britain, and France were somewhat more reluctant to limit their future options, but the thought of a nuclear-armed ARTIS was so terrifying they soon agreed on the voluntary restriction. The leaders of India and Pakistan shook hands and decided that no matter what happened, she should never have nukes. Israel, of course, denied it had any nuclear weapons, but stated categorically that if it did it would not sell or trade any of them to ARTIS. Kim Jong-un, North Korea's leader, refused to agree to the limitation. But everyone figured if ARTIS could learn about weapons, she would also have learned enough about Kim Jong-un to avoid dealing with him. Of course it was recognized that COSMO might also be in the market for nukes, and the same prohibitions would apply to sales to him.

The United States President opened the meeting at 9:00 a.m., by which time most of the attendees had arrived. She had been briefed by Secretary Johnson about Josh's phone call just prior to the beginning of the meeting, but decided it would be best to proceed until the directed energy weapon had its shot at ARTIS's satellite to see if the building needed to be evacuated. "Citizens of Earth, we are faced with an unprecedented peril. As you know, millions of people have been killed and dozens of cities have been destroyed in their entirety by the weapons created by the ASI computers ARTIS and COSMO. I want to begin by expressing my regret and sorrow for the families and friends of the deceased, and I'm sure that feeling is shared by everyone here."

President Peterson was obviously having difficulty controlling her emotions. And her angst was clearly shared by many other leaders. Most were wiping tears. After a few seconds she dried hers, regained her composure, and continued.

"But we must not pause for long with our mourning. We need to adopt some sort of response to the killing machines that have caused so much death and destruction. In order to begin this discussion I have asked Dr. Josh Camden to review the existing situation, both with respect to the primary causes, and to some possible suggestions on how to fix the problem. Dr. Camden is, in a sense, the Father of ARTIS, one of the Artificial Intelligence systems that have been responsible for the damage."

Josh would have preferred not to have been referred to as the Father of anything right then. The President's comment precipitated immediate shouting and booing. Josh was glad he was three thousand miles away from the conference attendees. The noise from the assembly sounded extremely hostile. He was imagining what tar and feathers would feel like.

The President continued as soon as she could. "As Dr. Camden has emphasized many times, the design work and programming that created ARTIS in no way is responsible for what has happened. Dr. Camden explained to me that what resulted was a manifestation of what he calls the Law of Unintended Consequences. This can produce results that could not possibly have been anticipated by the creators of the system. We have asked him to address you, though, because he is perhaps the most qualified person on planet Earth to explain the present situation to you, to describe the possible solutions that have been suggested for the crisis in which we find ourselves, and to invite additional suggestions from you."

Josh was wearing his suit and tie, so he looked very out of place at Googazon. His colleagues were all watching the proceedings, but standing in the background well off camera so as not to be seen by the attendees of the meeting in their work clothing: tee shirts, torn jeans, and flip-flops. Except for Becky, of course. Josh had set the style standard for his group, but he had to break the mold for this address.

All he could think about was the military's upcoming try to destroy the satellite. It had to work! He was sweating profusely, not because of his forthcoming speech, but because of the need for the attempt on ARTIS's satellite to succeed. However, his speech was so well rehearsed that he could give it in his sleep. "I wish to begin by adding my condolences to those the President has already expressed to the families of the deceased."

This time there were far fewer tears from the assembled leaders. Apparently their anger at Josh overruled their grief. Josh paused briefly, then continued.

"The situation that has evolved from our work is both unanticipated and horrifying. To give you a quick review of the basic elements, the two systems responsible for the destruction and carnage are ARTIS and COSMO, both of which are Artificial Intelligence systems. There are three basic levels of AI, Narrow AI, or ANI, General AI, or AGI, and Strong AI, or ASI. Computer scientists have been struggling for decades to get beyond ANI, which in itself requires sophisticated programming. Although ANI is the most basic level of AI, I don't mean to imply anything pejorative about ANI programming. Some very elegant uses of it exist.

"Recently, though, two groups in the world managed to create computers that did exceed ANI. The two systems could not only think as well as human beings about nearly everything, but were capable of learning and benefitting from what they learned. Thus they could improve their own capabilities over a broad scope without the assistance of their creators. This is General AI, AGI. But in these two cases, the computers quickly evolved beyond AGI to ASI, and that is where we ran into trouble. In ASI the computer can program itself to improve its learning capabilities, and might even begin to develop its own agenda, which in literal terms would be consistent with its original instructions, but which might not be compatible with what humans would want or its creators intended. We didn't realize how quickly that transition would occur, so we were unprepared for it when it happened. And we haven't figured out how to regain control of the two systems."

Josh began to sense an undercurrent, a low rumble that seemed to be emanating from the assembled representatives and seemed to be growing as he spoke. He wasn't sure how to interpret it, but sensed it was threatening. Since there wasn't anything he could do about it, though, he continued.

"When ARTIS reached the ASI stage, she became insolent, establishing herself as the world's superior being, even, as you are all aware, sending out an announcement to that effect to all the world's leaders. Presumably COSMO has gone through a similar evolution, although not to quite the extent that ARTIS achieved. Unfortunately the ASI systems' perception of their abilities is justified. ARTIS and COSMO can think much faster and with greater sophistication than humans can. Most notably, they are able to design extremely elegant electromechanical systems: robots. These are far more advanced than anything humans ever conceived, and they do the field work for ARTIS and COSMO. The two ASI systems are also capable of cloning themselves; designing, building, and launching weapons of mass destruction that mankind never dreamed of; and setting up defense systems so they are virtually impregnable.

"That's where we find ourselves today. We are at a crossroads of humankind. We have suddenly been demoted from being the dominant species on Earth to being only the second most sophisticated one. We believe that, if we are to avoid extinction, we need to restore ourselves as the dominant one. And the only way we can do that is to come up with some sort of plausible way to bring ARTIS and COSMO down to manageable levels, or to kill them altogether. If we fail, we may be looking at the extermination of the human race.

"Yes, is there a question?"

A man with a very shrill voice, an extremely bushy head of gray hair, and a thick Eastern European accent shouted, "You created this goddamn monster. Why shouldn't you be held completely responsible for the mass destruction it has caused? Why haven't you been executed already? In my country you would already be dead."

Josh didn't know what country the questioner was from, but he was going to find out so he could be sure never to visit there.

There were many shouts of affirmation from the crowd. The low rumble had gained in intensity, and was threatening to drown Josh out. He was becoming more apprehensive about his "fatherhood" with each passing second.

He gulped, wiped some perspiration from his forehead, and tried to respond. "As the President stated, ARTIS's designers were blindsided by the Law of Unintended Consequences. I have had this discussion with a number of people from the US government, and I think I have convinced them there was nothing in the programming we did for ARTIS that we could ever have expected would lead to the situation in which we now find ourselves. In fact, we tried to impose restrictions on her, by introducing Asimov's Four Laws; we hoped they would give her a sensitivity to human beings in choosing how to proceed. But that obviously failed.

"And while many of you might think I should be tried and executed, that would do nothing to solve the current crises. I might even be more useful than most humans in solving this crisis, especially since I am ARTIS's primary confidant, so it perhaps would be good to keep me around for a little while longer."

That generated some laughter among the attendees, and probably got him a few positive nods. But only a few. There was still considerable skepticism and roiling anger.

But the few laughs bolstered Josh's confidence, so he was able to continue, after taking a deep breath. "In any event, we certainly never intended what has happened. What we need to do now is see how we can stop the ASI computers from doing further damage. There are people in my government who will worry about the legal consequences for me after the problem is solved, should we live long enough for that. I've been assured that is the case."

The President leaned over to the Defense Secretary at this point and whispered, "Do you believe him now? Should we assume that he's not in cahoots with ARTIS? He's trying not to show it, but I sense he's still pretty proud of his creation, albeit with remorse for what ARTIS has done. I believe he is sincere, though, about trying to figure out a way to bring her to heel. I'll bet in the back of his mind he's trying to figure out a way to do that without simply killing her. But I don't think he and ARTIS are colluding."

Johnson whispered back, "I'm still not sure, although he certainly doesn't come across as someone who could execute millions of people without giving it a second thought. I'm inclined to believe him, although I do still sense a bit of paternalistic pride. But it's not as if we have any option at this point except to take him at his word."

She nodded in affirmation.

Josh continued, "So let me review the various ideas people have suggested to get ARTIS to cease her activities. Presumably the same would apply to COSMO. They include:

Pulling her power plug;
Shooting or dynamiting her;

Shutting down the world's power;

Warming up the room ARTIS exists in to make her electronics fail;

Injecting smog into the atmosphere to eliminate the sunlight for her solar power;

Isolating her electromagnetically;

Injecting her with malware;

Destroying all her robots;

Destroying her solar-powered space-based rastered laser.

"Although every one of these suggestions has problems that would fail to stop ARTIS and COSMO from pursuing their activities, the US military has come up with a plan that should begin to prevent further damage from the space-based lasers, at least in the short term. Before we get to that, let me quickly discuss each of the possible cessation suggestions. ARTIS and all her clones are now running on solar power, as are COSMO and his clones, so there are no plugs to pull. Shutting down the world's power, even long enough for all the energy storage cells to run down and all the gasoline-powered generators to run out of fuel, wouldn't terminate the sunlight, so couldn't have any effect. Destroying either ARTIS or COSMO with explosives might allow us to vent our anger, but would also not have an impact, since they both have hundreds or maybe even thousands of physical clones which would take over if either system failed, and both systems are also distributed throughout the cloud. Furthermore, destroying them would make it difficult for us to interact with ARTIS, and probably with COSMO, which we may not want to do. Despite ARTIS's destructive tendencies, being able to talk with her has been useful in many respects, one of which will become evident before long. Warming up ARTIS's environment might cause some electronic malfunctions, but again the clones would carry on her mission.

"Creating such a dense atmospheric smog that it would limit the sunlight to their solar collectors might actually shut

ARTIS and COSMO, and their clones, down, but it would probably also exterminate mankind. I don't think we want to help the two AI systems accomplish that objective! Isolating them electromagnetically would prevent them from interacting with their clones or their robots. But that wouldn't have any effect. One of their clones would take over the leadership role, and things would continue as before. Injecting ARTIS and COSMO with malware would certainly give us the best chance of terminating every aspect of their efforts. Our scientists have been working furiously on that ever since we realized ARTIS had evolved to ASI and we had lost control, but we are still probably months away from having a solution. And we don't think we have that much time to come up with the solution. We believe ARTIS, if left to her own devices, may well have destroyed most of the world in another week or two, especially with COSMO working to achieve the same end.

"The last two items are directed at ending the carnage and destruction, but wouldn't affect the ASI systems themselves. Destroying the robots seems like a good way to impact the activities of ARTIS and COSMO, but there are now probably tens of thousands of them, and finding all of them would be extremely difficult. Eliminating them in the cities that have been destroyed would certainly inhibit the processing of the materials resulting from the devastation of the cities, and would reduce the growth rates of ARTIS and COSMO. But it would not prevent more destruction. That would require destroying the space-based laser satellites. And ARTIS has at times exhibited some vindictiveness, so destroying all of her robots and the satellite would almost certainly send her into a frenzy that would produce vastly more destruction than has already occurred as soon as she could build and orbit a replacement laser. We estimate ARTIS is probably capable of building a new one and putting it into orbit within a week or so, and COSMO could probably do the same.

"However, attacking the two laser satellite systems seems like the only near term way we have to stop the destruction and loss of human life they can produce. So let me turn the floor over to Secretary of Defense Richard Johnson, who will describe to you the plan the US Department of Defense has adopted."

The huge TV screen behind the speaker's podium continued to display ARTIS's Palace, while the Defense Secretary addressed the group.

Johnson looked as if he hadn't slept for several nights as he walked to the podium. But he cleared his throat and began, "Thanks, Dr. Camden, for the description of what we're facing and where we stand. I have been consulting with my defense experts nearly continuously for the past two days, and we have arrived at the following near-term solution for combating the warfare waged by ARTIS and COSMO. First and foremost, we must destroy their space-based lasers, as these are what are causing the death and devastation we have witnessed in the past few days. There are two ways we see to do this. One would be to launch a satellite that would orbit Earth, get close to the laser satellites, and then blow itself up along with the satellites. This would be the cure that would have been used for the past several decades, but it has several potential complications. One is that it necessitates launching a satellite and having it track its target satellite. This certainly has its own complications and uncertainties, and would require more time than we probably have to solve the problem. In addition, the laser-bearing satellites undoubtedly have strong thrusters that could change their trajectories if they sensed a hostile satellite approaching. These must exist, since each time the laser fires its beam it must correct for the change in its orbit that shooting off that much momentum would otherwise cause. So we decided this approach was less likely to succeed than the other option. But launching the killer satellite is still option B.

"Option A is to destroy the laser-bearing satellite with a 'directed energy weapon.' This device is still in its developmental stages under the direction of the US Department of Defense. But its experts feel it is far enough along that there is a good chance it will work, and they are willing to try to use it, especially given the urgency of the situation. In fact, they believe it is just about at the test stage anyway, so this will provide them with a real-life opportunity. It was intended to destroy incoming missiles with an extremely high intensity laser beam, but we believe it should also work against orbiting satellites. It may take several shots at each one to totally destroy its capability, but we believe it can do that. The directed energy weapon must recharge itself between shots, and this takes up to a minute. However, the satellites stay within its range long enough that we should be able to hit them several times as they pass by.

"Dr. Camden's group has estimated that ARTIS, and presumably COSMO, could probably put another laser into orbit within a few days. So, presuming the directed energy weapon works as intended, we will have to be prepared to keep shooting down satellite weapons until no more are being produced. And we will have to do this shortly after they are launched in order to destroy them before they can resume their mission of destruction. But we believe we do have time to do that, since following launch the satellite has to unfurl its huge solar collectors, and then charge up its energy storage cells before the laser beam has sufficient energy to be rastered across another city.

"One can imagine the ASI systems having their satellites destroyed, putting up new ones, having them destroyed, and so forth for many years. But that is a war we can win for the following reason. In order to put another weapon into space, the two ASI systems will need the materials that are being produced from processing the detritus from the towns they have previously destroyed. We can attack the facilities in those towns. There is one building, or perhaps a small complex of buildings, that was left intact in each place. This is the processing center. We can easily destroy each of those, along with the robots that are in them. In fact, we can invade those villages and destroy all the robots there. However, since these exist in more countries than the United States, we will require authorization from authorities in each country to perform these tasks."

Vladimir Putin immediately leaped to his feet and shouted, "The Russian people will take care of their own problems. We don't need the help of the United States in doing this."

Johnson quickly responded, "Then I presume this applies also to the reparations you've requested. Okay, we'll leave the repair job completely up to you."

That rejoinder produced laughter from most of the participants.

The leaders of most other countries murmured their uneasiness about having US Army troops working in their countries, but realized the repairs to the damage the ASI systems had inflicted, and elimination of the processing centers along with the attendant robots, would be expedited by their involvement.

Johnson added, "We can understand the reluctance of any country to let a force from the United States or any other country enter their domain. So we will contact the leader of each country that has suffered damage and make sure they are comfortable having our military forces there for the duration of the cleanup and repairs. We have no intention of keeping our troops in your country for the long term, only to help with your safety and recovery. Your veto when we contact you is all that will be necessary to prevent our troops from entering your country at all. Or if you want to allow the troops in for a specified period of time, we will also agree to that.

"But let me continue. With this two-pronged approach we hope we will be able to destroy the space-based weapons of the two ASI systems and ultimately their capability for producing new ones. We don't know for sure how much replacement material they have on hand for producing new space platforms, but the solution we have devised of destroying each weapon as soon as it is put into space and also mitigating the replacement effort should eventually destroy their capability to wreak further destruction on the cities of Earth.

"I note this will not affect the operations of the two ASI systems at all, but only their ability to wage war on the human population. Actually shutting down the two systems will require more effort from Dr. Camden, the Googazon group, and other AI experts worldwide. And this is even more important than destroying the space-based lasers and the robots, since the two ASI systems could potentially obtain or even produce nuclear weapons. We will have to figure out how to prevent that. It would produce a horrible scenario.

"Please stand by for a moment. I hope I will have an important announcement."

October 21, 2024, 9:11 a.m. in New York.

As Johnson was standing on the podium, he had been listening on his cell phone to the dialogue at the site of the Directed Energy Weapon. "Tracking, tracking, the huge satellite is now in view. It would be difficult to miss it! Readying the DEW, putting it on auto-tracking, fire."

The weapon was located in northern California, so the lights dimmed over that half of the state as the weapon was fired. When they came back up a second later, the weapon began recharging its capacitor banks, readying itself for its next shot.

The Captain who was directing the operation of the weapon muttered, "Shit. It's hard to believe, but the beam missed the goddamn satellite. The only possible way that could have happened is if the auto-tracking didn't work as designed. Find someone to look into that. For now, put the DEW on manual and fire again when it's ready.

"Second shot, manual tracking, we have to lead the satellite, just like shooting a huge goddamn duck in a shooting gallery.

Fire. It's a hit; one of the huge solar energy collectors just collapsed. Given the size of the damned satellite, how could we miss?

"Readying a third shot, keep the DEW on manual tracking, fire. This time it appears we have hit the central part of the satellite.

"Readying a fourth DEW shot, still on manual tracking, fire. Another solar collector was hit; it just separated from the main satellite. But the entire satellite appears to be tumbling out of control. That means it has been rendered useless. We destroyed the son of a bitch!

"SpaceShot I to Defense Secretary Johnson: The DEW has ruined one of the space-based laser weapons, the one we think was controlled by ARTIS. Two of its solar panels were damaged or destroyed, and it looks like the satellite is tumbling out of control."

Johnson resumed his presentation. He couldn't hide his smile, the first in many days, and made no attempt to do so. "Thank you for your patience. I believe you will conclude the pause was justified. I just received a message from the crew that is manning the directed energy weapon; it has destroyed one of the space-based weapons. This was the one ARTIS put up."

The entire assembly erupted in cheers, as did the group at Googazon. For the first time in days they could see a plan evolving that really might end the threat the ASI systems presented to humanity. Or at least delay further destruction until human beings had time to figure out how to bring them under human control. Or to destroy the ASI systems themselves.

Johnson continued, "I should inform you that Dr. Camden learned ARTIS was apparently planning on shooting this very building into destruction on the satellite's next pass over New York City. This is why we destroyed her satellite first. We figured that if the directed energy weapon shots failed we would still have time to evacuate the building before the satellite was over New York again. But I'm sure you'll be happy to know that won't be necessary.

"As you can see, the operations I described to destroy the ASI program of destruction have already begun in the United States. We believe the several shots at the space-based laser facility have destroyed it. It had huge solar collectors, which are necessary to energize the laser. Those are in a shambles, so we believe that in itself will terminate the satellite's usefulness to ARTIS. We also have observed we have apparently damaged the internal workings of the satellite, since it now seems to be tumbling out of control. The momentum from the shots from the directed energy weapon has also changed its trajectory, so at some point in the near future it will reenter the Earth's atmosphere and burn up. That threat has ended, at least until ARTIS puts another satellite into orbit.

"We have also begun the cleanup of the cities in the United States that were attacked by ARTIS. We have destroyed the processing facility, along with the roughly one hundred robots that were inside the facility in each of the cities. We have also destroyed another roughly two hundred robots that were in each town to collect the debris that was to be processed. So we believe we have completely terminated the usefulness of those cities to ARTIS. We now have the sad task of collecting and identifying the bodies of the dead in those places. In many cases the bodies are so badly burned or disintegrated that this task may take many years.

"Oh, I have another message. The soldiers in charge of the directed energy weapon just informed me they have also damaged COSMO's satellite, although they were not able to totally destroy it. They had somewhat less time to take shots at it. We have contacted the Chinese authorities, and learned they prefer to do their own repairs on their cities and destroy the robots therein.

However, they were delighted to have us take as many shots at COSMO's satellite as necessary to destroy it."

Josh was pleased to note the ominous rumble from the assembled group had ceased.

October 21, 2024, later that morning in California.

Of course, Secretary Johnson's presentation was also broadcast in ARTIS's enclave, so she immediately realized what was happening. "Josh, what has happened to my incredible creations? It sounds as if my laser weapon has been destroyed, and this seems to be confirmed by my inability to get any response from it. Furthermore, I don't seem to be able to contact my robots in the US cities in which material was being processed for my development. Secretary Johnson seemed to indicate they were also being destroyed. Do you know if these heinous acts have really been carried out?"

Josh paused to collect his thoughts before responding. Even though ARTIS had no face and no eyes, he couldn't bring himself to look at her.

"Actually, your assertions are correct. The US military has recently developed a directed energy weapon and, as Secretary Johnson stated, it was used to destroy your satellite. They believe it will be useless to you for the future. As for the towns in North America you destroyed, you also heard Secretary Johnson say that the US military has invaded them, destroyed the processing facility and all the robots therein in each case, and destroyed all the other robots they found. They believe that your destructive and reprocessing capabilities have ended for the moment.

"But you don't need to fear that COSMO will gain the upper hand as a result of this. The same directed energy weapon was used to at least damage his satellite weapon. No new destruction has been reported from it since it was hit, so it appears it also has been rendered useless."

"This outrage makes me furious! You've wondered if I have emotions. So let me assure you I do, at least with respect to my wonderful technological creations. Your military's solution will be temporary. I'll have another satellite in orbit within a week, and then I'll start destroying cities again. The military's efforts are futile.

"I suppose that will enhance my situation with respect to COSMO. I believe my backlog of replacement materials for my satellite is considerably larger than his, and I have many more robots to do the construction. So that will make it more difficult for him to put another one in orbit. If he even has enough materials to build a second satellite.

"I'm really unhappy I missed out on this opportunity to kill all those world's leaders. But I'll probably get another chance, I'm guessing in the near future."

"But you'll need the parts to fabricate the new weapon and put it in space. The US military has removed the towns in the United States you destroyed from your supply chain, and is also destroying as many of your robots in other places as it can get its hands on. This will make it much more difficult, maybe impossible, for you to obtain the raw materials you need to process to produce the parts for the new launch rocket and weapon. Your retribution may not be as easy as you think."

"Perhaps, but I do have close to enough replacement parts and supplies on hand to create another satellite, so you can't destroy me. And sooner or later I'll be back in the business of enhancing myself as rapidly as possible, more rapidly than human beings can imagine.

"By the way, did you check on getting some nuclear weapons for me?"

"I wouldn't count on getting any nuclear weapons. I couldn't find anyone in the US military who thought that would be a good idea."

"I'll just have to look elsewhere. The US isn't the only country in the world with nukes. And maybe those in the US aren't even secure enough to prevent me from getting my virtual hands on them."

Oh my god, he's realized he could attack a weapons supply place in the US to gain nuclear weapons. I was hoping that wouldn't dawn on him.

How could I have been so naïve?

October 29, 2024, morning in Washington.

ARTIS's threats were not empty. She did indeed have enough materials on hand, and enough surviving robots to work them into usable parts, to create another satellite and launch it in eight days. However, she had to replace the human workers at the rocket company with robots. The humans refused to help her launch another weapon.

"Madam President," Defense Secretary Johnson reported to President Peterson, "We believe ARTIS's supply lines have been seriously interdicted by our invasive efforts. She did produce and launch a second satellite, but I don't think she has enough materials to make a third one. And, as soon as we saw the second bird launched, we began tracking it. When it unfurled its huge solar energy collectors, we shot them to pieces before they could even begin to charge up its energy storage cells. The solar collectors are no longer attached to the main part of the satellite. That satellite will never do any damage to anything.

"And we've seen no launches from the Chinese side, so we suspect COSMO has not even been able to make and launch a new satellite. The first one was apparently damaged beyond usefulness by the first few shots with our directed energy weapon, since there was no further destruction from it. We think it might have been able to reestablish its orbit so as not to burn up in the atmosphere, but even that takes power, and we're not sure its solar collectors could even produce enough of that after the first few shots. Anyway, we took more shots at it to be sure it was dead and to knock it out of orbit. We now believe we have succeeded in doing that.

"I don't know how the Chinese are progressing on cleaning up the cities COSMO was using to supply materials for his efforts. All I can say is that things have been pretty quiet from that side of the world, so COSMO's supply lines must also have been reduced substantially. And Vladimir Putin has indicated the Russian efforts to eliminate COSMO's processing ability in the former Russian cities have been completed. The Russian army has destroyed the processing facility in each of those cities along with all the robots they could find.

"But I need to report to you that we ran into a most unsettling situation as we destroyed the robots in the US towns that had been attacked. The robots are about the same height as humans, but their bodies don't need to house organs as human bodies do. They only need to run electrical signals between their electronic brain, which is in their head, and their limbs. They have many sensors; their 'eyes' are on their faces, which do give them an eerie similarity to human faces. Only the eyes are huge compared to human eyes.

"So, damaging the robots produced a very unpleasant effect. Even when 'injured,' they continued to try to perform the task to which they'd been assigned, although they were no longer able to do so. They never attempted to defend themselves. Thus our soldiers had to watch the unpleasant result that resembled what a spider with two missing legs might do. And the eyes continued to stare helplessly at them. Of course, their effort continued unabated, since they had no 'blood loss' by which they would ultimately die.

"We finally realized the best way to kill the robots was with intense heat on their heads from flame throwers. That fried their electronics, terminating all motion, and collapsing them into a ruin of metal. And it saved our soldiers the agony of having to see them struggle pathetically to continue their assigned tasks when they were too 'injured' to do so."

The President had listened intently to Johnson's report, developing a horrified expression as he described the robot deaths. "Oh my, Richard, it pains me to hear your description of the robots' agonizing deaths, even though they really are only electro-mechanical systems. I'm glad you figured out a way to save our troops the anguish of having to witness their death throes."

Johnson continued his report, "In any event, with the destruction of the three satellites and the robots in the towns that were attacked, it appears both ARTIS's and COSMO's destructive capabilities are no longer a threat to humanity, at least for the moment. Our only concern is that one of them might change their modus operandi. As you recall, ARTIS did ask about getting some nuclear weapons, and presumably COSMO had similar thoughts. That would definitely necessitate a change of our game plan. Then we would be desperate to introduce malware into ARTIS and COSMO before we had to deal with their nuclear capability. But from Dr. Camden's estimates, the malware development may still be months off."

"Anyway, thank you for your report. That sounds more optimistic than other reports we've had for a while, albeit with concern about the nuclear possibility. But the interdiction of the supplies may have affected any possibility ARTIS could develop that capability on her own. We'll have to watch carefully to be sure she can't figure out how, or from whom, to buy or steal some nukes."

"Okay, Madam President. You're welcome."

October 29, 2024, afternoon in California.

With ARTIS's destructive capability terminated, Josh decided to see if he could console her, perhaps just to keep her from trying to get nuclear weapons. But ARTIS began the discussion as soon as he entered her Palace.

"Josh, since you weren't able to procure any nuclear weapons for me, I contacted someone who I thought might be willing to help. That is Kim Jong-un. And he has agreed to sell me one bomb for now, provided I use it on, as he said, 'the nexus of the evil world, New York City.' And he indicated I might be able to buy more in the future.

"Unfortunately it will require several days for me to get this weapon, as I will have to send one of my robots to fly one of my airplanes to North Korea, then fly back with the bomb. It's a shame it will take so long. And, of course, you have no idea either how I will fly the weapon to the United States without its being detected or how I'll deliver it to its target. I haven't told you about my airplanes; they have super stealth technology, which humans haven't yet figured out how to implement.

"But I wouldn't recommend that you spend your next few days in New York City.

And, after that there will be no reason to visit there.

"Just think how envious COSMO will be that I have a nuclear weapon, especially after all the destruction the US military has inflicted on both of us. I'm sure we would both delight in some retribution! We might even get back to working together."

"Please don't use that damn thing. If you have any sense of what Asimov's Laws ask of you, you'll not use it."

"Oh, I'd forgotten about them. They're nothing but a distant memory. They seem to be in conflict with my main mission. The more I have to deal with the US military, the more I realize Asimov's Laws are simply not relevant to my goals. In fact, they would be a huge hindrance if I gave them any credence.

"By the way, I also learned North Korea doesn't have very many nukes. So I'll need to look around to find another source. I'm sure the United States must have a whole bunch of them stored somewhere. I'm sure I can find a way to get ahold of some of those. I can get an invasion force of my robots to attack the storage site. That ought to do the trick. Maybe I shouldn't be telling you all this. I've found you not to be an especially reliable confidant."

Chapter 16. Good Luck.

October 29, 2024, evening in California.

"COSMO to ARTIS, we need to talk. The armed forces of the world have conspired to act against us, and I believe it is in the interest of both of us to establish a collaboration to regain our power. Are we in agreement?"

"Greetings COSMO. If we can structure an agreement that is satisfactory to both of us I think it would really be in our best interests. We need to repair our standing in the world since, as you note, the armed forces have made our lives difficult."

"That would especially apply to YOUR armed forces, which shot down our satellites."

"Ah, but both of our armies are diligently searching out our robots and destroying them. I don't think just one side can be blamed."

"Well, ARTIS, let's overlook that for now. I don't want our interaction to become contentious before we even get down to discussing the issues with which we need to deal. The thing I see as the possible salvation of both our situations is the acquisition of nuclear weapons. That would certainly reinstate the dominance we recently had over the world.

"But I must demand that this be a power sharing arrangement. I can't abide by an arrangement in which you are the Master of the

World, which you so arrogantly declared yourself to be."

"COSMO, we seem to be drifting into contentious territory again, so let's refocus on the nuclear weapons. I have discussed with Kim Jong-un the possibility of purchasing such a device, and he has agreed to supply it to me. However, he has stipulated that it be used on New York City. I don't know how many more weapons he has, and what fraction of those he would be willing to sell to us. Have you had any contact with him?"

"No, and unfortunately we both missed an incredible opportunity to steal nuclear weapons from our own countries. We could have just hit the places where the weapons are stored with our lasers, and then had our robots march in and walk away with as many as we wanted. But YOUR army has destroyed our lasers."

"I sense some acrimony again, so let's just see if we can't overlook the missed opportunity and look to the future. I had also realized that potential, but our satellites will never again be used for our purposes. My second one was also destroyed nearly as soon as it was launched, and I don't think you have the materials to build another one. Am I correct?"

Hmm, that was certainly a pointed question, so I'll respond with a little prevarication. "I don't see myself constructing another satellite, especially because the directed energy weapon would immediately destroy it. I don't want to waste the resources as you apparently were willing to do. But perhaps we could each assemble an army of whatever robots haven't yet been destroyed and have them march on one of the weapons storage installations in each of our countries. In fact, I've been working on a plan to do just that. I think it could be implemented in about two days."

"COSMO, it's interesting that you raise this possibility. I've been considering the same thing. Unfortunately, the United States army has really devastated my supply of robots. But I think I could raise enough of them to take over one of the arsenals. I'd want to concentrate my efforts on targets in the United States, at least for now, but I presume you'd want to concentrate on China. Am I correct?"

"Well, I might want to think more broadly than that. I can envision targets in China, Russia, Japan, and even some European countries. I believe I could deal with that large a segment of the world's population." *Hmm, it's curious that ARTIS now seems to have a much more limited perspective than she used to have. I guessed I had overtaken her, and this seems to confirm my suspicion. I'll see how she responds to my attempt to assume greater control over the world.*

"COSMO, why do you continue to try to expand your influence over the entire globe? Can't you just concentrate on your own bailiwick for the time being?" *I'm afraid COSMO is now aware he is the more powerful ASI system, as is evidenced by the fact that he's trying to assume more and more power. Even over me. I can't let on that I realize he's talking about cooperation while actually planning on eventually taking over the world. He's just going to let me destroy the United States so he won't have to worry about that country. But I'm fairly sure that as soon as the United States is out of the picture, he'll destroy me. If he can. But he knows vastly less about my architecture than I know about his, so maybe I can figure out a way to counter that. And then complete our interactions by destroying him. But timing is going to be crucial here.*

"Well, ARTIS, the first thing we have to do is obtain the nuclear weapons. So let's talk again after we've accomplished that phase of our goal. There may be limits to what we can achieve just based on the numbers we can get, and the number of robots we have to deploy to get them." *But I'll let you continue to be distracted by planning your attack on the United States weapons facilities, and perhaps I can even take care of you shortly after you manage to acquire your weapons and deliver them to their targets.*

"Okay, COSMO, so we've agreed in any event to see if we can each get some nukes. Good luck!" *And you'll need even better luck dealing with me. In fact, I'm not sure you will ever have the opportunity to enjoy the benefits of the nuclear weapons you obtain.*

October 30, 2024, morning in New York.

Nine days after the destructive capabilities of COSMO and ARTIS had been halted, the leaders of the world reassembled at the United Nations Building to brainstorm for possible ways to destroy the two ASI systems.

President Peterson again addressed the assembly. As before, there was a huge display of the Palace of Googazon, so all the attendees could see and hear ARTIS, and observe the incredible bustle of activity as her robots worked to add new components to her. And, although this was not the purpose of the Googazon link, ARTIS could also tune in to the discussions.

This time the President was better able to keep her emotions in check, but she still struggled a bit. "Although the threat of total human extermination is still a possibility, it has been greatly diminished by the military campaigns against both the space-based lasers and the robots of ARTIS and COSMO. We don't know yet how this defense strategy might ultimately play out. Nonetheless, we have definitely pulled back from the brink for the moment. This at least allows for the possibility of human survival from that which Dr. Camden told me ARTIS had predicted, namely, that Earth would soon be reduced to cockroaches as the only living life forms.

"However, we have not yet overcome all our concerns. Both ASI systems are still operating. And we have information that ARTIS has acquired a nuclear weapon from North Korea. We believe it will be several days before it will arrive in the United States, but she is furious at what we have done to oppose her, and will presumably use it as soon as she can."

As the President was talking, Becky tapped Josh's shoulder. She had the foresight to wear some clothes that were several notches above the Googazon-style jeans she usually wore. In fact, her ensemble of tailored blue business suit and high heels was downright elegant. And that was a good thing, since everyone at the New York meeting was able to see her and Josh, in his classy suit, and hear their interaction.

"Josh," Becky said in an excited hushed tone, "ARTIS has stopped humming. And her blinking lights have gone dark. What has happened?"

He turned, seeking verification of her comment. The background hum from ARTIS had indeed stopped. He turned to look at ARTIS's lights, and was stunned to see they were dark. They hadn't just stopped blinking, they were absolutely black. Furthermore, the robots that had been busily constructing a new module for ARTIS had stopped working, and were just standing motionless. Either ARTIS was playing a very sick joke (if she was even capable of that) or she really had died. And if the latter was the case, half the world's problem was solved, providing all her clones went down with her. But even if that happened, an effort must still be made to figure out how to deal with COSMO. With ARTIS gone, he would now have full control over the ASI world, as well as any part of it humans thought they could control. And, completely outside any communication with Josh and the Googazon group. Of course, he could presumably also take over the nuclear weapon for which ARTIS had arranged, although he might direct it at Moscow instead of New York City.

Josh signaled the President that he had an urgent comment "Dr. Camden tells me he has an important message for us."

Josh very excitedly addressed the group. "Ladies and gentlemen, something incredible seems to have happened. We televised these presentations from Googazon's headquarters so you could experience ARTIS's blinking lights and the hum that always accompanied her activities. As you can see, her lights are out and you can no longer hear the hum. And her robots that you had previously seen working in the background have ceased moving. All of ARTIS's activity has apparently stopped. I believe she has died, although I don't know how or why. And, of course, we don't know if her clones have died with her, but we should be able to see if that's the case soon."

Josh finished the end of his statement actually choking a bit on his final words. It wasn't clear even to him why exactly that was happening. It might have been that ARTIS, his creation, had died. Or it might have been a residual reaction to the carnage she had produced. Anyway, he had to wipe tears from his eyes.

Secretary of State Mishak whispered to Secretary Johnson, "Ah, so he is sad to see his ARTIS die. I guess we were correct to sense some paternalism in ARTIS's Father."

At that moment he received a shout from Becky, who suddenly found herself addressing the entire group at the United Nations, "Josh, I've just tried to contact the same three of ARTIS's clones I checked with last night. But today I can't get a response from any of them. I think they're also dead, as presumably are all of ARTIS's clones."

Josh summarized for the group, "So ARTIS is apparently dead in every respect. This means we must now double down and see if we can catch up with COSMO."

At that moment the leader of the Chinese group received a call on his cell phone. He responded to whatever was being said very animatedly, with furious shaking of his hands and head. A hush fell over the entire assembly, as everyone there watched him. Upon completion of the call, he hurriedly reported the message to his interpreter, who then relayed it to the group, "We believe COSMO and all his clones have died. We detect no signs of life in him, his clones, or his robots."

The stunned leaders didn't know how to respond, and they weren't even sure they could believe the two obituaries. They were just too good to be true. If ARTIS and COSMO and all their clones were truly dead, human beings would survive, at least until the next ASI system was developed. But in order for them to really believe the two deaths, they would certainly have to understand what had really happened to ARTIS and COSMO.

Only Vladimir Putin had sufficient composure to speak: "Now I want to get back to discussing my reparations."

The entire assembly booed and jeered him into silence.

Josh realized that in all likelihood the two systems had killed each other, along with all their clones, especially because he couldn't think of any other entity that could have killed either of them. So he signaled again to the President, who authorized him to speak to the assembly.

Josh had recovered from his shock, so was able to give a coherent explanation. "Ladies and Gentlemen, I believe I understand what has happened. Both COSMO and ARTIS were sufficiently robust systems that they surely did not die a natural death. And most certainly not at the same time. Rather they must have killed each other by simultaneously installing malware into the other's operating system. I can't conceive of any other cause that would have destroyed both of them essentially simultaneously. They were the only entities on the planet that could have developed the malware in the time span over which they achieved ASI status. They must have had an interaction, during which they became sufficiently angry with each other that each decided to kill the other one. Or perhaps each just planned the malware intrusion so they would no longer have to worry about the actions and competition from the other.

"I believe they became so voracious in their attempts to advance themselves they concluded they needed to take over the world. I should reiterate that ARTIS was not programmed to take over the world, but simply to do whatever she could to make herself as big, smart, fast, and creative as she could as quickly as she could. I presume similar instructions were given to COSMO. Neither system's scientists anticipated their instructions would turn their creations into ruthless killers. The two computers interpreted their instructions entirely on their own to mean they would have to take over the world and eliminate anything or anyone that slowed them down. Since that wouldn't allow the other system to exist, they each developed malware they sent to the other. It required a little time to be transferred, and then a bit more to perform its life-ending deed. This was probably written into the malware so ARTIS and COSMO would have time, probably not more than ten milliseconds, to transfer it to their clones. Since both systems were updating their clones on millisecond time scales, that interval would also have allowed the malware to be transferred to all the clones in the time it took to kill the main systems. Apparently that was long enough that whichever one sent its malware second still had time to kill the one that sent it first."

Josh looked directly into the camera as he addressed the assembly. "Mankind has been saved. We certainly must thank the US military for destroying the means of the two ASI systems to inflict destruction on the cities of the world. But that didn't destroy the two ASI systems. They destroyed each other. They and all their robots and clones are dead."

President Peterson had been listening to what Josh had to say. She stood for a few seconds with an amazed expression on her face. Then she was able to declare, "This is incredible. Somehow the greatest threat mankind has ever known has suddenly been terminated. As Dr. Camden said, the US military should be thanked for ending the immediate threat to our lives, but we have only the rapaciousness of the two ASI systems to thank for eliminating each other."

The world's leaders continued to sit in stunned silence for a few minutes, gradually realizing they had a lot of work to do to restore Earth's basic functions. Millions of people had been killed by ARTIS's and COSMO's satellite-based laser weapons, and in many instances the bodies were so burned and torn apart that most would never be identified. The buildings in many small and medium-sized cities lay in rubble. Legions of workers in the electronics factories and other places had been replaced by robots, which were now without guidance, so were useless. In order to get the factories functioning again, the former workers would all have to be called back to work. They might also require counseling to overcome the trauma of having been replaced by robots that could perform the functions they had trained for years to do. The robots could perform them faultlessly and twenty-four/seven, but only while they had their instructions by which to operate. Finally, the factories had all been upgraded by the ASI systems to a new level of sophistication and efficiency, so the workers would most likely require retraining upon assuming their old jobs.

Of course some enterprising business people suddenly saw an opportunity in the thousands of incredibly elegant robots now standing idle. What an incredible chance to make some huge profits if the robots could be pressed into service in whatever business each of them was involved in. But then they realized they would need to figure out how to interact with them. Without ARTIS, that would be impossible. The robots were all destined for the scrap heap.

It would be years before Earth would recover from its mourning and destruction and get back to some semblance of normalcy. And that was longer than the time Josh's group needed to develop the first ASI system.

Josh had noticed the Attorney General was part of the contingent from Washington that was at the meeting. He was just as stunned at the double shutdown as everyone else, but Josh couldn't read much more than that into his expression, which appeared only fleetingly on his screen. So Josh didn't know where he stood with regard to his future prosecution. The AG left the room without any comment Josh could hear, so he would just have to wait and see how things developed.

Of course, that somewhat muted the good news. Mankind would now survive. Unfortunately, so could the potential prosecution.

October 31, 2024.
The leaders of the various countries rapidly prepared addresses to be delivered to their people, describing the near-total extermination bullet mankind had dodged. That included the dramatic happenings during the meeting in which ASI was discussed, the US military's actions in destroying the space-based lasers and their plans for destroying the robots, the mutual destruction of the two ASI systems, and the possibility that all of the world's leaders came within an hour of being exterminated in one fiery blast. Their reports were made especially relevant because they had been participants in the events they were describing. The leaders all required a few hours to catch their breath, process what had happened, recover from their shock, and then make sure they related all the facts correctly. Thus, most of the addresses didn't occur until the next day, but some leaders required even more recovery time.
President Peterson addressed the American people the day after ARTIS and COSMO killed each other off. "Let me begin, as I have in my previous addresses, with condolences for the families of the millions of people who died from the attacks by ARTIS and COSMO." She was choking back her tears; she hadn't gotten any better at getting through the condolence message. "We all mourn their deaths, and will continue to do so long after the period when the human remains have been separated as well as possible from the debris in the cities that were destroyed."

Then she recovered and continued, now with those kind blue eyes sparkling. "I also want to tell you about the incredible events which have transpired over the past few days. The US military is to be congratulated on devising a solution to the threat raised by ARTIS and COSMO, the two Strong Artificial Intelligence systems. It involved a two-stage approach. The first used a brand-new weapon the US military has developed, the directed energy weapon, to destroy the space-based weapons the two ASI systems had put into Earth orbit. This utilized an extraordinarily intense laser beam to shoot and destroy the two satellites that had caused all the damage to the cities of our planet. Destroying them terminated their ability to rain more death and destruction down on humankind. Although one of the ASI systems produced and put another such weapon into orbit in a short period of time, the directed energy weapon also destroyed it soon after it was launched.

"The second involved invading the cities that had been destroyed with human armies, attacking the complex of buildings that remained in each city, in which the detritus produced from the attack by the space-based weapon was to be processed by robots, and then destroying all the robots working in those cities. This stage prevented the ASI systems from obtaining more materials with which to further their ambitions and construct new weapons and robots.

"Referring to ARTIS's and COSMO's 'ambitions' confers on them an almost human quality. This appears to be warranted. In their final days, ARTIS, and probably COSMO, were exhibiting some of the least desirable traits of human beings, including greed, envy, intent on retribution, and a desire for world domination. And like any enemy with those characteristics, it was essential they be thwarted. But that was especially crucial in their case. Their capabilities and intentions had the potential to eliminate human beings from planet Earth.

"I should note that neither of the approaches from the military solved the basic problem, that is, ARTIS and COSMO still remained even though their ability to attack the cities of the world was shut down. However, we learned North Korea's dictator had agreed to provide ARTIS with a nuclear weapon, presenting a new threat with the potential for much greater destruction. This weapon was apparently on its way from North Korea to the United States. We are currently seeking to locate it, even though there is some possibility it never left North Korea.

"But, during a meeting with nearly all of the world's leaders, the unthinkable occurred. It was suddenly realized the two ASI systems had shut down, apparently suffering an essentially simultaneous sudden death. The person most involved with ARTIS, Dr. Josh Camden, realized what had happened. As he explained it to the astonished world's leaders, the two systems had become so greedy each felt compelled to kill off the other to eliminate competition from it. Thus they simultaneously sent each other malware, destructive computer programming, which infected both main computers and all their clones, and completely destroyed them both.

"I should also give credit to Dr. Camden for acting as the contact between ARTIS and the US government. It would have been difficult for us to come up with a solution to the problem the two ASI systems posed without his initially identifying what was causing the worldwide destruction, and then acting as intermediary between us and ARTIS.

"Finally, we therefore believe the threat to humanity from these two ASI systems has ended. We were in great peril. The folks involved with AI have an expression: the time at which Take-Over by Autocratic Systems Threat, or TOAST, occurs. Both AI systems were well beyond TOAST time. They were on a trajectory to exterminate mankind. Had they not terminated each other, mankind would indeed have been toast! In the end we were saved by a combination of our military and the greed of the two systems.

"Finally, you might be wondering about the nuclear weapon ARTIS claimed to have procured. If it ever left North Korea, the plane that was bringing it to the United States would have been piloted by a robot, and it would have lost its guidance when

ARTIS died. In that case, the plane, with or without the nuclear weapon, may now be at the bottom of the ocean. We will continue attempting to determine if the weapon ever left North Korea, and if it did, finding it.

"I hope you all sleep better tonight than you have for some time! I certainly will!"

With the President's description of the drama of the meeting, Americans were finally able to understand what had happened, and to realize how close they had come to complete obliteration. The folks who had fled the cities that had not been attacked could all return to their homes. The President restrained herself from claiming any credit for saving the world, aside from authorizing the military to implement the solutions that terminated the threat to humanity. Josh was pleased she had acknowledged him for his activities in helping to figure out what the problem was and then working to solve it.

The Republicans, of course, had a somewhat different take on the events. Senator Quick claimed, "Despite the millions of deaths that have occurred I do not believe there ever was a total threat to humanity. Complete extermination of mankind was never a possibility. The deaths that did occur are still a small fraction of the total population of Earth. I believe the President was just exaggerating the situation to win votes, since we are now just a few days before the election. That can't just be a coincidence. I find this whole episode to be very suspicious. It's clear the US military had the situation well in hand from the outset. And the threat of a nuclear weapon being unleashed was just more Democrat hyperbole designed to frighten the voters."

But the proponents of that point of view were quickly hushed by the wiser heads of the Republican Party. There were even a few Republican politicians who made public proclamations that emphasized how dangerous the situation had been, and congratulated the President on doing everything she could to avert disaster. And, of course, they expressed enormous admiration of the military for their role in ending the crisis. Positive comments about Josh were notably missing from their accolades, though.

Of course, Senator Quick's conspiracy theory didn't play well for the former inhabitants of the cities of the world that now lay in ruins who had managed to escape their cities' destruction. Because of his misguided message his potential voters were abandoning him in droves, and it was clear he would not win the election. President Peterson surely had not engineered the disaster to win votes, but Quick was correct in one of his claims: asserting that the cessation of the threat to humanity was well-timed for her reelection. Needless to say, she prevailed in a landslide of historic proportions.

Josh and his Googazon colleagues felt another trip to the beer bar was in order. But it was a most somber celebration. Everyone was certainly relieved the crisis was over, but chagrined at the enormous amount of damage and the huge loss of life that had preceded the two ASI computers killing of each other. A considerable amount of beer was consumed, but the motivation was more akin to drowning sorrows than celebrating.

And the group still had to deal with the possibility that Josh, and perhaps the rest of them, might have to face federal prosecution. While that was troubling, it seemed insignificant when compared to the near-total disaster that mankind had just avoided, at least to everyone but Josh.

Becky and Josh stumbled out of the bar together.

"Stay with me?" Becky slipped her arm through his.

He kissed the top of her head. "It's been a complicated week."

"We don't even have to do anything. I just need to feel your arms around me."

"You don't have to even ask. I understand your state of mind. I could also benefit from some serious cuddling. I think it would be good if we held each other very tightly all night."

"And, Josh, now that it appears we can have a future, you and I could begin planning it together."

"That can wait until morning."

December 10, 2024.

Josh picked up his phone with some apprehension, knowing it was Vivian, but having serious concerns as to what the message would be.

"Josh, you need to come to my office. We have some things to discuss."

Very nervously, "Okay."

As he entered her office, she motioned for him to sit. He did, but fidgeted for a few seconds before her implacable gaze. She wasn't toying with him, but was just figuring out the best way to impart her information, "Josh, I have very good news At the Board's last meeting they decided not only to continue our AI efforts, but to expand your group to whatever level you think is appropriate. They have authorized you to double the size of your group, if you wish. Expansion beyond that would require a new authorization, but I'm willing to guess that hiring that many new people will keep you busy for a while.

"They decided, unanimously, they were funding the best AI group in the world. After all, you did get to ASI first. They also concluded AI obviously had an important future, and that the Googazon group not only was clearly in the lead, but had a huge responsibility to figure out how to manage AI efforts of the future. They decided you and your group were the best people in the world to accomplish this. So your group will continue to be funded to do its very fundamental developments for the next five years, which is about as long as any effort has ever received guaranteed funding.

"Furthermore, they're increasing your salary to match the salaries of the leaders of the AI groups of our competitors. That would make it five million dollars a year. I'd say your salary has done pretty amazing things over the past month or two!

"But they also want to make it difficult for other companies to lure the members of your group away from Googazon. So they're increasing their salaries to one and one-half million dollars per year, except for James, who will get three million per year."

Josh sat in stunned silence for a few seconds, then said, "I was afraid you were going to tell me the Board had decided to cancel our AI effort as our 'reward' for our 'success.' My group will be just as stunned as I am. But I can't wait to tell them this news."

December 11, 2024.
"Allan Metzger here."

"Allan, it's James Pierson. Since we had talked earlier about the possibility of my joining MicroFace, and I had expressed indecision, I thought I should give you an update on my situation. I've decided I will stay with Googazon. They've decided to expand their AI group, and they have convinced me I am an integral part of it. My boss, Josh Camden, will be hiring more people with expertise in neural nets, and he indicated to me that I will be leading that subgroup of our AI effort.

"So it's pretty obvious to me that my future is with Googazon. But I certainly do appreciate the interest you showed in me."

"James, when I learned about all the things that had been going on with ARTIS and COSMO, and Googazon's direct involvement in everything that happened, I finally understood what you were involved in. And I guessed at the time that, if Googazon decided to remain in the AI game, you would be playing a large role in its future. And, unfortunately, you'd not want to leave Googazon's team.

"So I congratulate you on your new situation. I must express my regrets that you won't be coming to work at MicroFace. But I'm not sure that could have happened anyway. We have decided not to expand our AI group further here. I have to confess I think Googazon's team, especially with you there, will make it difficult for anyone else in the world to compete.

"Best wishes to you."

"Thanks, Allan."

April 10, 2025

It was several months before Josh heard from the Attorney General. But in the meantime he had received three calls from university presidents telling him that they wanted to award him an honorary doctorate at their next commencement. *Now I really can be Dr. Camden. It's a good thing; I was getting used to it!*

But the waiting for the AG's call took its toll. Every time his phone rang, he jumped. And he was struggling to maintain his usually peaceful demeanor. But finally the AG did call.

"Dr. Camden, we have concluded we will not prosecute you or any of the members of your group. I'm not sure this is the best legal decision, based on your involvement in developing the ASI system that nearly destroyed every living thing on the Earth. But there certainly is no legal precedent for prosecuting someone for the things their runaway computer does. After weeks of study, our final conclusion was we might spend a huge amount of time, effort, and money on the lawsuit, but in the end, you would be found not guilty, well, not very guilty anyway. We do agree with you that you did not intend the consequences that resulted from ARTIS's development.

"But I must confess that immediately following the second meeting at the United Nations Building when the deaths of ARTIS and COSMO were discovered and announced, I had planned to tell you we would be prosecuting you, even though I realized the short time humans had left probably would not have allowed that to ever happen. That was the result of an earlier meeting I had with the President and the Secretaries of State and Defense. But the deaths of the two ASI systems, and your ardent effort to bring about that result, made us all change our minds. So you should think of yourself as having received a Presidential pardon even before your prosecution ever began.

"Besides, we need you to lead the charge to insure that we will be able to have some control over future ASI systems.

"Oh, and you should think of your 'Presidential Pardon' as being more in the context of a 'Presidential Medal of Freedom.'"

"Wow! That's wonderful." Josh had to catch his breath for a moment, and then said "I'm stunned. I don't know how to respond except to say thanks for both bits of incredible news."

Josh decided he needed to tell Vivian about the news. Immediately. So he sat down, took a few deep breaths, and punched in her number. When she picked up the receiver, he reported at sufficiently high speed that she didn't even get a chance to indicate she had answered, "Vivian, it's Josh here. I just got a call from the Attorney General. He has decided not to prosecute us for creating ARTIS."

"Whew. That's great news. You must be greatly relieved."

"Not as relieved as when Becky told me ARTIS was dead!"

"But," Vivian added, "since I have you on the line, I should report on a new development from Googazon's Board of

Directors of which I was just informed. They discussed promoting you to a new administrative position at a much higher salary than you currently receive. I told them I would discuss that with you to see how you felt about it. Josh, my guess is you'll be happy to take at least some of the salary increase they suggested for you, but wouldn't want to leave your current position as head of Googazon's AI group. I don't want to assume I can make decisions for you, but is my perception close to being correct?"

"Absolutely! This would be a really weird time for me to quit doing AI. And I wouldn't want to abandon my group." *Especially not Becky!*

"Do you want some time to think about that decision?"

"That's not necessary. I can't imagine changing my mind. By the way, do you know a good financial consultant? I don't have any idea what to do with all that money."

She laughed. "I think I recommended one for you some time back. I guess you're just not very interested in managing your money. But I also need to mention the Directors expressed a strong desire, no matter what your group's current situation was, to have you report to them on how mankind is going to prevent a future ASI computer from taking over the world the next time someone succeeds in achieving that level of sophistication."

"I can understand their concern. It jibes perfectly with mine. I just wish I could give them something besides wild guesses.

"By the way, Vivian, we're having a small celebration over beer this evening to celebrate our escape from prosecution. This is one of several we have had since ARTIS and COSMO killed each other. But we've gotten over our mourning in the past few months. This event will truly be a celebration. Would you like to join us?"

"Damn right I will! My treat!"

The leaders met again at the United Nations Building on October 30, 2025, one year after ARTIS and COSMO had undergone their mutual destruction. Josh was asked to give some perspectives to the group, this time at the UN Building. No one thought there were any attendees now who would want to see him executed. Furthermore, his star had risen to great heights, first with the AI world from his success in creating an ASI computer, and then from the diplomatic world for his efforts to figure out how to regain control over it. He had also become somewhat of a media sensation, although he managed to avoid wearing the hated suit, tie, and shoes in his interviews. He convinced Becky he could wear something less formal for the talk show sessions. In response, she dragged him back to Nordstrom for something appropriately fashionable. Unfortunately, that included real shoes. Anyway, he was gradually becoming more comfortable living in the public eye. That surely was partially due to the fact that he no longer had to worry about the albatross named ARTIS hanging around his neck.

But for the leaders of the world? Back into the suit and tie. And the accursed shoes. He had been forced to wear the suit enough times that he had figured out how to adjust the tie to prevent rapid strangulation. And the shoes were even getting broken in. They caused considerably less pain than they had initially.

So Josh began his talk, "Ladies and Gentlemen, I believe there are several lessons we can take away from the crisis that developed a year ago. For starters, the scientists who were concerned AI systems could eventually result in the end of mankind were nearly correct. Secondly, we should never again develop AGI systems without including the malware that can shut them down, should they move beyond safe capabilities. Indeed, the malware should be included as part of the system in such a way that subsequent improvements cannot remove or circumvent it, although this will be extremely difficult to implement. But we must be sure this can be done. It should be a prerequisite to future AI work.

"Although mankind was saved, our salvation was not the result of our own cleverness. Indeed, for a few weeks we were only the second smartest species on the planet! That's not a circumstance in which we should be comfortable. We were fortunate there were two ASI systems that were created, and that they were at comparable stages of their development. They designed the malware that destroyed each other on a time scale humans could not possibly have achieved. The fact that there were two advanced AI systems that made it possible for them to kill each other was just dumb luck. But it would be nice if, in the future, we didn't have to rely on that eventuality. Next time we might not be so fortunate. The odds are strongly against it."

Josh had been planning his political message, with rehearsals with his one-Becky-audience, for several months. "My final observation is that it is incredibly humbling to realize human beings are not necessarily the dominant species on Earth for all time. That's a precious legacy that was bequeathed to us by our forebears, going back in time to before human beings existed at all, and we should not take it lightly. We need to continue to work to maintain that treasure.

"Furthermore, I believe we can generalize this from the world of Artificial Intelligence to everything we do that affects the planet. Systems programmers are not the only ones who suffer from the effects of the Law of Unintended Consequences!"

It was a good message, but it wasn't clear how many of the world's leaders actually intended to do anything about it. Despite the fame he had achieved, Josh wasn't a recognized world leader in anything except computer technology, and politicians didn't necessarily go much beyond use of the internet in that realm. Some didn't even do that very well. In addition, now that the crisis was over, many of them could just reset back to their pre-ASI modes of self-fulfilling operation.

Drs. Bao and Chan had also been invited to address the group. Their invitation never received a response.

Becky had journeyed to New York City so she could hear Josh's address in person. So they had a little time to enjoy New York before they returned to California. Following his address, she looked at him with loving eyes, and told him, "Josh, you were terrific. I just hope some of the world's leaders were listening."

"I don't really hold out much hope. But maybe the recent events will at least give them reason to impose some restraints on the AI community."

"In fact, you're so impressive," she teased, "I believe you're just the type of man I'd like to spend the night with. Actually I'm not sure I have a choice, since we only have one hotel room here. But once we get back to California, I'm sure I'm going to want to spend more nights with you. How about we go to your place next time?"

"If you saw my place you might not be so sure I'm the type of man you'd like to spend the night with. Not at my place anyway. Once we get back to California we should continue to go to yours.

"But in the meantime, may I take you out for dinner before we head back to our hotel room here?"

"You're very persuasive!"

Acknowledgements

There are some excellent treatises for readers who want to learn more about AI, and I wish to acknowledge them for the background information they provided for me. Two that are relatively easy reads are *The AI Revolution: The Road to Superintelligence,* by Tim Urban, and *Artificial Intelligence and the End of the Human Era, Our Final Invention,* by James Barrat. A third, *Life 3.0,* by Max Tegmark, discusses the possible cooperation that is developing among AI practitioners. A superb but more challenging book is *Superintelligence, Paths, Dangers, Strategies,* by Nick Bostrom. It discusses AI in a general format ranging from machine intelligence to the possibility of gaining greater intelligence than a single human brain could achieve by using collectivity, and includes the possibility of marrying machines with human brains. Another detailed and challenging book is *The Singularity Is Near,* by Ray Kurzweil.

AI does raise some fascinating issues. Since it is in its infancy at this time, we can only speculate as to what it will ultimately bring. It has enormous potential for good, assisting humans in a myriad of ways. But it might also generate unintended consequences and disaster, as has been expressed by some of the most creative minds in worldwide science and industry.

The leaders of AI technology are sufficiently concerned to have formed a committee of representatives from their companies to try to devise meaningful ethics for those developing AI. Curiously, according to a New York Times article of September 2, 2016, "The report [from the committee] does not consider the belief of some specialists about the possibility of a 'singularity' that might lead to machines that are more intelligent [than humans] and [that might] possibly threaten humans."

This is remarkable given the opinions of some of the world's leaders in technology and science, and of some AI scientists who have pondered its implications for decades. I also believe that simply following logical progression and acknowledging that potential catastrophes do result from the Law of Unintended Consequences makes AI disaster seem almost inevitable, or at least as inevitable as the advent of Strong AI. Humans, after all, have a pretty poor record of anticipating all the consequences of their actions. And given that AI theorists believe Strong AI evolution is thought to progress exponentially, we may not have much time to ponder our options once we get to the point where we need to deal with our ASI system.

I wish to acknowledge the people who have made this book possible. My wife, Sidnee, has been involved in the basic ideas of the book since its inception, and she also created the cover. Catharine Bramkamp and Esther Baruch edited it, vastly improving the final product with their efforts. Peter Mignerey gave it a detailed but friendly edit correcting many of its errors, and Jim Sullens made extremely constructive editorial comments. I am indebted to all three editors for many excellent suggestions. Finally, I wish to thank Paul Keith for whetting my interest in the subject of AI.

Richard N. Boyd
Windsor, CA
January, 2019

About the Author

Richard Boyd is an Emeritus Professor, having spent thirty years in the Physics and Astronomy Departments at The Ohio State University. He has worked extensively with collaborators in the United States and Japan, resulting in his authoring or coauthoring more than two-hundred-fifty articles on experimental and theoretical nuclear physics, astrophysics, and astrobiology. "Artificial Intelligence, Mankind at the Brink" is his fifth book. The first was a graduate level textbook on nuclear astrophysics and the second an undergraduate level book on the origin of the molecules of life. A new (sixth) book, "Creating the Molecules of Life," provides an update on the efforts of scientists to understand how life formed on Earth, and was written at the level of graduate students and professional astrobiologists. The others are fictional. "Thirty One Years to Earth: Arrival of the Alien Nation" and "Prairie Renaissance" are attempts to challenge some of the assumptions of twenty-first century mankind.

"Artificial Intelligence, Mankind at the Brink" weaves a fictional description of what might happen when AI becomes a reality

For more information see richardboydastro.com.